I turned around to face him . . .

My knees were weak. I almost fell. He caught my shoulders, supporting me. A great shudder went through me. I closed my eyes again, whirling, and when I opened them I looked up at him and tried to speak. I couldn't. Although we stood in the shadows, he was perfectly visible, wearing a robe of dark, gleaming satin over trousers and shirt. His handsome, rugged face was a mask of anger, mouth stretched tight over his teeth, eyes dark with fury, raven locks spilling untidily over his forehead. His hands gripped my shoulders savagely, and he looked as though he wished they were gripping my throat.

"What the hell are you doing here!" His voice was low, but it seethed with rage.

I was painfully aware of my scanty attire, the frail cloth barely concealing my bosom. I folded my arms around my waist, shivering. A gentleman would have offered me his robe, but then Lyman was no gentleman . . .

Midnight at Mallyncourt

JENNIFER WILDE

writing as Edwina Marlow

A DELL BOOK

Published by
Dell Publishing
a division of
Bantam Doubleday Dell Publishing Group, Inc.
666 Fifth Avenue
New York, New York, 10103

ISBN: 0-440-20901-3

Printed in the United States of America

Published simultaneously in Canada

July 1992

10 9 8 7 6 5 4 3 2 1

OPM

To Marilu

One

*I*NOTICED him immediately. He was tall and blond and strikingly handsome, and there was a rakish air about him. As he stared at me, quite openly, a faint smile curled on his wide mouth, and the vivid blue eyes were filled with that thoughtful assessment I had long since grown accustomed to seeing in men's eyes when they looked at me, as though I were something they were thinking of buying. I had grown accustomed to it, one had to in my profession, but I still didn't like it. This particular man made no effort to conceal what was on his mind. Tilting my chin haughtily, I walked on past him. He lifted his elegant beaver top hat. The smile broadened. The blue eyes seemed to dance with secret amusement.

I walked down the promenade, my long silk skirts rustling, the ostrich plumes on my hat billowing. Perhaps he wouldn't follow me. Perhaps for once I could enjoy a simple stroll without having to fend for myself. I was accustomed to that, too, and quite adept at warding off tipsy young gallants and boorish middle-aged roués. It was something I had learned that first year with the Gerald Prince Touring Company, and now, after four years, I no longer cringed inside every time I saw that look in masculine eyes. It was an occupational hazard, Laverne had explained, poor Laverne, who hadn't had that problem for years, reduced to playing minor character roles, finding what solace she could in the gin bottle now that her looks were a thing of the past.

"A pretty little thing like you, ducky," she had said, "the men'll go wild. You'll have to fight 'em off, all kinds of men, and one of these days you'll meet one you won't *want* to fight off. Take my advice, ducky, make sure he's rich. With your looks, your breedin'—why, Jenny luv, you could have yourself a bloomin' earl if you was a-mind to—"

I hadn't had an earl. I hadn't had anyone. That was some kind of record for the Gerald Prince Touring Company. Most of the girls came from the slums, pretty, vivacious, determined creatures who chose the stage instead of the brothel. Only last week Daisy had eloped with a dashing young student from Oxford, and Chloe was debating whether or not she should let her current gentleman friend set her up in a flat in London. I liked the girls, all of them, but my background had been different. Perhaps that was why I still clung to my virtue. Influenced by her pious, straitlaced German husband, our Queen set rigid standards for her subjects, and in drawing rooms all over the country young girls blushed modestly at the least suggestion of anything improper. Strict propriety was rampant, in public, on the surface, but in my profession I saw another side. Nevertheless, I was still as virtuous as any well-bred maiden in white organdy and blue sash, despite the worldly wisdom I had had to acquire in order to survive. The girls couldn't understand my attitude, but they respected me for it, particularly as I passed no judgments on their own morals. I was virtuous, but I was no prude. One couldn't be in the theater.

The theater, I thought wryly. That was hardly the word for it. Fifteen years ago Gerald Prince had been one of the stellar attractions in the London theater, dazzlingly handsome, incredibly magnetic, compared by critics to Garrick, to Kean, but his arrogance, his lack of discipline had brought an early eclipse. Now, at forty, he was still handsome, though inclined to stoutness, and still magnetic enough to play romantic heroes convincingly, but the shabby, tattered touring company he hauled around the provinces was but an echo of what he had once known. I had joined the company at eighteen, and Gerry had assured me we would play London the very next season. Four years had passed. We were in Brighton now, and it was the nearest we had ever come to London.

Brown velvet reticule swinging from my wrist, topaz silk skirts fluttering crisply, I strolled on down the promenade, savoring the salty air, the sound of waves crashing over the shingles, the shrill cry of gulls as they circled overhead. Fine carriages and elegant curricles rumbled up and down the street, and the pavements were crowded with fashionably dressed men and women, men in frock coats and top hats, women in silk and velvet, smiling, laughing, enjoying the sunshine and the aura of vitality that prevailed. It was The Season, and Brighton was at its best, the hotels full to overflowing, the expensive shops doing remarkable business, the plush restaurants invariably crowded. It was rumored that Her Majesty intended to spend a few days at the Royal Pavilion, even though she claimed it was an atrocity and added that Prinny must have been out of his mind when he built it. But what could you

expect from a man who would take up with a creature like Mrs. Fitzherbert, she asked. Whether or not
the Queen decided to grace us with her Royal Presence, Brighton was decidedly festive, sparkling with
gaity, ablaze with color. I felt some of that excite-
ment now, delighted to be here, forgetting many of
the problems that beset me.

Although I had grown accustomed to hardship,
to tension, to constant friction, I could still take
pleasure in life. I could still smile, still experience a
youthful exuberance as I did now. I could still believe that things would get better. I hadn't lost hope,
and I hadn't become cynical. Not quite. Four years
ago, when my parents died in the influenza epi-
demic, leaving me destitute, I had made my decision, and I didn't regret it. Not entirely. As the
daughter of a country squire, brought up in a ramshackle though comfortable old house and given an
exceptional education, there were two choices left
open to me when I discovered that all the money
was gone, that the house and all its furnishings
would have to be sold to pay off my father's debts: I
could become a governess, or I could marry one of
the dull, pleasant young men eager to rush to my
rescue. I detested the idea of going into service, and
I detested the idea of marrying Stephen or John or
Reggie just for security, without love. I was young
and impetuous and eager to savor life to the fullest,
and I saw no reason why I should have to make
either choice.

At that genteel, much-too-expensive school I
had attended from twelve to seventeen, I had ex-
celled at amateur dramatics. Both Misses Penn-
ifords had adored putting on plays, and I had always been given the leading roles. I was good, very,
very good, even the other girls admitted that, and

they said it was a shame the stage was such a wicked place, so improper. If it weren't, they claimed, I could become a great actress. I was as scandalized as they were at such an idea, but when my parents were dead, when the house and all that lovely old furniture was about to go on the block in public auction, I couldn't have cared less about scandal. The Gerald Prince Touring Company was playing an engagement in York. I went to the theater. After the performance I went backstage. I was interviewed by the great man himself. He agreed to audition me. When, five days later, the company left town and I left with them, friends and neighbors were as horrified as any of those giggling schoolgirls would have been. Jennifer Randall had been a respectable young woman, an ornament in York social circles, admired by one and all. Now, I felt sure, Jennifer Randall was a name mentioned only in shocked whispers after the servants had left the room. I would never be a great actress. I had no illusions about that. I had been a gifted amateur. I was a competent professional, competent enough to climb from dress parts to ingenue roles to Gerald Prince's leading lady, a somewhat dubious honor. I might shine in his shabby troup, but in the real theater in London I would have quickly sunk into oblivion. I had come a long way since that day backstage in York, I thought, watching a small boy in a blue suit frolicking on the beach with his brown and white terrier. My salary had increased in proportion with my roles, and this in itself was remarkable, for Gerald Prince was not a man celebrated for his generosity. I might have to mend my own costumes and do my own hair styling, but five pounds a month was an enormous sum.

I was saving almost all of it. There were a number of expenses, but the extra money I earned sewing for the girls usually took care of them. I loved to sew, was extremely adept at it, and while the other girls were out on the town with their gentlemen friends, dancing, drinking champagne and eating oysters, I could usually be found in my hotel room, mending a pair of tights for Chloe, making a velvet gown for Annabel, trimming a bonnet for Louise. Soon—two more years? Three?—I would have enough put away to open my own modest dress shop in London. It was something I longed to do, one of the reasons I was able to endure the backstage squabbles, the strain of too many performances, the privations of dusty third-class railroad carriages and fourth-class hotel rooms in dismal little towns.

Two more years, I thought, and then I can give this all up. If only I can keep Gerry at bay.

Gerald Prince was a ladies' man. Most of the girls found him both seductive and fascinating and were delighted to share his bed, and, sensing my abhorrence of such conduct, he had been content to carry on a mild, jocular flirtation with me, never pressing for more. It was only recently that he had grown more persistent, more determined. The roles we were playing had something to do with it. *Lucrezia Borgia* was the most daring production Prince had ever attempted. I played Lucrezia, and he was Cesare. There was a violent, passionate love scene in the fourth act. Of late he had played it for real, seizing me brutally, leaving me bruised and shaken after the curtain fell. He had taken to lingering in my dressing room, too, lounging against the wall with arms folded over his chest, those magnetic brown eyes with their heavy lids never leaving me as he made idle chitchat in his husky voice.

We were doing *Lucrezia Borgia* again tonight. I dreaded it. The play never failed to bring out the worst in my employer. Gerry had left me alone for four years, content to dally with the merry, chattering creatures who gladly made themselves available. He was bored with them now. Now he wanted something more challenging. Everyone in the company was aware of it. Some of the men were even betting on whether or not he would succeed. I prayed he would find someone else to amuse him. I prayed we would drop the Borgia play from our repertory and go back to drawing room comedies and melodrama. Gerald Prince could dismiss me at a moment's notice. I had seen him dismiss others without the least qualm. I needed my job. I needed those five pounds a month.

Leaving the promenade, I strolled up one of the side streets and soon found myself across the street from the Royal Pavilion. Standing beneath a leafy shade tree, I stared at it. With its turrets and domes and oriental windows, its ornate pillars and colorful gardens, it was like something out of an Arabian Nights adventure, a pleasure palace unlike any other in all of England. The interior, I had heard, was even more bizarre and exotic, all done in Chinese style with fabulous colored glass chandeliers and handpainted wallpaper. Queen Victoria's room, however, was more modest, as prim and decorous as the lady herself, done in shades of lavender, blue and white with none of the oriental gimcrackery she considered so vulgar. Many a scandal had exploded within those walls while Prinny and his fellow rakes drank and gambled and dallied till dawn. Perhaps because I was so worried about the present, I wondered what it would have been like to have lived in those not-so-distant days.

"Miss Randall?"

I turned, startled. The man I had noticed earlier on the promenade was standing beside me, the elegant beaver top hat in his hand. So he had followed me after all. I should have known it.

"Go away," I said. My voice was sharp.

"I want to talk to you," he replied, totally unruffled.

"Nothing you could say would possibly interest me."

"You're wrong," he drawled.

"Shall I summon a Bobby?"

He shook his head slowly, watching me with those vivid blue eyes. He was tall, over six feet, with a superb, muscular build. His brown leather knee boots were polished to a high sheen. His tightly fitting tan trousers and matching frock coat were obviously the work of a master tailor, and the white and brown striped satin waistcoat was the latest word in fashion, as was the black silk ascot. He was a gentleman, I could tell that from his beautifully modulated voice and superior manner, but to my eyes he was no better than the robust young students and flashy businessmen who thought any woman on the stage was easy prey. I stared at him haughtily, ready to demolish him with my tongue. He smiled, as though anticipating it. A lock of dark blond hair had tumbled over his forehead.

"I suppose you've admired me from afar," I said peevishly.

He shook his head again. "I saw you last night for the first time. A most inferior performance, I thought. The second act—you threw away your best lines. You let Prince upstage you in every scene. Any actress worth her salt would have put him in his place."

"You're a critic, I take it?"

"I rarely go to the theater," he replied. "My name is Edward Baker, Miss Randall. I have an interesting proposition to make—"

"I've had a number of propositions, Mr. Baker, and none of them have been interesting. You're wasting your time."

"I think not," he said.

He continued to stare at me, completely at ease even though he could see me bristle. He was in his early thirties, I judged, and he was incredibly handsome. The wide, curling mouth was both sensual and cruel, and the dark brows were decidedly unusual, one almost straight, the other arching, giving him a roguish, inquisitive look. There was an arrogance about him, a certain aloof quality that made a striking contrast to the potent virility. Irresistible to women, I thought, and vastly experienced. Obviously wealthy, too. Any of the girls would have been immediately enthralled, delighted to have been accosted by him like this, yet I felt nothing but irritation. Still, there was something different about him. I couldn't decide what it was, but I sensed it immediately. He was interested in me, and the interest wasn't entirely physical.

"Did you get the roses?" he asked idly.

"So you're the one who sent them," I said.

"A token of my esteem."

"Even though I gave a wretched performance?"

"Even though you gave a wretched performance," he agreed.

"You're terribly insolent, Mr. Baker."

"It's one of my more attractive qualities."

"I suppose you expect me to thank you for the roses."

"Not especially."

"One of the girls, Sally, also received a bouquet of roses last night. There was a diamond bracelet attached to hers."

"You feel you should have received a bracelet, too?"

"Not at all," I said icily, "I merely wanted to point out that sending me a dozen long-stemmed red roses gives you no right whatsoever to approach me in this—in this insufferable manner."

"Most women enjoy being approached by me," he said lazily.

"I don't doubt that. I'm not 'most women,' though. I'm an actress, Mr. Baker. I'm not a prostitute. I perform on the stage—exclusively."

The wide mouth lifted at one corner in a sardonic grin, and the vivid blue eyes were amused. There was a cold, steely quality about the man that was strangely attractive. His serene composure, his quiet, silken voice merely emphasized it. Edward Baker, elegantly, almost foppishly dressed, calm, confident, seemed, because of this, far more masculine than the more aggressive, robust types who swaggered and flaunted their virility. I was attracted to him, in spite of myself, and he was perfectly aware of it. That irritated me all the more.

"I had a reason for approaching you, Miss Randall."

"I'm certain of *that*," I snapped.

"You're intrigued. Admit it."

"Mr. Baker, I—"

He scowled, his features suddenly hard, the blue eyes cold.

"Enough!" he said sharply. "I intend to talk to you. I'm wearied by all this banter."

"If you think—"

"I think you'll listen to me!"

"You're mistaken about that!" I retorted.

I started to move away. He seized my wrist. His fingers wrapped around it like tight steel bands, and when I tried to pull away they tightened even more. I winced. He was hurting me. He knew it. He was a man used to having his own way, a man who would brook no opposition. There was cruelty in that handsome face, and I sensed that Edward Baker was totally without scruples. Sapphire blue eyes icy cold, features impassive, he gave my wrist a savage twist. I had to bite my lip to keep from crying out.

"There's no reason for you to be so skittish," he said, and again the voice was calm, silken. "I have no intentions of raping you here in broad daylight. I have no designs on you whatsoever, Miss Randall. I want to discuss a business proposition, and, by God, I shall, whether you like it or not. Come—"

He moved briskly toward the small park at the end of the street, still holding on to my wrist, and I could do nothing but stumble along after him, tottering on my high heels. My skirts billowed in the breeze. The ostrich plumes waved. I had never been so humiliated in my life, my anger mounting with each second that passed. Reaching the park, he pulled me over to a small gray wooden bench in front of a clump of rhododendron bushes abloom with brilliant purple and purple-red blossoms. He shoved me unceremoniously onto the bench, and, seeing the expression on his face as he stood in front of me, I didn't dare attempt to get back up. No man had ever intimidated me before. This one did.

"Now," he said, "we'll talk."

"You must be very pleased with yourself," I told him. "Terrorizing helpless women—"

"Certain cases call for stronger measures than

others," he replied in that smooth voice. "You're a very stubborn young woman, Miss Randall. I'm not accustomed to meeting such determined opposition."

"You're accustomed to having your own way."

"Naturally," he said.

"If I were a man, Mr. Baker—"

"If you were a man, Miss Randall, I'd probably have murdered you for the insolence you've shown. As is, I've had to curb a terribly powerful urge to throttle you with my bare hands. I might yet, if you don't stop babbling on like the hysterical schoolgirl you most assuredly are not. Are you going to behave, or shall we fight some more?"

I didn't deign to answer. I was on the verge of tears, and the mere thought of displaying such weakness in front of him was appalling. My chin held high, I gazed across the street at the pavilion, fighting back the tears. Ordinarily I was strong and self-reliant, hard, even, because I'd had to be for the past four years, but this man made me feel weak and vulnerable. He made me terribly conscious of being a woman. He stood two or three feet away from the bench, legs spread wide, arms folded across his chest. The black silk ascot rustled against his throat. Locks of dark blond hair fell across his brow.

"You make five pounds a month," he said.

"How did you know that?"

"I know everything I need to know about you, Miss Randall. You're a competent actress, well worth that salary, but you're worried about your job. You hope to open a dress shop in London. You're saving toward that goal. Recently there's been a certain amount of tension. It seems Gerald Prince has suddenly developed an interest in you, and Prince is another man accustomed to having his own way. If foiled, he's been known to take severe measures. If you continue to reject his suit, you might well find yourself out of work."

"You—you've been talking to members of the company."

"Never mind that. Am I correct?"

"I see no reason why I should confirm or deny anything you might—"

"I'm correct," he continued. "You're in a rather ticklish situation. After observing your conduct this afternoon, I believe I'm safe in assuming that you *will* continue to reject his suit. That means dismissal —tomorrow, next week, next month, whenever Prince finally sees the futility of his pursuit."

"I'm perfectly capable of taking care of myself, Mr. Baker."

"I disagree, Miss Randall. You are, alas, a woman, and a damnably attractive one at that. Your reputation went up in flames the moment you left York with the company. No respectable man would marry you after you've been on the stage—sad but true in this age of ours. Nor could you find employment as a governess. You've saved enough to keep you for a while, but as soon as that money is gone—" He shook his head, making a slight gesture that somehow managed to describe imminent doom.

"How could that possibly concern *you?*"

"Under other circumstances, it wouldn't concern me at all. I'm not a bleeding heart. I couldn't care less about the suffering masses. The plight of the poor, the slum dwellers, the downtrodden and exploited factory workers—let Mr. Dickens and his ilk bleed for them. I haven't the slightest interest. Quite frankly, I find the victims of society a tedious bore. I'm interested in your own plight because I can make use of it. If that weren't the case, you could go to hell in a carriage and I wouldn't lift a hand to help you."

"Your frankness is overwhelming."

"It's another of my more attractive qualities."

"I've never met a man so—so—"

"Dastardly?" he suggested.

"Totally ruthless!" I snapped. "You seem to take pride in it."

"Alas, you're right," he said, apparently downcast. "I have very few of the redeeming virtues, but one must accept oneself as one is, and I, it seems, am a thorough cad. You agree with me. I can see it in your eyes. Cad I am, but at least I don't pretend to be a saint. Hypocrisy is one of the few bad traits I don't possess."

He spoke with gentle mockery, painting himself as a blackhearted villain, unfeeling, unscrupulous, but I wondered if that was entirely the case. He was cold and selfish and insufferably arrogant, but I was sure there was more to the man than met the eye. Even though I loathed him, even though I longed to fly at his face with nails unsheathed, I couldn't help but be fascinated, and I was extremely eager to hear about the 'business proposition' he had in mind. However, I would have gone to the stake before letting him suspect it. Chin still haughtily tilted, I tried to maintain a frigid dignity.

Edward Baker gazed at me thoughtfully.

"You make five pounds a month, Miss Randall," he said. "I'm willing to pay you five hundred pounds for one brief engagement."

"I can't be bought, Mr. Baker."

"I don't wish to buy *you*. I wish to buy your skills as an actress."

"You want me to—to perform?"

He nodded slowly, studying my reactions. Those peculiar eyebrows, one so straight, the other arching wickedly, gave his countenance a decidedly satanic cast, and Satan himself could hardly have been more devastatingly handsome. Edward Baker was unlike any man I had ever met. I was frightened, and intrigued. I felt emotions I had never felt before, and I wasn't at all sure what they signified.

"In a theater?" I asked.

"No. I want you to pretend to be my wife for a month or so—six weeks at the most."

"Your—your wife?"

Again he nodded. "It would be simple enough. I would introduce you as Mrs. Baker, and you would maintain the role only as long as necessary. It would be a role—nothing more. You would dress the part and act the part, displaying a modest, subservient affection toward me whenever anyone happened to be around. In private, you could hate me all you liked. I would make no physical demands on you, I assure you of that."

"This is—incredible," I said, dignity vanishing. "I've never heard anything so preposterous in my life!"

"There's nothing preposterous about it," he continued smoothly. "Let me explain further. I have an uncle, you see, and he is very rich. Very ill, too. He has only two male heirs, myself and a certain cousin of mine. He intends to leave his estate to one or the other of us. My cousin is a sullen brute, moody, temperamental, thoroughly unworthy, but, oddly enough, my uncle feels I am even more unworthy of the inheritance. Fortunately, he hasn't yet drawn up his will. Time and again he's told me that I need the influence of a good woman, that a suitable marriage would be the making of me. As you may have surmised, I'm not at all inclined to marry just to please him, so—"

"So you want to deceive him," I interrupted. "You want to make him believe you're married, and when he makes the will—"

"Precisely," Edward Baker said.

"A very clever idea."

"I think so, yes."

"Exactly the sort of thing a man like you would think of. You'd have no scruples about deceiving a sick old man."

"None at all," he assured me.

"What made you select me for the part, Mr. Baker?"

"Because, my dear, you were brought up as a gentlewoman. Despite your rather sordid surroundings, you have class, breeding. It shines through, even when you're playing a Cockney tart as you were in that deplorable drama I witnessed last night. It's a quality no actress could simulate unless she had a background similar to yours. You wouldn't have to act, really. You could discuss literature, music, the arts with perfect ease, and you could do needlepoint, pour tea properly—you could be the young woman you would normally have been had fate not intervened four years ago."

"You *do* know a lot about me, don't you?"

"As I said before, I know everything I need to know about you."

"A pity you wasted all that effort, Mr. Baker."

"Then you refuse the offer, I take it?"

"Nothing on earth could induce me to consider it."

Edward Baker smiled to himself, as though he knew better. He stepped aside as I stood up. I brushed my topaz silk skirts. I adjusted the tilt of the wide-brimmed tan straw hat adorned with brown and white plumes. The smile still flickered on his lips. As I started to leave, he made a mock bow, one arm folded across his waist, the other outstretched. It was a parody of courtly manners. I wanted to slap his face.

"Pleased to have made your acquaintance, Miss Randall."

"The pleasure's not mutual, I assure you."

"No? Pity. You and I would have been good together."

I moved across the grass toward the pavement.

"Oh, one other thing—" he said.

I turned, staring at him with cool disdain.

"I'll be here, at this same spot, tomorrow afternoon at two o'clock. Sharp. I'll be waiting. I fully expect you to give my offer more consideration, Miss Randall. I shouldn't be surprised if you decided to accept it after all."

I didn't reply. I moved briskly down the street, away from the pavilion, away from the man with the dark blond hair and magnetic blue eyes. I didn't look back, but I could tell that he was watching me. I had never been so humiliated, never so insulted! My cheeks burned at the thought of his insolence, his unmitigated gall. How dare he suggest I be part of such a wretched intrigue! My anger grew, steadily mounting, but there was another emotion as well.

It was even more disturbing.

Two

IT WAS twenty minutes before time for the curtain to go up, and backstage was in chaos as I stepped through the door that opened from the dingy alley I had just traversed. The stage manager was yelling at the crew who were raising the brilliantly painted backdrop depicting the interior of the Vatican. Girls clad in wrappers, their hair in paper curlers, raced up and down the flimsy metal staircase leading to their attic dressing rooms, and our chief character actor, Donald Hampton, was throwing a tantrum because the robe he wore as Pope Alexander VI had a great tear down one side. Gerry, cheeks flushed, brown eyes venomous, was fiercely admonishing one of the stage hands who had misplaced a prop needed for Act One.

I stepped over ropes, moved past stacks of painted flats that leaned precariously against the damp brick walls. Despite the din, I could hear the orchestra playing beyond the dusty blue velvet curtains and a low buzzing noise that I knew was the audience beginning to arrive. Sally, who was to play Guilia Farnese, was still in the pink satin gown she had worn to dinner, her blond hair in becoming ringlets, and she stood at the foot of the metal stair-case, chatting vivaciously with a tall, slender mid-dle-aged man in gleaming formal tuxedo and a black opera cape lined with white satin that swept the floor. He was the man who had given her the diamond bracelet last night, I knew, and with such an affluent protector on the scene, she wasn't at all perturbed when Gerry left the poor stage hand in a state near nervous collapse and strode angrily over to the staircase, bellowing that it was high time she got into costume. Sally made a face at him, gave her gentleman a peck on the cheek and moved indo-lently up the steps.

It was always like this, always noisy, always frantic, the very air charged with a frenzied excite-ment. I had loved it once. Once I had found it vastly stimulating, and I had been enchanted to be a part of this larger than life world of high color and glit-tering magic, but the magic had long since van-ished. I saw the dust, the dirt, the soiled costumes, and flaking paint, and what I had in the beginning considered artistic temperament I saw now for what it really was: nasty temper, petty jealousy, senseless outbursts over trifling matters. Perhaps it wasn't like this in the real theater, where profes-sional pride and professional ethics took first place, but here in our tatterdemalion company the glamor survived only for those who were snugly ensconced on the other side of the footlights.

"So there you are!" Gerry thundered, storming over to me. "I was beginning to think you wouldn't *get* here!"

"I've never missed a performance yet," I said calmly.

"Don't get cheeky! I've taken all the cheek I can take for one night! That bloody stage hand—" He curled his right hand into a fist, slamming it into his left palm. Gerry was always melodramatic. He never stopped acting, onstage or off.

"Curtain's about to go up," he cried, "and you're just getting here! Acting as insolent as that slut, Sally. *She* hasn't long to last, I don't mind telling you! When we leave for Chester, we'll be short one blond ingenue, mark my words! Thinks she can sass *me*—"

I gave a weary sigh. "I'd better go change, Gerry."

"Tonight is very important!" he continued. "A number of influential men from London'll be in the audience. I understand Richard Mansfield's being difficult again—" he added, rage abating. "They may want to replace him. That could be the reason they're here, Jenny. Mansfield's a pedestrian actor. I'd be superb in that role he's doing at the Drury Lane. More than superb—I'd be magnificent!"

Poor Gerry, I thought. He still clung to his illusions, still believed this touring company was merely a stop-gap in-between grander things. Although his fame had once surpassed even Mansfield's, that eloquent actor currently the darling of London, Gerry would never be asked to replace him. He would never be asked to replace anyone, but he had to believe, he had to posture, he had to bolster up that incredible ego that was still as towering as his talent once had been.

"I really must get to my dressing room—" I began.

"Hold on a minute," he said. His handsome, aging face was petulant, dark eyes glowering, mouth curling at one corner. "I want to know about that chap who came around last night, Jenny."

"What chap?"

"The one who came backstage, after you'd gone. He collared everyone in sight, asked the most impertinent questions about you. Took Laverne off to a restaurant—God knows what she told him! Who is he, Jenny?"

"I haven't the faintest idea," I lied.

"I didn't like his looks, didn't like 'em at all. What's he want to ask all those questions for? What's he got in mind? He comes 'round again tonight, I intend to have the stage manager throw him off the premises." He was watching me closely, his eyes full of suspicion.

"Do that," I said, totally indifferent. "The curtain *is* about to go up, Gerry. I'd best hurry—"

I left him standing there with his legs spread wide, fists resting on his thighs, a majestic figure in his Borgia costume and short golden goatee. Moving down the narrow stairs to the basement, passing the damp brown walls, I stepped into my dressing room. The sofa, dressing table, wardrobe and tall screen took up almost all the floor space, and the room smelled of greasepaint and stale powder, of dampness and soiled, dusty velvet. Gowns hung on pegs. A feather boa was draped across the screen. The roses Edward Baker had sent set on the dressing table in a tall silver vase, their rich red petals already beginning to wilt.

Stepping behind the screen, I took off my street clothes, slipped into a wrap and sat down at the dressing table. I felt unusually low tonight, weary, depressed. Ordinarily I was immune to the tensions backstage, but tonight they seemed to have affected me deeply. The squabbling, the flaring tempers, the confusion: All had taken their toll. Or was I merely deceiving myself? Were they the cause of my mood, or was it something else? I gazed at the roses, touched one of the blooms. Petals shattered and fell on the table like crimson scraps. After leaving him there in the park across the street from the pavilion, I had determined to put all thought of Edward Baker out of my mind. I had gone to my dreary hotel room, and I had taken dinner in the even drearier dining room downstairs, but I hadn't been able to forget him, no matter how I tried.

I remembered his words, the fate he had predicted in such vivid terms. Everything he had said was true. I couldn't deny that. If anything happened and I lost this job, I would indeed be in dire straits. Other ages might admire actors and heap them with honors, but in our own age, with the exception of those rare few like Mansfield who became the playthings of society, people on the stage were considered little better than charlatans and harlots. It would be impossible for me to find a decent job, and the only men who would have anything to do with me would be rogues like Sally's current admirer, middle-aged, married, eager to toy with me for a few months before thrusting me aside for a newer amusement. The money I was saving toward that dress shop wouldn't last long. I frowned, hating Edward Baker for making it so vivid, bringing it so close.

What if Gerry dismissed me? He was bound to do so if I refused to submit. I was on the verge of tears again, and that alarmed me. I hated any sign of weakness in myself. Tears were for those without stamina, without spirit. I wouldn't think about it. I wouldn't! I'd get through tonight, one more day behind me. Tomorrow would come, and I'd get through it, too. I had given up self-pity a long time ago, and I bloody well wouldn't start pitying myself now. Damn Edward Baker!

Peering into the dressing mirror, I studied my face. There were faint shadows about my green eyes, eyes that seemed even darker because of those thick, black lashes, and the skin seemed to be stretched tautly over my high cheekbones. My features were too classic, too cold to be considered beautiful in this age when plump, pink and white prettiness was the mode, and my waving auburn hair gleaming with copper-red highlights was not the favored shade of blond, but I was arresting, if not beautiful, unusual, if not the standard ideal. Tall and slender, my figure elegant instead of full-blown, I lacked the immediate allure of girls like Sally, but men turned to look a second time nevertheless. Edward Baker had looked, and he had liked what he had seen.

What a strange, enigmatic man, I thought, applying a light coral pink salve on my lips. Was he really as cruel, as ruthless as he seemed, or was that merely a façade? I smoothed soft mauve-gray shadow over my lids, then thickened my lashes with mascara. He was smooth, poised, thoroughly composed, but one sensed a cold, savage quality just beneath the surface. I remembered the way he had twisted my wrist, his blue eyes frosty, features impassive. A dangerous man, I told myself, and yet he had something that seemed to draw one to him, made one long for just that sort of danger. I supposed there were many men like that, but I had never encountered one before. It was just as well that I'd never see him again. Any kind of affiliation with a man like Edward Baker would only bring disaster.

I looked up as Laverne stepped into the room, resplendent in the dark green velvet dress embroidered with gold that she wore as Vanozza dei Catanei, Pope Alexander's mistress. Artificial rubies at throat and wrists clattered as she moved, and I noticed that her long golden wig was slightly askew. There was an unmistakable odor of gin, and her fleshy cheeks were much too pink. Laverne was a plump, cozy soul, forty-five years old, with only the pathetic remnants of what had once been great beauty. Generous, ever ready to open her heart or her pocketbook, she was sentimental, bawdy, garrulous and cheerful, my closest friend in the company. She loved gossip almost as much as gin, and her attitude toward me was that of a clucking mother hen who loved to fuss over her chick.

"Ten minutes to curtain and you're not even in costume," she scolded, plopping down onto the sofa. "You'd better get a *move* on, ducky."

"You sound like Gerry."

"Lord, is *he* in a state tonight! Raising hell right and left. Thinks them gents from London come to see him, he does. La! What a fool! Gerald Prince might still stir the hearts of middle-aged matrons, but they'd laugh 'im off the stage in London! You look a bit peaked tonight, luv."

"I have a headache."

"Worried about Gerry?"

"Not particularly."

"Think he'll come round to your dressing room again tonight?"

"I—I don't know."

"Bastards! All of 'em! Never was a man born worth the powder it'd take to blow 'im up. Gerald Prince is the worst of the lot. Why can't he be satisfied with those silly tarts chattering up in their attic dressing rooms? Jenny, luv, what are you going to *do?*"

"I don't know," I said calmly.

"Any other girl, she'd shrug 'er shoulders and give in for the sake of 'er job. I mean, what's another quick tumble more or less? But you, you're different. That's why he *wants* you. Lord, if I wudn't so worried about my own job I'd give 'im a piece of my mind, tell 'im off good and proper, I would, but he's my boss. He pays my wages. This company ain't so much, luv, but it's the only security I got."

"I can fight my own battles, Laverne."

"I wonder, ducky. I really do. You got breeding, you got principles, but where're they gonna get you? All them swells you turned down—" Laverne shook her head, fingering the chunky ruby necklace. "This ain't no life for a lass like you, God's truth. Both of us know that. If only you had enough saved to open that dress shop—"

"I'll manage somehow." My voice was crisp.

"I worry about you sometimes. I couldn't love you more if you was my own daughter, you know that, ducky, but sometimes I worry. You're hard, Jenny. You're tough. You've had to be, true, you've had to fight every step of the way, but sometimes I'm afraid you'll grow even harder. When I think of the innocent young sprig you was when you joined the company—it breaks my poor heart."

"Innocent young sprigs have a very poor chance of surviving."

"I know, ducky," she said forlornly. "More's the pity."

I stepped behind the screen and began to change into the sky-blue velvet gown I wore in the first act. Embroidered with silver and pearls, it had a formfitting bodice and wide, puffed sleeves slashed with silver, a magnificent garment just beginning to show signs of wear and tear. Laverne shook her head again as I moved around the screen to stand in front of the mirror.

"A vision of loveliness, God's truth," she said. "One of these days some man is gonna be mighty lucky."

I smoothed the material over my thighs. "Think so?" I asked idly.

"That gent last night—he was very interested in you, luv. He took me out to a proper restaurant full of swells, just like I was as respectable as anyone else, fed me roast duck in orange sauce, kept refilling my wine glass. All those waiters hovering around! I wudn't half-pleased, I don't mind sayin' so."

"I'm glad you enjoyed yourself."

"Oh, I knew what 'e was after, all right. Wudn't interested in *me*, not by a long chalk. He wanted to know everything about you, ducky, kept askin' the most personal questions. I got a mite tipsy, probably talked too much, but he was so charmin'. A handsome brute, too, that one, though a mite too chilly and reserved."

"I'm not really interested in Edward Baker, Laverne."

"You've *met* him, then?" she exclaimed.

"I've met him."

"Lord, ducky, and you never said a word! Just like you to let me babble on like that. A gent like him could do a lot for you, luv. He's got to be rich with them clothes 'e was wearin', and—"

"Curtain!" the stage manager bellowed.

"*Already?*" Laverne complained, disappointed at having to give up such a fascinating subject. "I'll just have time to dart into my dressing room for a quick nip. Is my wig all right? Lord, these talky historical epics! They'll be the death of me yet—"

I found it difficult to concentrate on the performance. My head still ached, and my mind was on other things. Fortunately, for the first three acts I had little to do but stand around and look beautiful and innocent as Gerry and Donald Hampton, as Cesare and Pope Alexander, plotted intrigues and planned murders, each striving to outdo the other in histrionics. I had one major scene in the third act when, six months pregnant and wearing a flowing black gown that failed to conceal it, I stood before the assembly of purple robed cardinals and claimed to be *virgo intacta* so that the marriage to my first husband could be annulled. It was the last act I dreaded. In the climactic scene, Cesare, driven out of his senses with incestuous lust, finally declares himself to Lucrezia who, in this play at least, is more sinned against than sinning and attempts to ward off his advances. It was always difficult to play, even more so now that Gerry was striving for such total realism.

The third act ended. The curtain fell. I went to my dressing room and made my costume change, replacing the black gown for one of white velvet embroidered with gold. I felt lifeless, moving as though in a trance. It was going to be worse than ever. I could tell that. Gerry had had that look of anticipation in his eyes all during the first three acts, and in our scenes together he had been more fervent than usual, barely repressing that surging desire, touching me, speaking in a husky voice. The audience was thrilled, stunned into shocked silence, anticipating the final confrontation as eagerly as Gerald Prince himself.

Why? I asked myself as I made my way backstage. Why does it have to be this way? I had worked so hard, and now everything I had worked for was about to be destroyed because of one man who refused to take no for an answer. I stood in the wings, holding onto a rope as I watched the stage hands changing the sets. I could hear the audience beyond the curtain chattering and laughing gaily. A cold rage welled up inside. It wasn't fair. Damn Gerald Prince! Laverne was right. All men were bastards, and women were their victims.

"Great house tonight," Gerry said, strolling up to join me. "They're loving every minute of it."

I didn't answer. The backdrop was up. The furniture was in place. The stage hands were applying the finishing touches.

"I'd like you to try to put a little more into the last scene tonight, Jenny," he remarked casually. "You've been holding back—I've noticed that the last few times we've played it. This kind of thing doesn't work unless you give it all you've got. It's not drawing room comedy, you know."

"I know," I said stiffly.

"Try to loosen up a bit, will you? You've been like a zombie all evening. The leading lady has a certain responsibility to her audience, and you've definitely been holding back. I'd hate to have to re-place you."

"Is that a threat, Gerry?"

"A threat?" He was the picture of surprised in-nocence. "Of course not, luv, of course not, but you must understand that, as head of the company, I have certain responsibilities, too, and can afford to keep only the best people on the payroll. Keep that in mind, Jenny luv."

The curtain rose. Donald Hampton was pacing about in Papal robes, a fierce expression on his face as he awaited the arrival of his son. Gerald Prince swaggered onstage, looking splendid in black silk

tights and black velvet doublet embroidered with
silver and pearls, the wide sleeves slashed with red
satin panels. He and Donald played their scene, and
then Laverne tottered onstage as Vannozza, tipsily
pleading with her son to abstain from his unnatural
desires. Her wig was still askew. She forgot several
of her lines. Gerry was seething. From where I
stood, I could see his nostrils flaring. Laverne made
her exit, and he was alone on stage, delivering his
impassioned soliloquy.

I heard my cue. I made my entrance. The footlights seemed brighter than ever, flickering in a
smoky half circle. I could smell the oil burn. I could
see the great mass of upturned faces like miniature
half moons in the darkened auditorium. I forgot the
unpleasant smell. I forgot the audience. I was a professional actress, and I would do my best no matter
what personal stress I might be under. Jenny Randall and her problems vanished. I became the tragic
Lucrezia, her beloved second husband brutally murdered by her insanely jealous brother, torn between
the hatred she felt for that brother and the unnatural love equally as strong. As Lucrezia, I listened to
my brother's declaration of passion. I shook my
head, I wept, and when he seized me, I fought,
breaking away from him.

"No, Cesare!" I cried. "It can't be—"

"It *must* be," he said with rumbling menace.

The audience was hushed, taut with suspense,
waiting for that final, shocking kiss that brought the
curtain down. Weeping, I stood beside the scarlet
sofa, watching my brother approach. He stopped.
He leered. He stroked the short golden goatee.
Strong, majestic, he was the very incarnation of
cruelty and vice. When he crushed me to him for the
last time, I was to yield and melt against him as the

curtain fell. Shoulders rolling, lips curled in an evil sneer, Cesare approached, and suddenly I rebelled. Something inside snapped. I was no longer Lucrezia, I was Jenny, and the man in the magnificent costume was no longer Cesare Borgia, he was merely a man who filled me with loathing. He stood in front of me, so near I could feel the heat of his body.

"Relax!" Gerry whispered angrily.

He stroked my cheek with his fingertips. Suspense mounted. The whole house was silent, not a paper rustling, not a soul stirring. Looking over Gerry's shoulder, I could see half of the company watching from the wings, Sally, Chloe, Donald Hampton, Laverne with a worried look on her face. All were aware of the real-life conflict so grippingly illustrated here in this scene. All were eager to see what the two of us would do. Gerry touched my hair, winding one of the coppery locks around his finger. He was breathing heavily. Seething with rebellion, as rigid as a statue, I looked up at him. His handsome, middle-aged face was beginning to sag a bit. The cruel smile still curled on his lips. His eyes were filled with a lust he didn't have to simulate.

"The time has come, my fair one," he said in a powerful voice.

"Don't touch me!" My own voice was stony.

Gerry started. Those words weren't in the script. Momentarily flustered, he frowned, completely at a loss, and then he threw back his head and gave a loud, rumbling laugh. He cut the laugh short. He took a deep breath. He reached for me. I drew back my hand and slammed it across his face with all the force I could muster. There was a resounding smack, and my palm stung fiercely. Everything seemed to be shimmering with haze. I saw the pink hand print beginning to burn on his cheek. I heard the loud rattle of the curtain coming down. I was moving rapidly across the stage, past the group in the wings, and there was a thundering noise that I realized must be applause.

Thoroughly shaken, trembling, I reached my dressing room. I closed the door behind me and stood there for several moments, leaning against it. My heart was beating rapidly, and the air still seemed to be filled with shimmering haze. Gradually, it cleared. Composure returned, and I was filled with a strange, icy calm. It was over now, and I didn't care. I simply didn't care. I took off the white velvet gown and hung it on a peg. I removed the makeup and washed my face with cold water. In the mirror, my face was hard. It might have been chiseled from stone. My green eyes were flashing. Calmly, I brushed my long auburn hair. I was standing behind the screen, wearing only my petticoat, when the door opened and Gerry sauntered into the room.

I expected him to be seething with anger. He wasn't. He was as cool, as composed as I was myself. A faint half smile played on his lips. He was still wearing the elaborate costume of Cesare Borgia.

"You didn't take your curtain calls," he said casually.

"No."

"There were seven," he told me. "The audience loved it. You gave our little play a—uh—somewhat different ending, but fortunately few of them were aware of it."

"Indeed?"

"It could have been disastrous, of course. For your sake I'm glad it wasn't. You've been under a great deal of stress lately, Jenny. Something has been bothering you. You didn't know what you were doing tonight—I understand that. I've decided to forgive you."

"That's generous of you, Gerry."

"Oh, I can be exceedingly generous," he replied.

"I don't doubt that."

I had pulled on my brown linen dress. Reaching behind me, I fastened it up. Gerry was watching me, a thoughtful look in his eyes as he stroked the Borgia goatee. Calmly, I moved around the screen and sat down on the dressing stool to put on my slippers. Skirts rustled crisply as I did so. Ignoring him, I buckled the slippers and stood up.

"This play," he said, "it demands a—uh—certain experience. You're uncomfortable in the role, and that's because you lack the experience that would enable you to fully understand it. I'm aware of that, and that's why I've decided to overlook your —peculiar conduct tonight."

I didn't reply. Opening the wardrobe, I took out my brown velvet reticule and the dark golden shawl I had crocheted myself.

"I could give you that experience, Jenny."

"I'm sure you could."

"I've had my eye on you for some time now."

"I'm fully aware of that."

"The other girls—they're shallow, frivolous, a waste of time. I realize that now. For four years I've been a blind fool, expending all my energy trying to make something of greedy, foolish little hoydens while all the time you were right there, waiting."

"Waiting?" I said.

He ignored the question. "You're different, Jenny. You have an indefinable quality—there's something noble in your makeup. You and I would make a smashing team. Together—why, we could scale the heights.''

"Do you really think so?''

"I'm certain of it,'' he said earnestly.

There was an expectant look on his face. Gerald Prince was a petty tyrant, accustomed to having everything his own way. The other girls had succumbed willingly enough, and he simply couldn't grasp the fact that I might not succumb as well with certain dismissal in store if I didn't. I gazed at the man standing before me, his fame a thing of the past, his good looks fast fading, his career on the downhill slide, and I no longer felt any anger. I felt only pity.

"I'm sorry, Gerry.''

"You mean—'' He looked stunned.

"The answer is no.''

"You ungrateful little—you can't—''

"Oh, but I can,'' I said calmly. I wrapped the dark gold shawl around my arms and picked up my reticule. "I'll save you the trouble of dismissing me. I quit. As of now. I have half a month's wages due. I'll send for them. Goodbye, Gerry. It's been an interesting four years.''

He was incredulous. His cheeks flushed. He started to say something, but before he could get the words out I left, closing the door behind me. I went up the narrow steps and crossed the deserted stage. I could hear the merry chatter of the girls drifting down from their dressing rooms. There would be no fond farewells. I would see Laverne at the hotel, and she would be horrified, yet she would understand. As I left the theater I felt no regrets.

I felt, instead, a curious exhilaration.

At one forty-five the next afternoon my bags were packed. I left them with the hotel clerk, telling him I would send for them before the day was over. Wearing my best maroon and black striped frock, pulling on a pair of black silk gloves, I stepped out into the bright afternoon sunlight. I was filled with a sense of adventure. Laverne had burst into tears when I told her what I had done. Thoroughly crushed, she had sobbed and dabbed at her eyes with a handkerchief, claiming she'd never see me again, predicting I would starve. I promised her I would write. I assured her that I had no intentions of starving. I knew what I had to do, and any reservations I might have would simply have to be thrust aside.

I walked briskly down the promenade. The water sparkled with silvery spangles of light, washing over the shingles in glittering waves. Gulls circled overhead, filling the air with their raucous cries. Fine carriages clattered down the street. The ornate white brick hotels with their marble porticoes rose along the front in majestic splendor. I turned up the side street. Ahead, I could see the turrets and domes of the pavilion rising above the emerald green treetops. I saw the small park. He was standing in front of the rhododendrons, wearing a trim gray suit and a white satin waistcoat embroidered in black. A tall gray top hat was on his head, and one hand gripped a pair of white gloves. He looked cool and aloof. When he turned, he didn't seem at all surprised to see me approaching.

Three

HE JOURNEY by train had been long and tiresome, but Edward Baker showed no signs
of exhaustion. He was as composed, as distant and polite as he had been when we boarded the
train in London early in the morning. When we finally alighted at the station at Mallyn Green, a shiny
black phaeton upholstered in padded blue velvet
had been waiting for us, a servant wearing the dark
blue Mallyn livery perched up on the high front seat,
ready to drive us to the great house two miles from
the village proper. A cart bearing all our luggage
had gone on ahead, and we were on our way to
Mallyncourt now, the two sleek, muscular grays
spanking along at a steady pace down the wide dirt
road. My "husband" sat back with a remote expression, engrossed in his thoughts, ignoring me. He
might have been alone in the carriage.

We had been together for almost two weeks
now, and he was as much of an enigma as ever. We
had left Brighton for London immediately, moving
in to a grand, imposing hotel as man and wife. We
had a plush suite, and I was rather alarmed when I
saw the master bedroom. Edward put my fears to
rest immediately, cooly informing me that he would

sleep in the tiny room ordinarily assigned to mi-lady's abigail. He had done so, taking breakfast with me every morning in the richly appointed sitting room. He sent word of his marriage to his relatives as soon as we were installed in the hotel. I had assumed we would be departing in a day or so, but that wasn't the case. Edward had business to attend to in the city, and I must have a complete new wardrobe. Jenny Randall's clothes were all very well for an actress in a fourth-rate touring company, but they would never do for the wife of Edward Baker.

My days were spent in shops and at dressmaking establishments, and our suite was soon a chaos of boxes and tissue paper, bolts of material, pins, tape measures, ribbons. Madame DuBois, the Parisian dressmaker, came to fit me herself, marveling at my slender form, my titian red hair, exclaiming that it was a joy to dress such an unusual beauty, declaring she would outdo herself. I was amazed at the quantity of things Edward felt I should have, amazed at their splendor, too. When I mentioned how frightfully expensive all this must be, he told me that the clothes were a necessary investment and added in a bored voice that I would naturally keep everything after our charade was over.

Although he came to pass approval on everything purchased, I saw very little of him during the day, and my evenings were usually spent alone in the suite, admiring my new clothes, reading, writing letters to Laverne. Edward did take me to dine at a few fine restaurants, and one night he took me to see the great Richard Mansfield perform at the Drury Lane, but for the most part he left me to my own devices, apparently bored by my company. He was always polite, true, but that icy reserve was always maintained. I should have been relieved. I wasn't. I wondered if he would be as remote and unfeeling once we arrived at Mallyncourt.

The phaeton rumbled over a particularly nasty rut, and I was thrown against Edward. He put out a hand to steady me. I murmured an apology and settled back on my own side of the seat. Behind the low gray stone walls on either side of the road were rich farmlands, each field enclosed in its own gray wall, making a brilliant patchwork over the rolling hills of emerald, brown, red-brown, gold. I saw small, tidy farmhouses with thatched roofs, chickens scratching in front of the barns, black and white cattle roaming about in the fields beyond. This was a rich agricultural area, I knew, and the Mallyn dairy products were famous all over England.

"Tenant farms," Edward said, observing my interest. "All part of my uncle's estate."

"He must be extremely wealthy."

"Filthy rich," he retorted. "My uncle was the second son, seventeen when his brother inherited Mallyncourt. He shipped out for the orient. He was ambitious and unscrupulous and greedy, worked for the East India Company for a while, went into business for himself at the age of twenty-three. Import-export. By the time he was forty, he was one of the ten wealthiest men in England. His brother, my Uncle Frederick, died without children, and the old rascal inherited Mallyncourt. The place was in a shambles when he took over, the house tumbling down over his head, the farms a steady drain on the estate. He spent almost half his money improving conditions, renovating the house, revitalizing the farms, setting up the dairy. That was twenty years ago. He's more than doubled in income what he sank into it in the beginning. Shrewd old codger, my uncle."

"Is he a bachelor, too?"

"A widower. My Aunt Sarah died when I was a child, and he never remarried. Never had any legitimate heirs, although there're a dozen or more bastards roaming the countryside who bear an embarrassing resemblance to my uncle. He was a randy one in his day, a real hell raiser. Hasn't changed much, either."

The liveried servant clicked the reins, his back ramrod straight. He couldn't have helped but overhear Edward's remarks, but Edward didn't seem to care. To him, I realized, servants were like so many objects, there to wait on him when needed, to be completely ignored the rest of the time. I had noticed this attitude in London. The people who served us there might as well have been invisible so far as Edward was concerned. I supposed it was the way he had been brought up. No matey chats with the stable boys for him, no friendly words to the parlor maids.

"You make your uncle sound formidable," I remarked.

"He is," Edward replied calmly. "Sly, devious, wily, hot-tempered, headstrong, as vindictive and sharp-tongued as a fish wife. He's seventy now, still a tyrant, still delights in terrorizing the household from his sick bed."

"I don't imagine he terrorizes you."

"Not at all. I caught on to his tricks before I put on my first pair of long trousers. Others might cringe and tremble, but I realized that he was nothing but a lonely, disappointed old man who craved attention. I know how to handle him, always have. Unlike Lyman. They're constantly at each other's throats."

"Lyman?"

"My cousin. He lives at Mallyncourt with his wife and daughter, acts as Uncle James' chief bailiff, manages the estate now that the old man is no longer able to do so himself."

"I—I know so little about these people I'm about to meet."

"I suppose I should give you a bit of background," he replied. "After all, a wife would have learned something about the family. Frederick and James had two sisters, Clarissa and Jane. Jane had a grand debut in London. She could have had her pick of the most eligible bachelors of the day. She promptly came back to Mallyncourt and scandalized the countryside by marrying Angus Robb, the son of a tenant farmer, an uncouth lad with whom she had been having an affair prior to her debut. Lyman was the outcome of the match. His parents are both dead now. Uncle James took him in when he was thirteen."

"You were living there at the time?"

"My mother, Clarissa, made a more suitable match. She married a young lieutenant, Jeffery Baker, the wealthy scion of a prominent London family. I was born a year later. My mother died bearing me. My father went away to India where he quickly succumbed to cholera. I was raised at Mallyncourt." He paused, shoving a dark blond lock from his brow. "My uncle never had any legitimate children, but he was saddled with two young nephews early on. He loved to pit us against one another. Still does. That's why he's being so obstinate about the will."

"You and Lyman obviously don't get along," I observed.

"That's an understatement," he replied. His voice was icy. "Lyman is an uncivil brute, churlish, disrespectful, the upstart son of a tenant farmer and a dizzy-headed young trollop who had neither sense nor morals in spite of her family name and respectable upbringing. Lyman and I have always been at odds."

"Is he your age?"

"Three years older. He's thirty-four."

"You mentioned a wife and child—"

"Vanessa is one of the most beautiful women in England," he informed me, "and undoubtedly one of the most depraved. At eighteen she was a professional beauty, the delight of London society, her portrait painted by Whistler, by Millais, by Holman-Hunt. Her background was impeccable, and she could have made a spectacular marriage. She didn't. My cousin went up to London on estate business. They met, and she promptly cast aside all her eligible suitors. Aristocratic women, you'll observe, are frequently attracted to the brusque, brutal type of male. Lyman is as virile and rough as his father was before him, and, like my Aunt Jane, Vanessa considered the world of polite society well lost for such a rugged specimen. They eloped. Lyman brought her back to Mallyncourt, and Lettice was born seven months later. That was ten years ago. Vanessa is twenty-nine now, more beautiful than ever."

"Is the marriage a happy one?"

A thin, sardonic smile curled on his lips. "Hardly that," he said in an emotionless voice. "Her elopement with Lyman was an adventure, a madcap escapade worthy of a spoiled, pampered young beauty, but unfortunately it backfired. She tired of him quickly—that was inevitable—and found herself a prisoner in the country, isolated from the society she had reigned over at one time, with a masterful, dominating husband who refused to let her have her way. Vanessa has been taking her revenge on him for a number of years now—"

He didn't elaborate. It wasn't necessary.

"And the child?" I inquired.

"Lettice is a thin, pale, bitter little thing, prickly and thoroughly antisocial. She keeps to herself, preferring the company of her dolls to that of real people."

"That's terribly sad," I said quietly.

"Don't waste any sympathy on Lettice, my dear. At ten she's already an accomplished shrew. On the rare occasions when she's forced to abandon her dolls and join company she can be utterly scathing. She has no friends, naturally. The other children in the neighborhood detest her."

I was silent, thinking about this strange assortment of people I would soon be acquainted with. We had left the farmlands behind and were now passing through a wooded area, branches joining overhead to make a leafy green canopy through which only a few thin rays of sunlight sifted. Edward's face was in shadow. He sat stiff and erect beside me as the wheels of the phaeton whirled over the hard uneven dirt road, the sound of the horses' hooves echoing with the dense woods on either side.

"It's a rather unusual ménage," Edward remarked, almost as though he were reading my mind, "but you needn't feel intimidated. I'm sure you'll be able to hold your own."

"I wonder about that," I said nervously.

"You're no vapid, timorous maiden, Jennifer. You've got spirit. That's one of the reasons I—er—selected you—" Although he couldn't have cared less what the servants thought, he was careful to avoid saying anything that might have given away our game. The coachman might have been some mechanical robot perched up on the high front seat, but he could hear every word we said.

"I hardly know what's expected of me," I said.

"You're to be a well-bred, obedient wife, and you're to charm my uncle."

"From the way you've described him, that hardly seems possible."

"The old man still has an eye for the ladies," he replied. "He may be on his death bed, but he still appreciates a beautiful woman."

"Does he appreciate Vanessa?" I asked.

"He finds her amusing," Edward said idly.

"I see."

The woods were behind us now. We passed through two tall, weathered brownstone portals, a wrought-iron arch spanning across them with a large, ornate M worked into the center of the design. The road wound around splendid green lawns with tall, majestic trees spreading their boughs, and a few minutes later we passed under the archway of the weathered brown gatehouse elaborately decorated with pinnacles and strapwork. Ahead, beyond the deliberately untidy and multicolored walled front gardens, I could see the house itself. It was a magnificent sight, making a proud silhouette against the darkening sky. The rooftops were adorned with the same pinnacles and elaborate strapwork I had observed on the gatehouse, and the walls, once a soft tan, were now a streaked, mellow brown, the dozens and dozens of windows a gleaming silvery blue that reflected the last rays of light in brilliant sunbursts. I was amazed at its size, its imposing yet strangely unassuming grandeur.

"Queen Elizabeth once stayed here," Edward told me, "and Mary Queen of Scots was, briefly, a

prisoner in the west wing, but I shan't bore you with
the history of the place. There are a number of
books in the library you may consult if you're interested. It's a draughty pile, impossible to heat properly, an aged dinosaur of a house incredibly surviving the centuries and totally incongruous in this day
and age."

"It's—beautiful," I said in an awed voice.

"It has beauty, yes, but it's highly impractical."

"You don't love Mallyncourt?"

"I have no love whatsoever for it," he said,
bored. "If I inherit, I'll sell. There are any number
of wealthy Americans who'd snap it up without a
moment's hesitation."

I found this attitude incredible, but it was in
keeping with his character. Family tradition would
mean nothing to a man like Edward Baker, nor
would he be moved by the historic splendor repre-
sented by a house like Mallyncourt. I wondered idly
what *would* move him. He couldn't be as unfeeling
as he seemed.

"Your uncle must require a whole fleet of servants," I remarked.

He nodded grimly. "There is a butler, a housekeeper, a governess for Lettice, a personal valet for
my uncle, a cook, six footmen, a gaggle of maids,
two gardeners, a coachman, half a dozen or so stable boys, all of whom are fed and maintained by the
Mallyn estate. The butler and housekeeper have
quarters in the basement, as does the cook, the governess has a room in the nursery, and the other
house servants have rooms in the attics. The rest of
them sleep over the stables."

Circling around the exotic, wildly beautiful gardens, the phaeton drew up in front of the wide, flat
steps. Six slender brown columns supported the or-

nate portico, and there were pots of red geraniums on the posts of the graceful balustrade. Edward alighted and helped me down, his face impassive as the coachman drove away toward the stables. The two of us stood in front of the great house, momentarily alone. I was extremely nervous, a prey to all sorts of apprehensions, and Edward noticed it. Some of his remoteness vanished. My nervousness amused him.

"From this moment on, you're my wife," he told me.

"It's not a role I fancy," I said acidly.

"My loving wife, I might add."

"That will be the most difficult part to simulate, I assure you."

"Oh? You find me unlovable?"

"Distinctly!"

"That's because you don't know me," he said lightly. "I've no doubt you'll warm to me in time."

"I shouldn't count on it, Mr. Baker."

"Edward," he reminded me. "You'll play your role nicely."

"I'll try."

"You'll do more than try, my dear. Five hundred pounds are at stake, remember. There will be no slipups. Not only would you lose the five hundred, but you would also incur my wrath. You wouldn't want to do that, Jennifer."

"You don't intimidate me."

"No?"

"Not at all!"

"Try to curtail your venom, Jenny dear. You're in love with me. We had a whirlwind courtship, a simple, private wedding and have just returned from an ecstatic honeymoon. An occasional lovers' quarrel might be in keeping, but certainly not the animosity I currently detect in your eyes." He took my arm, tucked it under his and escorted me up the steps. "You're an actress, luv. The curtain is about to go up."

The great doors opened as if by magic. Two footmen in the Mallyn livery stood back, and the butler approached. Severely dressed in black, he was tall and thin and extremely grand, more aristocratic than the bluest of blue bloods.

"Afternoon, Jeffers," Edward said crisply.

The imposing Jeffers nodded, barely glancing at me. The footmen stood rigidly against the wall, as motionless as statues. I glanced around at the great hall, trying to conceal my awe. It was square in shape, two stories high, and although a gallery ran around three sides on the first story, I saw no staircase. The enormous fireplace was of gray marble, the Mallyn coat of arms worked in moulded and gilt plaster above the mantelpiece. Faded Brussels tapestries depicting hunt scenes in shades of tan, gray, green and indigo hung along three of the stone walls, and the fourth was paneled in dark wood, displaying a collection of pikes, enameled shields and ancient weapons. A huge brass chandelier hung from the ceiling, and though the room was sparsely furnished, the furniture remaining was both lovely and majestic. There was a great chest which, I knew, would have been used as a safe for money and jewels during previous ages. Henry VIII might have dined at that long, narrow table. Ladies in farthingales might have sat on those immense, elaborately carved chairs with their high backs and threadbare crimson velvet seats. The black and white marble floor gleamed.

"My letter arrived?" Edward inquired.

"It arrived two weeks ago," Jeffers replied,

showing neither interest nor surprise. "The west wing apartment has been readied for you and your wife, Master Edward. Your luggage arrived some time ago. Everything has been arranged—satisfactorily, I trust."

"And my uncle?"

"Still in a poor condition, though, I might add, as easily riled as ever—if you'll pardon my saying so. The doctors are quite alarmed. Lord Mallyn *will* demand his bottle of port every night."

Edward smiled, pleased. "I've been away two months, and the old devil hasn't changed a bit. Still hanging on. What did he have to say about my marriage, Jeffers?"

"I shouldn't care to repeat that, sir."

As Edward chuckled to himself, I had the strong and unmistakable impression that someone was staring at me. Looking up, I saw two small hands gripping the railing of the gallery. A thin, childish face peered down at me, the eyes dark and hostile. There was a faint rustle of skirts and then the slender form disappeared through one of the doorways opening onto the gallery. That would be Lettice, I thought.

"Shall I show you to the apartment?" Jeffers inquired.

"That won't be necessary," Edward retorted, suddenly curt. "Come, my dear. I'll take you up. You must be fatigued."

We moved down a long, low-ceilinged hallway with rooms opening off on either side, affording me brief glimpses of more splendor, and eventually arrived at a much wider hallway that extended along the length of the house in back. It was stark, with only a few benches and chairs, and the tapestries here were even older, less splendid, patched in several places. Tall windows looked out over a rolled, emerald green back lawn enclosed by neatly trimmed hedges, and an extremely wide staircase of flat stone steps led up to the first story.

"There're more splendid staircases in both wings," Edward said. "This one was built for the horses."

"Horses?" I was incredulous.

"The early Mallyns were enthusiastic horsemen, had to ride every day, and, English weather being what it is, that wasn't always feasible. The gallery upstairs is one hundred and seventy feet long, fifty feet wide, so they rode there on inclement days, leading the horses up these steps."

"Incredible," I said.

"You needn't look so alarmed. The practice was abandoned over a hundred years ago."

Just as we started up, there was the loud retort of a door slamming at the east end of the hall. Loud, impatient footsteps rang on the bare stone floor. Edward paused, his hand on my elbow. I could see a man striding briskly toward us, slapping the side of his boot with a riding crop. His head was lowered, and he was muttering something to himself, obviously unaware of our presence. Still a few yards away, he looked up and saw us standing there on the second step. He stopped abruptly, startled. Edward laughed softly to himself.

"Cousin," he said, nodding.

"So you've come back!"

"But of course." His voice was gentle, with only a faint hint of mockery in those silken tones. "Let me present my wife. Jennifer, this is Lyman Robb, the esteemed cousin of whom I have spoken so frequently. Lyman, Jennifer—Mrs. Edward Baker."

"How do you do," I said.

Lyman Robb was glaring at his cousin with lowered brows, a thunderous look on his face. He didn't acknowledge my greeting. He barely glanced at me. Never before had I seen such hatred made visible as that that burned in those dark, flashing brown eyes as he stared at Edward. They were murderous eyes, I thought, instinctively moving back a step. Edward's hand held my elbow in an even tighter grip, warning me.

Lyman Robb looked as though he wanted to lunge at his cousin and slash him across the face with his riding crop. With a visible effort, he controlled his rage, though the hatred burned as hotly as ever. Not quite as tall as Edward, he was nevertheless a large, powerfully built man with enormous shoulders, wide chest and lean waist, his legs long and shapely, tightly encased in clinging tan buckskin breeches. His brown boots were splattered with mud, and his thin white cambric shirt, tucked in carelessly at the waist and open at the throat, was sweat stained, the sleeves full and billowing, gathered at the wrists.

I stared at him with a kind of horrified fascination. I had never seen a man so vital, so bursting with life. One could sense the red blood coursing through his veins, and he seemed to seethe with animal vigor. There was a deep cleft in his chin, and his mouth was full, the lips curling savagely at the corners. His nose was Roman, a pugilistic ridge between his dark, arching brows, and with his broad, rather Slavic cheekbones, his wildly unruly black locks and those murderous brown eyes, he looked like some primitive Hun bent on rape and plunder. Robust, aggressively male, smelling of the stables, he was excessively handsome in a crude, rough-hewn fashion. I could understand now why the aristocratic Vanessa had been ready to throw everything else aside to elope with him.

"Your marriage was very timely," he remarked. The words seemed to come rumbling up from his chest. His voice was rough, with none of the refined accent of his cousin's.

"Exceedingly so," Edward replied.

"It was love at first sight," Robb said sarcastically.

"Naturally." Edward's voice was smooth.

Lyman Robb looked at me fully for the first time, taking in every detail of my dress and person. I wanted to shrink back, but Edward was still holding me firmly by the elbow. Both repelled and fascinated, I held my chin high as those smouldering brown eyes studied me. Robb finally looked away, turning his attention back to Edward.

"*She* may not know why you married her, but I do. I know all too well. It's not going to work, Edward."

"That remains to be seen."

"The old man almost had apoplexy when your letter got here. He raged for a full week—the servants were afraid to go near him. You thought you would please him, but the reverse is true. He wanted you to marry, yes, but he fully intended to select your bride himself. You gambled, Edward, and you've lost."

"I doubt that, cousin. You see, he hasn't yet met Jennifer."

Robb gave a short, crude laugh. "If you think she'll win him over, then you're a bigger fool than I thought."

Edward ignored the comment. "Speaking of wives," he said, "where is the lovely Vanessa? I should have thought she'd be on hand to greet her new cousin-in-law."

"I haven't the slightest idea where she might be," Robb replied, and his tone indicated that he hadn't the slightest interest, either. "Perhaps one of the footmen has taken her fancy, or perhaps she's out riding with one of the local gallants who find her so intriguing. Radcliff's son has been spending a lot of time at Mallyncourt, a worthy addition to her throng of suitors. I'm far too busy to keep track of my esteemed wife. I've been working in the fields all day."

"That's more than evident," Edward replied, his fine nostrils giving a barely perceptible sniff.

"My odor offends your delicate sensitivity?" Robb threw back his head and laughed, a rich, full laugh this time. "Forgive me, cousin, and let me apologize to your wife as well. You see," he said, turning to me, "Edward is the aristocrat in the family. He went to Oxford, while I attended a humble agricultural college. He leads the life of a fashionable gentleman, and me, I work, I'm content to toil like the farmer I am to keep the estate in hand. Your husband wears the fine clothes. He has enough polish for both of us—I wouldn't have it any other way."

With that, he strode briskly on down the hall, his shoulders rolling, once again slapping the top of his boot with the riding crop. A moment or so later we heard another door slam loudly. I looked up at Edward. His vivid blue eyes were filled with hatred, icy, controlled, but equally as potent as that I had seen in Lyman's eyes a few moments ago. I sensed that only their uncle's presence had prevented physical violence from exploding between them a long time ago.

After a long, tense moment, Edward mastered his emotions, and when he turned to me again, he was as cool and unruffled as ever.

"Engaging chap," he remarked.

"He's—rather overwhelming."

"Yes, that's quite true. Strangely enough, he's quite popular in the neighborhood. The tenant farmers worship him, perhaps because he's willing to work side by side with them. The local gentry consider him 'the salt of the earth.' As he's Lord Mallyn's nephew, they're more than ready to make excuses for his—uh—rather boorish exterior. I trust you weren't too appalled, my dear."

"I managed to survive the encounter."

That familiar thin smile curled on his lips. "You handled yourself rather nicely. Come," he said, "we'll go on up to the apartment, and after you've rested a spell and changed out of your traveling clothes you can meet the rest of the family."

"I can hardly wait," I said bitterly.

Still smiling, Edward led me up the wide, flat steps.

Four

"THE GREEN, I think," Edward had said nonchalantly, and then he had left me alone in the bedroom, sauntering through the sitting room that connected this room with the other, smaller bedroom. The arrangement, obviously, was to be similar to the one we had had in the hotel. Now, an hour and a half later, rested, refreshed, I could hear him moving about in his bedchamber as I stood in front of the full-length mirror critically examining my reflection.

Even though Edward had told me we dressed for dinner at Mallyncourt, I wondered if this particular garment wasn't a bit too splendid. A rich emerald green satin, it had great puffed sleeves, off the shoulders, and an exceedingly low neckline. The bodice was formfitting, the waist tight, and the skirt made billowing cascades of emerald over starched crinoline petticoats. "No ornaments," he had informed me, and I saw now that he was right. My eyes, surrounded by long, soot-black lashes, were as green as the material, and my rich auburn hair, gleaming with copper-red highlights, fell in abundant waves. Perhaps I wasn't beautiful, but I had never looked more striking.

Edward will be pleased, I thought wryly.

He was to take me to meet Lord Mallyn, and then we were to join the others downstairs for dinner. I wasn't nearly as nervous as I had been earlier. I was fully into my role now, the costume, the setting giving me a confidence that had been lacking as we rode to the house. I was Edward's wife now. Jenny Randall would exist only in those moments when I was offstage, alone, free to indulge in the luxuries of privacy and emotion. As I glanced around the spacious room, it was hard to believe that it wasn't actually a stage set.

The lower half of the twenty-foot walls were paneled with white wainscoting, the upper half with creamy white plaster work with designs picked out in gold leaf. The gilt work was continued on the white ceiling, making circular designs around the crystal chandelier that hung down with hundreds of pendants glittering with violet-blue facets, for all the world like diamonds. The towering bed with its purple velvet hangings embroidered in gold and matching counterpane was fit for a queen, and Edward had casually informed me that Mary, Queen of Scots had slept in it for two weeks when she stopped at Mallyncourt en route from one stately prison to another. A rich blue carpet covered the floor, and there was an immense wardrobe, a dressing table, elegant chairs upholstered in violet. Above the vast white marble fireplace was an alabaster frieze depicting the wooing of Helen. A fire burned merrily, orange-blue flames devouring a stout oak log, and candles shed a warm golden glow from blue and white porcelain wall sconces. There was, I knew, a servant whose sole duty was to attend to the lighting and extinguishing of candles, another who tended the fires.

"Impressed?" Edward inquired.

I turned to find him lounging in the doorway, resplendent in a black broadcloth suit and white satin waistcoat embroidered with dark blue fleurs-de-lis. Although impeccably attired, black leather boots gleaming, sky blue ascot perfect, there was, nevertheless, a certain carelessness that augmented the total effect. He might have been wearing any old thing, as comfortable in this attire as he would have been in frayed hunting jacket and soiled jodhpurs. An errant lock of dark blond hair had tumbled over his brow, and his expression was slightly bored.

"It's an incredible room," I said.

"The carpet's threadbare," he remarked. "The upholstery's faded, and the plaster's beginning to flake. The room is too large to heat properly. There's an icy draught, you'll notice. You mustn't let all this crumbling splendor overawe you, my dear."

"Your wife wouldn't be awed?"

"Not at all. Indifferent, rather."

"Even though Mary, Queen of Scots slept in that bed?"

"It's full of wormholes. Pray the whole thing doesn't collapse on top of you one fine night."

"You have no romance in your soul. None whatsoever."

"I'm probably the least romantic chap you'll ever meet. I'm a realist, my dear."

"And entirely mercenary," I retorted crisply.

Edward Baker made no reply, but I could see he hadn't liked my remark. I was rather pleased about that. For some reason I hoped to goad him out of that aloof, distant poise he maintained. Even anger would be better than his chilly remoteness. He studied me now, lids at half-mast, mouth set in a tight line. I thought he was going to make some cutting comment, but he didn't.

"Come," he said tersely, "the old man will be waiting."

Neither of us spoke as he led me down a narrow hall and then along a much wider one with windows looking out over the front gardens. He held my elbow in a firm grip, a habit that was beginning to irritate me, and his handsome profile might have been sculptured from marble. Nearing the end of the second hall, he stopped, turning to me with a grim expression.

"I think we should set one thing straight," he remarked. His voice was calm though exceedingly chilly. "You're my employee. You were brought here to perform a role. We've had our little verbal spats— I've rather enjoyed them—but henceforth, you'll show respect. Is that understood? Even when we're alone together, you'll show the proper respect."

"The respect due an employer?"

"Precisely."

"And if I don't?"

The question seemed to amuse him. His lips curled in the thin smile I was beginning to know so well. There was something chilling about it, and I felt a slight alarm, almost afraid of him. I managed to conceal it, however, meeting his gaze with one of cool disdain.

"I admire your spirit, my dear, but don't push me too far. The consequences might not be at all pleasant."

"You don't intimidate me."

"You've made a point of telling me that on more than one occasion. Methinks the lady doth protest too much."

"I wish—"

"I know," he said wearily. "You wish you'd never agreed to this. You did agree, Jenny luv, and there's no turning back now. Forget your personal feelings. Do your job like the competent little actress you are, and the reward will be more than ample."

Never before had the folly of my decision been brought home so sharply as it was at that moment. I must have been mad to have accepted his offer, mad to have come here, and I wanted to rush madly down the hall, out of the house, to forget Edward Baker and everything connected with him. I could feel tears welling up inside. I had never felt so alone, so vulnerable. Edward gazed at me with level blue eyes, fully aware of my emotional crisis, calmly waiting for it to subside. I hated him for knowing me so well, hated myself for displaying signs of weakness. For several seconds I seemed to be torn asunder, and then I braced myself, mentally as well as physically. The tears never materialized. I summoned strength from a hard core inside, and when I spoke, my voice was as cool as his own had been.

"Very well, Mr. Baker."

"I wasn't mistaken in you," he replied idly. "I sensed the stuff you were made of. You've got strength—fire. You're going to do a splendid job."

"I'll do my best."

"Your best, I'm sure, will be superb."

"Let's not keep Lord Mallyn waiting any longer."

Opening a door near the end of the hall, Edward ushered me into one of the most bizarre rooms I had ever seen. It was vast, almost barnlike, the walls paneled in varnished golden oak, long yellow silk drapes hanging at the tall windows looking out over the west side of the grounds. Although a fire roared lustily in the immense fireplace, the room was icy cold, and it was filled with an amazing clutter of furniture. Vivid Chinese screens stood behind Regency sofas, Oriental tables of beaten brass beside Chippendale chairs. There were great brass gongs and delicate wind chimes, red lacquer chests, piles of colorfully embroidered pillows. Persian carpets were scattered over the parquet floor, and ornaments jostled one another on every available surface: delicately carved ivory figures, tiny jade idols, lacquered boxes inlaid with mother-of-pearl and semiprecious gems, exquisite Ming vases, small crouching dragons of red and silver. A large golden Buddha with a ruby in its forehead sat complacently beneath one of the windows, and there was a veritable forest of dark green plants in ornate brass urns. The place was incredibly dusty, thick coats of it on all the furniture, balls of it under the sofas and chairs. Half a hundred candles filled the room with brilliant light.

"Mementos of my uncle's travels," Edward said. "He used to be quite a collector."

"What beautiful things—"

"Some are quite valuable, some mere trash. He refuses to let the servants touch them—won't allow the maids in the room. Another of his little eccentricities."

"I can hear every word you're saying! I'm not deaf, Edward! Thought maybe you'd be afraid to show your face—and who's that trollop with you? Red hair! Never liked a woman with red hair! Bring her closer, you scoundrel! Let me get a good look!"

Totally unruffled by this harsh outburst, Edward held my elbow tightly and led me across the room toward a huge bed that might have belonged to an Eastern potentate. It was hung with fraying Oriental tapestries, piled high with colored cushions against which the sharp-faced old man was propped. He wore a crimson silk robe and, incongruously enough, had a patchwork quilt of multicolored squares spread over his legs. The quilt was old, decidedly mothy, and might have been made by some farmer's wife. The table beside the bed was piled high with dirty dishes, bottles, jars, a magpie's nest of papers and magazines and paraphernalia. There was the unmistakable odor of medicine, of old age, and another, stronger odor that was explained when three ancient, decrepit Pekinese scrambled from their nests of bedclothes and filled the air with shrill, agitated barking.

"Silence!" the old man thundered.

The Pekinese whimpered and scurried back under the covers with remarkable alacrity. Lord Mallyn heaved himself up higher against the cushions. His long, scrawny fingers were festooned with rings. He was very thin, his skin like fine old parchment, and his hair, still profuse, was the color of tarnished silver, spilling over his high forehead in unruly, sweat-damp locks. There were deep hollows beneath his high, bony cheekbones. His nose was beaklike, his mouth a thin white slit. He must once have been an exceptionally handsome man, I reflected, but he showed every one of his seventy years now. Nevertheless he was still imposing, would still dominate any gathering without the least effort. His eyes, dark brown, almost black, seemed to snap and smoulder, showing now venom, now amusement, now impatience as he regarded us.

"I see you're as feisty as ever," Edward remarked dryly.

"You expect to find me cringing under the covers like a frightened old woman? You expect me to whimper and whine? You know me better than that,

my boy! When I go, it won't be with a whimper—
it'll be with a bang, the loudest bang you ever heard!
Not that I'm about to go. Far from it! These bloody
doctors are out of their minds, all of 'em! Well, boy,
this is quite a stunt you've pulled! What have you
got to say for yourself?''

"I think my letter said it all," Edward replied,
his voice cool. "I met Jennifer and fell in love with
her. I married her. There's no more to say, is
there?''

"You know bloody well I had my eye on Meg
Stephenson for you, planned to match you up with
her!''

"Meg Stephenson is a simpering bore."

"Be that as it may, she's also one of the wealthiest heiresses in this part of the country. After I kick
off, boy, you're gonna *need* a rich wife! This one—I
suppose she hasn't a penny to her name."

"Not a penny," Edward said.

"But breedin'! She's got that. I can tell. Cool,
aristocratic, right down to 'er fingertips! Looks, too.
You may be a dyed-in-the-wool bounder, you may be
the bloodiest, most impudent pup in captivity, but
you've got taste. Jennifer, eh? That your name,
girl?''

"That's my name," I said crisply.

"Oh, la! She's got a temper, too. Figures, with
that red hair. Don't like me, do you, lass? Think I'm
an abominable old man, a preposterous old cross-
patch who should be taken out and shot. Don't
bother to disagree with me! I can tell what you think
of me. It's there in those eyes. Green eyes! Whoever
heard of anything so outlandish!''

"Really, Uncle," Edward began, "I think—"

"Get out of here! Go on!" Lord Mallyn stormed.
"Who needs your grim face? Out! Jenny and I want

to get acquainted—Jennifer is too formal, my girl. Jenny it'll be. Come closer, girl—ah, no doubt about it! You're a beauty all right—"

"I'll meet you downstairs in the drawing room, Jennifer."

"You still here!" Lord Mallyn cried hotly. "Thought I told you to get out! I'll brook no insubordination, boy, nor from that cousin of yours either! Think they can defy me just because I'm on my deathbed," he told me. "Think they can run all over me, both of 'em. Begone, boy, or I'll turn the dogs loose on you!"

Completely unperturbed, Edward made his exit with cool dignity. His uncle let out a loud, hoarse cackle, gripping the edge of the quilt with scrawny fingers. One of the dogs peeked out, gave his master's hand a rapid lick and then burrowed back under the covers. Once the door was closed behind his nephew, Lord Mallyn seemed to relax. He chuckled to himself, a wry amusement snapping in those dark eyes. He looked up at me, grinned and told me to sit down. I obeyed, sweeping a pile of magazines off the chair at the side of the bed. The old man studied me with his head cocked to one side, making soft clacking noises with his tongue.

"Love to keep 'em jumpin'," he confided. "Fools! He and Lyman both. They think I'm about to die—you never saw such a rubbin' of hands, such greedy looks. I may cut 'em *both* off. I've had a fierce bout with the flu, lass—it's hung on for weeks —and my gout bothers me somethin' terrible, but I'm not on my deathbed. I've got another ten years in me, and I intend to relish every one of 'em!"

"That's an admirable resolution," I said.

"He tell you I was dyin'?"

"He said you were gravely ill."

"A lot *he* knows! I'll be up and about in another week or so. Just you wait and see! Never sick a day in my life till this crept up on me. Those damned doctors think just because I'm seventy I'm headed for the graveyard! I'm bedridden, true, have been for months, but that last journey is a long way in the future, let me tell you!"

He looked up sharply as the door opened and a plainly terrified footman entered carrying a silver tray on which set a glass and a bottle of red liquid. Mouth tight, eyes narrowed, Lord Mallyn tensed, crouching back against the cushions as though ready to spring. All three dogs had leaped out from under the covers and were jumping about in a frenzy, barking furiously as the footman, his face pale, approached the bed. His hands shook visibly. Glass and bottle rattled on the tray.

"Time for your medicine, Lord Mallyn."

"Out! This instant!"

"But—"

"Are you *deaf*, man!"

The footman began to back away, trembling. Lord Mallyn threw out his hand, seized a jar from the bedside table and hurled it across the room. It barely missed the man's head, shattering into a dozen pieces as it crashed against the wall. Dropping the tray with a loud clatter, the footman darted for the door and slammed it behind him before his employer could hurl something else. Lord Mallyn clapped his hands together, delighted with himself, exactly like a thoroughly spoiled and devilishly mischievous little boy. One of the dogs leaped up to lick his face. He let out another roar. All three dogs vanished promptly, although one feathery brown tail remained outside the covers, wagging vigorously. It was, obviously, a game all four of them enjoyed immensely.

"I suppose you think that was dreadful of me?" he said slyly.

"Isn't that what I'm supposed to think?"

"I have to have *some* fun," he pouted. "It's so damnably *boring*, being cooped up in bed all day. Nothing to do, day in, day out. The servants know what to expect, lass. They enter at their own risk. That chap—" He chuckled, shaking his head. "Did you see the look in his eyes? Thought he was a goner, he did! Damme! Quite invigorating! Clark, now—he's my valet, stuffy chap, stiff as a poker—he won't take a bit of it. I'm as meek as a lamb with *him*."

"I find that hard to believe."

"You don't think I can be meek? I can be angelic if I'm a-mind to be. Just don't feel like it very often. You don't approve of me, do you?"

"Not in the least."

"What? You're not *afraid* of me?"

I shook my head. He looked disappointed, then delighted. Slapping his knee lustily, he let out another hoarse cackle.

"I *like* you, girl. You've got spunk! Vanessa, now, she indulges my every whim. Flirts with me. Teases me. Loves to humor me. You're not about to, I can see that right now. Refreshing, most refreshing! Maybe Edward wasn't such a fool after all."

"Do you enjoy being a terror?" I inquired.

"Love every minute of it," he admitted. "I see it won't work with you, though. Damme! You're exactly what this place needs! You and I are going to be *friends*, Jenny!"

"Indeed?"

He nodded, and once more I was reminded of a

mischievous child, a little boy with a bright new plaything. That ruined, sunken face with its beak nose and thin lips looked almost youthful with the damp silver locks plastered across the forehead, the dark brown eyes twinkling merrily. He wrapped the crimson silk robe closer about him and settled the quilt more snugly over his legs. The dogs came out, two of them snuggling in his lap, the third resting languorously at his feet. Lord Mallyn and I took stock of each other. He was an outrageous old fraud, but I found myself warming to him just the same.

"You're going to *need* a friend, too," he said.

"Oh?"

"You've stepped into a hornet's nest, you know. Edward probably didn't bother to warn you. The others—they're gonna hate you. Lyman. Vanessa. Lyman's set on inheriting the estate, thought he had it neatly sewn up, as he knew I wouldn't leave it to a bachelor. Then Edward showed up with *you*. Lyman's right back where he was to begin with. Most frustrating for him, poor fellow—" He shook his head, apparently forlorn, and then his thin mouth spread into another grin. "No, lass, they're not going to take you to their hearts, not at all."

"I'm sure I'll manage," I said calmly.

"I'm sure you will, too! Edward's chances of inheriting have just increased by a good fifty per cent."

"You love pitting them against one another, don't you?"

He nodded, still grinning. "Rascals, both of 'em. Lyman's a damned hard worker—the whole county respects him. He manages the estate far better than I ever did, though of course I'd never let *him* think that. Works like a farm hand himself,

Lyman does, loves the soil. He's always pestering me to make even more improvements, introduce new methods, plant experimental crops. He's a deserving lad, but, unfortunately, as surly as a bear, hotheaded—can't see myself leaving the estate to *him!*"

"And Edward?" I inquired.

"He's just as bad," the old man said, thoroughly enjoying himself. "Cold as an iceberg, that one, unfeeling. Elegant, polished, a gentleman worthy of a fine old house like Mallyncourt, but no fire, no feeling! Sometimes I wish he had some of Lyman's hot blood, wish he'd let loose and fight with me, but no, he's always controlled. He knows how to get around me, he thinks, thinks he has me fooled, thinks he's the favored one just because the two of us don't have shouting matches like Lyman and I do."

If he hoped to rile me by criticizing Edward, he was mistaken. Lord Mallyn's opinion of his nephew could hardly be lower than my own. I stood up, my emerald satin skirts rustling, and calmly informed him that I had best go on down to the drawing room. The old man looked disappointed, but he looked tired, too, his face sagging, weary lines about those remarkable eyes. The conversation and his virulent outburst at the footman had taken their toll, his vivacity ebbing away. Leaning back against the cushions, idly stroking one of the dogs, he looked up at me, frail, withered, but still curiously majestic. In his youth, he must have been a dynamo, I reflected. Even now he still retained that incredible presence that made everything else seem pale and lifeless.

"Do you play cards? You do? We'll have some rousing games together. Lettice says I cheat—that child, my one consolation. I'm a lonely, miserable old man, surrounded by souvenirs of the past—" He made a sweeping gesture, indicating the objects cluttering the vast room. "Once I lived to the fullest, savoring each day. There was adventure in my soul! I loved, I fought, I traveled, I dared, and now— now I cling to a mothy old quilt my beloved Sarah made, I look at my treasures, remembering days full of color and excitement when I was young and robust. Now, alas, the only fun I have is bullying the servants and taunting my nephews—" He sighed, looking sad and abject.

"You expect me to pity you, Lord Mallyn?"

"I was hoping you *might*," he said slyly, eyes twinkling.

"I don't, you know. I think you're a wretched old faker."

"Really? You're a lass after my own heart! You come back, you hear? We'll chat. We'll play cards. I *do* cheat—I may as well admit it—but I doubt I'll be able to put anything over on *you*, girl!"

"I rather doubt it myself."

"Go on, desert me," he said, playing the abject old man again. "Leave me alone with my misery. No one wants to spend any time with a senile old fool doddering on the edge of the grave. You're eager to get back to that handsome husband of yours, I can tell. Jenny—"

"Yes?"

"Be careful, lass," he said quietly.

"Careful?"

He nodded, frowning. "Edward—you don't know him. You're too good for him. Knew that the minute I laid eyes on you. I like you, lass, and I wouldn't want to see you get hurt. There's going to be trouble."

He wasn't playing a role now. There was genuine concern in his eyes. He looked almost frightened.

"What—what makes you say that?" I asked.

"Those boys hate each other. Always have. Things have been building up between them for years. Tension's been steadily mounting, and now— I have a feeling you're going to be a catalyst. I shouldn't be surprised if there was actual bloodshed. Vanessa, you see, and—"

"Vanessa? What—"

"Greedy. Worse than either of them. It's all gone too far. It's my fault. I should never have—"

All the energy seemed to drain out of him. Leaving the sentence dangling, he shook his head and sank back against the cushions, pulling the multicolored quilt up over his chest. The dogs stirred, peeking out with disgruntled expressions.

"You'll be careful?" he whispered.

"I—I'll be careful," I said.

"I'm an old sinner. It doesn't matter about me, but the child—and you, girl. You should never have come—"

"Lord Mallyn, what are you trying to tell—"

"Weary," he said, "so weary. Sleep. Oblivion—"

He closed his eyes, his chest rising and falling as he let out a deep, raspy sigh. Extremely frustrated, I looked down at that thin, emaciated face, and then I moved slowly across the long room. At the door, I turned. Lord James Mallyn was already asleep, snoring quietly, looking much older in repose, looking painfully frail and defenseless. He clutched the quilt in his sleep as though for protection, and the dogs were nestled comfortably about him, one on his legs, one on his shoulder, the third snuggled up in the curve of his arm.

I left the room, closing the door softly behind me.

Candles burned dimly in the hall, casting flickering shadows over the ancient walls. The house was very still, silent. It seemed to be holding its breath, waiting. Something was wrong. Something was very wrong. The old man had seemed almost senile those last few moments, his mind wandering, but he had hinted at something far more sinister than a feud over the inheritance. As I stood there in the hall, frowning, I had a strong premonition of danger. It seemed to hang suspended in the atmosphere like an almost physical substance, heavy, oppressive, clinging to the walls. The candles sputtered. Outside, the wind roared, causing the windows to rattle in their frames. You're being absurd, I told myself. You're imagining things.

But no matter how I tried to shake it, the feeling of imminent danger remained.

Five

I HAD no earthly idea how to get down to the drawing room. The house was so large, with so many winding corridors, connecting rooms, sudden twists and turns that one unfamiliar with its peculiarities was apt to get lost. I had visions of myself wandering up and down strange halls, going through a labyrinth of rooms, moving up and down narrow, unexpected staircases, but I managed to retrace our steps back to my bedroom, and from there I found my way to the long gallery Edward and I had passed through earlier on, on our way to the west wing apartment. I paused, wanting to compose myself a bit before going down to join the others.

The gallery was surely one of the largest and most impressive rooms in all of England, I thought, awed by its immensity and splendor. Over one hundred and seventy feet long, fifty feet wide, it provided ample room for horseback riding, and I could visualize those earlier Mallyns galloping up and down its length. The ceiling, thirty feet high, was a creamy ivory with connecting scallops and circles molded in pink plaster, now faded a light brownish orange, and four majestic brass chandeliers hung down. The floor was covered with a mat of woven rushes, yellow beige, that made a crinkling noise as one walked over it. The south wall, ivory plaster, had two great brown and gray marble fireplaces, intricately molded, and the rest of the space was taken up by family portraits: seven Vandykes, three Holbeins, a number of Romneys and Gainsboroughs, all in heavy, ornate gold frames. On the north wall were six great window recesses, each one like a small individual room jutting out, canopies of dusty yellow velvet and tarnished cloth of gold hanging above the entrance of each recess. The room was very sparsely furnished, although the chests, tables, the chairs upholstered in yellow velvet were all Chippendale, exceedingly elegant. Candles blazed in twenty or more many-branched wall sconces, but the room was shadowy nevertheless.

Rush mat crackling underfoot, I moved across the room and stepped into one of the recesses, like many-paned glass cages suspended on the back of the house. The recess was dark, and there was a wide window seat stretching around all three sides. I sat down on the padded yellow velvet cushion, causing flurries of dust to rise, and, leaning my cheek against one of the thick, leaded panes, peered out at the immense square of rolled green lawn enclosed by hedges. It was awash with moonlight, the grass silvered, the hedges black, the treetops towering beyond like dark rustling giants in back.

My earlier apprehension had vanished almost entirely. Common sense had finally prevailed. The old man had a sure sense of drama. He was like an audacious, rather hammy old actor, playing his character role to the hilt, and I realized now that his "warning" was probably nothing more than simple playacting. He loved to shock, to startle. Bored, lonely, fretting at his bedridden state, he created his own drama to relieve the tedium, and he had probably hoped to frighten me simply to satisfy a perverse sense of humor. I had been thoroughly duped and, leaving the room, had experienced exactly what he had hoped I would experience. The old rogue probably hadn't been asleep at all. He was probably cackling to himself even now, satisfied with a prank well executed.

The glass was cool against my cheek. I smelled dust and old velvet and damp, crumbling stone. Behind me, the long gallery seemed to yawn like a great cavern. Pensive now, rather melancholy, I thought about these past two weeks. Everything had gone according to plan, and the old man liked me. I sensed that. Edward would finally be able to persuade him to draw up his will, and the five hundred pounds would be mine whether it was in Edward's favor or not. In just a few weeks I could leave, go to London, finally buy that small dress shop and lead a life of complete independence, an unusual feat for a woman in this day and age.

The future was promising, and if one certain element seemed to be missing, I could do very well without it. Romance might seem all important to some, but I knew better. I no longer dreamed of a dashing, handsome cavalry officer on a fine white steed who would sweep me up into his arms and carry me off into a misty never-never land of high passion and eternal devotion. I had known too many men, and I was far too levelheaded. Love was a luxury for pampered young girls who didn't have to worry about making a living. If I still sometimes felt these vague, disturbing yearnings, like I did at the moment, I could accept them for what they were. It was only natural for one to feel this subtle, elusive discontent, and it had nothing to do with love. I certainly wasn't in love with Edward Baker. I loathed the man. I was pensive, true, but not because of him.

The sound of footsteps brought me out of my revery. I sat up, tense. Someone was coming down the gallery, no, more than one person. There were at least two sets of footsteps. I heard voices now. They seemed far away, muted, growing more audible as the speakers drew nearer the recess. Should I step out? Should I make my presence known? I hesitated, not knowing what to do, and then it was too late.

"—those diamonds and that gown rather too grand?"

"I thought they would be appropriate, darling. After all, I wouldn't want Edward's little sparrow to outshine me."

"She isn't a sparrow, Vanessa. Far from it."

"Oh? You've seen her?"

"I've seen her." Lyman's voice was rough, disgruntled.

"And she's beautiful?"

"You might say that, yes. Striking."

"Most unlike you to notice a woman, darling. Usually you're much too boorish and preoccupied to know whether she's fat, thin, short or tall. I wonder about that, luv."

"What do you mean?" he growled.

"Why you noticed this particular woman. You never notice *me*, pet. I have to resort to all sorts of wiles to make you even acknowledge my presence."

"Does my indifference disturb you?"

"Not in the least," she said gaily. "I have my little consolations."

"Yeah," he grunted.

"It would be rather *nice*, though, to have you notice me now and then, pet. You're still a fascinating virile creature—quite appetizing. I frequently find you irresistible—like tonight."

"Forget it, Vanessa," he said harshly.

"We used to have—"

"What we used to have has been dead for years."

"I know. It's sad."

"Sad? You've hardly been consumed with grief."

She laughed. It was a bright, tinkling, silvery laugh, enchanting, yet there was nevertheless a certain sharpness to the sound, an undercurrent of bitterness. Holding my breath, I saw their shadows on the floor in front of the recess, and, a moment later, they came into view, stopping a few yards away from where I sat. Her back was to me, and Lyman was facing me. I prayed he wouldn't look over her shoulder and see me.

"It's been a long time, Lyman," she said. Her voice was, a rich, seductive voice. "It's quite a blow to my vanity, luv. You haven't slept with me since—"

"Since I found you with—Reggie, wasn't it? Or was it Clive? It's difficult to keep track of them all."

"I have the same problem," she said lightly.

Lyman scowled. He was wearing an ill-fitting pale blue broadcloth suit and an embroidered black waistcoat, managing to look unkempt even in this attire. His tall black boots needed shining, and his mustard yellow ascot was already rumpled. He was, nevertheless, a splendid male animal. Vanessa laughed again. Sculptured ebony waves were stacked elegantly on the back of her head. Her blue velvet gown was cut very low in back, leaving an expanse of naked ivory flesh, and her wide blue velvet skirts fell to the floor in puffed scallops caught up with black velvet bows. Her waist was small, surely no more than twenty inches. Even with this partial view, I could tell that she must be breathtaking, a creature of remarkable beauty and glamor.

"You look disturbed, pet. Don't tell me it still bothers you?"

"It did, once. Now I'm totally immune."

"I wonder—" she said provocatively.

"Save it for someone else, Vanessa."

"You could have given me a divorce years ago, darling, but no, that would have alienated your dear uncle—a Mallyn divorced? Un*think*able. Immorality didn't bother him, but divorce—it's simply not *done*."

"After he dies, after I inherit—"

"Then you'll be a very wealthy man, pet. I wouldn't *want* a divorce. Besides, we must think of Lettice."

"You couldn't care less what happens to her."

"That's putting it rather strongly, don't you think? Let's just say I'm not a devoted mother. I'm far too young, far too selfish."

His face impassive, Lyman looked over her shoulder. He saw me. For perhaps half a minute his dark, smoldering eyes held mine, and then he looked away, his face as hard and impassive as ever.

"We'd better get down to the drawing room," he said gruffly.

Vanessa sighed, lifting one slim white hand to pat the ebony waves at the back of her head. "I suppose we had," she said. "Really, Lyman, you do bring out the worst in me. I don't know what brought all this on. I suppose I pitied you. You looked so lonely, so moody. I suppose I thought you might appreciate a little wifely—"

"Come along, Vanessa."

Lyman started toward the wide staircase, and, after a moment or so, Vanessa followed him. I could hear the sound of their footsteps echoing up the stairwell, and then there was silence. My cheeks were burning. I felt thoroughly humiliated to have been caught in such an awkward position. Lyman hadn't seemed surprised to see me sitting here. He had shown no emotion whatsoever. He must despise me. He must think I was deliberately eavesdropping. Wretched, my cheeks still flushed, I stepped out of the recess and moved slowly toward the staircase, wondering how I could possibly face him again tonight.

More footsteps rang up the stairwell. Edward stepped into the gallery, looking rather worried.

"There you are. I thought perhaps you'd lost your way."

"No—I—"

"What's wrong? You seem upset."

"N-nothing. I'm perfectly all right."

"The old man fluster you? Is that what it is?"

"Yes—" I lied.

"Don't worry about it. He does it deliberately. How did it go?"

I managed to compose myself. "I think he likes me," I said.

"Indeed?"

"He wants me to play cards with him."

"Splendid," Edward said, visibly pleased. "That's a good sign."

"I—I really don't feel like eating anything," I said. "I'd like to go back to my room."

"Nonsense. The others are waiting."

Taking my elbow in a firm grip, he led me down the staircase. Faded, patched tapestries hung on the cold stone walls, flapping slightly in the currents of air that swirled up the well. It was extremely chilly, the air like ice water, and I shivered. Passing down the long hall immediately beneath the gallery, we turned through a doorway, moved down another hall and stepped into the drawing room near the front of the house. The walls were covered with bright mulberry silk, and there was much dark, polished woodwork. A fire burned in the gray marble fireplace, crackling briskly, and candles burned in the elaborate brass chandelier.

Lyman was slumped on a long gray velvet sofa. He stared into the fire with a sullen expression, making no effort to rise as we entered. A plump, nervous-looking middle-aged woman with mousy brown hair stood near the piano, a pale, thin little girl in white organdy beside her. All three of them were merely a backdrop for the radiant creature in dark blue velvet who came forward to greet us, hands extended.

"There you are!" she exclaimed. "I've been longing to meet you. You're Jenny! I'm your cousin Vanessa, darling."

She took my hands. She smiled a dazzling smile. I smiled, too, hating her as strongly as she hated me. Vanessa kissed my cheek and then released my hands, turning to Edward with a delicious pout.

"Cruel of you to keep her from us so long, Edward," she said, tapping his arm. "You can't imagine the excitement your letter created. It was so *unexpected*, you see. I, for one, was positively delighted."

"I've no doubt you were," he said coldly.

"Dear, dear, are you going to sulk, too? These men—" she said, turning back to me. "Impossible to live with! You and Edward must have fallen in love at first *sight*, darling. It happened so quickly. Or has he been keeping you secret for much, much longer?"

"Careful, Vanessa," Edward warned.

"Whatever do you mean? I was just trying to be friendly with my lovely new cousin." Her voice sparkled with charming malice. "I can't understand why you're so *touchy*, pet. It isn't as though you have anything to *hide*. Men! I'll never understand them."

Vanessa Robb was the most beautiful woman I had ever seen. I couldn't deny that. Tall, slender, elegant, her features were sheer perfection: the shell-pink mouth beautifully molded, the nose classic, the cheekbones high and aristocratic. Her eyes were a deep sapphire blue, lashes long and curling, dark brows perfectly arched. With her creamy complexion and gleaming ebony hair, she was a vision of loveliness. In another woman such beauty might be cool, unapproachable, but Vanessa glowed with a warm animation, and there was a strong seductive allure no man could fail to notice.

"But I'm being a *wretched* hostess," she exclaimed. "Let me introduce the others. My husband you've already met, I believe. This is our dear little Lettice—say how do you do, dear, curtsy like you've been taught—and this is Miss Partridge. Such an appropriate name! She *is* a dear plump little partridge—we all adore her."

Flustered, extremely uncomfortable, the governess bobbed a greeting, but Lettice merely glared at me with hostile gray eyes. She had inherited none of her mother's beauty, none of her father's vitality.

Much too thin, much too sallow, Lettice was undeniably plain.

"Hello, Lettice," I said quietly.

She didn't reply. She merely glared, bristling.
Openly hostile though she was, there was still something touching about the child, something vulnerable and curiously poignant. Her life couldn't be a
very happy one, I thought. She was obviously miserable, lonely, and her belligerence, her stiff, unyield-
ing manner was like a protective shell.

"They won't be dining with us, of course," Vanessa continued. "They always dine in the nursery,
but I wanted to have you meet my dear little girl.
She'll play for us."

"No," Lettice snapped.

"Chopin, I think, pet. That would be lovely."

"I won't!"

"She's been taking music lessons for three
years now. I do feel girls should be accomplished,
particularly when they're not going to be pretty.
Lettice is already skilled at a number of things. She
can do water colors and sew and—"

"I'm glad I'm not pretty!"

"What an absurd thing to say, pet."

"I'm glad! And I'm not going to play, either!"

"Really, Lettice, I don't intend to tolerate—"

"Leave the child alone, Vanessa," Lyman
growled.

"Everyone seems to be in league against me,"
Vanessa remarked. "Very well, you may go to your
room, Lettice. Take her away, Partridge."

The child marched out of the room with stiff
shoulders, the governess scurrying along behind
her, more flustered than ever. There was a moment
of silence. Vanessa smiled, examining her diamond
bracelet. Lyman slumped on the sofa, scowling. Ed-

ward was aloof, completely oblivious to the ugly little scene that had just been played. I couldn't believe a woman could be as unfeeling toward her own child as Vanessa had been. She had deliberately humiliated the girl, had seemed to take a perverse satisfaction in doing so.

"I must apologize for my daughter," she said.

"I quite understand," I replied.

"Do you, luv?" She knew exactly what I meant.

"Thoroughly," I said.

We looked at each other. Vanessa smiled.

"She really should be sent away to school," she remarked. "It would do her a world of good, but Lyman won't hear of it. I can't see why he's so obstinate about it, but, after all, he *is* my lord and master, and I must bow to his will."

Edward smiled his thin smile. Lyman stared into the fire, his expression unaltered.

"Well, then," Vanessa said, "I guess you and I should get to know one another, Jenny. We're going to be *such* friends, I feel. Tell me all about yourself. Where did you and Edward meet?"

"She was staying with her aunt in London," Edward said icily. "I met her at Lady Ashton-Croft's reception."

"I don't *know* any Randalls. The family must be obscure—"

"I was raised near York," I said. "My father was a country squire."

"Oh yes, I believe Edward's letter mentioned something to that effect. It must have been dreary, but you don't *look* like a country mouse. That gown, for example. It might have been designed by Worth. Worth does all my gowns. I delight in buying new clothes, if only to hear Lyman roar when the bills arrive. Dear Uncle James doesn't complain, though, and he's the one who pays. Lyman, of course, is merely his bailiff."

Her husband completely ignored this sly dig, climbing heavily to his feet, moving over to prod the fire with a poker. He and Edward made quite a contrast, I thought, the one so cool and urbane, the other so rough and volatile. Vanessa continued to chatter, brightly, gaily, hurling subtle barbs now at me, now at Edward, now at Lyman. Her bitchiness was extremely polished, sly, never blatant, an integral part of her vivacious prattle. It was interesting to note that, although she was obviously a fascinator of men, both men in the room loathed her, both looking as though it would have given them great pleasure to throttle her with their bare hands. Knowing this seemed to delight her, spur her on.

Jeffers appeared to announce dinner. Edward escorted me into the dining room. Crystal and silver sparkled on the long, polished table. Vivid blue and violet flowers formed a centerpiece. Candles shed a bright golden light. The meal seemed endless. Lyman sulked, ignoring everyone. Edward was silent, and I was still too unsure of myself to return Vanessa's bitchy remarks in kind. Lyman never looked at me, not once, and I kept wondering what he was thinking. Did he believe I had been deliberately eavesdropping? It shouldn't have bothered me, but it did. I was vastly relieved when the meal was over.

Lyman stormed out of the room without a word. Edward remarked that he wanted to go over the estate accounts and would join me upstairs in an hour or so. Smiling prettily, Vanessa took my arm in hers, patted it, and said that I simply must join her in her private sitting room where we could have a nice, cousinly chat together. Reluctantly, I went with her, praying I would be able to restrain my animosity.

It was a pretty room, much smaller than any of the others I had been in, all done in gold and white, intimate, elegant, especially redecorated for her, Vanessa explained. A fire burned cozily in the white marble fireplace. The ivory white walls had panels of gold leaf designs, and crystal pendants dangled from the ivory wall sconces. Vanessa stepped over to the window, lifted back the long white silk drape and peered out at the night. In the gorgeous, seductive blue velvet gown, her rich ebony waves so artfully arranged, she made a breathtakingly lovely picture. I granted that. In an earlier age she would have captivated kings, driven poets to suicide, caused revolutions in the Balkans.

"Well," she said, turning, "here we are."

"Here we are," I agreed.

"You really *are* a strikingly attractive creature, Jenny. I'm quite sick with jealousy."

"You have nothing to fear."

"Oh, *any*one can be merely beautiful, but you're different—you have a certain arresting quality. I've always felt that's more important than *beau*ty. I can see why Edward fancied you."

"Can you?"

"It was really quite clever of you, getting him to marry you so quickly. Dozens of others have tried and failed. I really never thought Edward was the marrying kind, although he's had some very interesting arrangements over the years."

"Oh?"

"Lush, frivolous creatures, actresses and such. I believe he has a cozy little house in London he reserves for them. None of them ever dwelled there for long, though. He's easily bored, quite merciless when he tires of a woman. Of course, *you* have nothing to worry about, pet. He *mar*ried you."

"Indeed he did," I said, smiling. "I've always felt a man should be experienced when he takes a bride."

"Oh, yes," she agreed. "That's *very* important."

Neither of us bothered to sit. We stood facing each other like two sleek tigresses, sizing each other up, claws momentarily sheathed. The air between us seemed to crackle with animosity, yet both of us were smiling, both polite.

"You know *why* he married you, of course?" she said.

"I believe I do, Mrs. Robb."

"Oh, you must call me Van*essa*. No, you're not a naive, gullible little fool smitten with love. I can see that. Edward must have told you everything."

I acknowledged this with a cool nod.

"And yet you married him just the same, knowing full well he didn't love you, was merely using you. I appreciate that. It's something I would have done myself. After all, you have every reason to believe that Edward will soon be fabulously wealthy."

"I have every reason to believe that," I said.

Vanessa smiled, examining her diamond bracelet again. When she looked back up at me, her eyes sparkled with malicious amusement.

"He's not going to be, you know. Edward isn't going to inherit. Lyman is. No doubt your husband thought you might be able to win the old man over, influence him. Any such effort on your part would be wasted, I assure you. Dear Uncle James has no illusions about me, true, he knows me for what I am, and it amuses him. I've had him eating out of my hand for years now."

"Indeed?"

"My affairs delight him. He admires my spirit, my boldness. And, too, there's Lettice. He adores her. Marrying you was an act of last minute desperation on Edward's part. The will shall be made in Lyman's favor."

"You're very sure of yourself, aren't you?"

"*Very* sure, pet. I've been working on the old man for years, waiting. I've no intentions of letting it slip out of my hands now. Well, then, I just wanted to make sure we under*stand* each other, Jenny."

"I think we understand each other perfectly."

"Marvelous. Now we can re*lax*. You must tell me all about Edward. Is he superb in bed? He's such a cold, formidable creature, so aloof—I've often wondered how he'd be as a lover. Quite exciting, I imagine. Do sit down, Jenny dear. Shall I ring for tea? It's going to be so nice to have someone to chat with. We must *plan* things, pet. I think we should give a ball in your honor—"

"No tea, thank you. I think I'll go on up to my room."

"Yes, of course, you must be exhausted. It's been a trying day. Well, luv, we'll get together later. I'm serious about that ball. It's been a long time since we've had any festivity at Mallyncourt, and I'm sure Uncle James will agree to it just to please me, even though he won't be able to come down himself—"

I smiled politely. "Good night, Vanessa."

" 'Night, luv," she said sweetly. "I'm so *glad* you're here."

I took my leave of her, making my way slowly toward the back of the house. Many of the candles had been extinguished, and the hallways were dim. I passed a footman. He nodded, moving on toward the drawing room with his candle snuffer. Reaching the wide back hall, I paused, not quite ready to go back up to my room. I was tense and overstimulated, and I knew it would be impossible to sleep for some time. The hall was icy, filled with the smells of damp stone and dust and ancient, fraying cloth. The tapestries covering the walls billowed gently with a soft, flapping noise. Candles threw long shadows across the bare stone floor. I decided to go outside for a while. An evening stroll might relax me.

Finding a door near the west end of the hall, I stepped out onto the veranda. Paved with flag-stones, it extended the length of the house in back with swirled brown stone pillars supporting the low roof. Across the stone balustrade I could see the immense back lawn, gilded with moonlight. Dark leaves rustled. A bird warbled sleepily in one of the trees. Leaving the veranda, I strolled across the grass, my satin skirt billowing against my legs. The sky was an ashy gray, and moonlight spilled over the dark clouds building up around the moon. It was a world of black, brown, silver, gray, with only the faintest suggestion of green. Nearing the line of shrubbery at the foot of the lawn, I turned and looked back at the house. Mallyncourt was a towering brown-black mass, shrouded in shadows, with hazy orange-gold squares where candles burned in windows.

Life-sized marble statues stood at various points along the shrubbery, mellowed with age, more gray than white, sad sentinels with broken bodies and sightless eyes. Finding a white marble bench, I sat down, oblivious to the damp and the icy chill that caressed my bare arms and shoulders. I wondered if Edward was still in the muniments room, going over the estate books and domestic accounts, and I wondered if he was pleased with the way I had handled myself at dinner. I hoped so. For purely professional reasons, I told myself. I had been hired to perform a role, and I intended to perform as skillfully as I was able to. Personal feelings had nothing to do with it. Edward Baker was my employer, as he had so sternly pointed out, and I owed it to him to do my best, no matter how I might loathe him as an individual.

I could hear water dancing in the wild, overgrown gardens in back of the lawn, beyond the line of shrubs. There were fountains there, I knew, and lily ponds and a hidden grotto. Water made splashing night music, and a frog croaked. It was growing late. I really should go back inside. Rising, I began to stroll slowly back toward the veranda, thinking about Vanessa now. I wondered how long we would be able to keep up that formal, strained politeness, how long the hostility could be kept contained behind a pretense of civility. Each of us knew exactly where the other stood, yet neither of us wanted to declare open warfare. When that happened, I would be ready. Four years in the theater, with its infighting and jealousies and daily bitchery had more than prepared me to hold my own.

Lost in thought, I stepped into the nest of shifting black shadows that filled the veranda. My skirts rustled stiffly. My heels tapped noisily on the flagstones. I stopped, abruptly. My blood seemed to run cold. Someone was here. Someone was watching me. I could feel hostile eyes, sense a presence. Very little moonlight spilled over the balustrade. The veranda was dark, layer upon layer of shadows spilling down like a misty black fog. I peered down the length of it, my hand to my heart, trying to still the rapid palpitations. I thought I saw a darker black form leaning against the wall a few yards ahead, the outline barely visible, black on black. As I watched, the form moved. A loud scratching noise broke the silence. A match blossomed into sizzling yellow-orange flame, and the burning blossom moved, rising, touched the tip of a slender black cigar. Briefly, before the light vanished, I saw Lyman's face. Heavy lids concealed his eyes as he concentrated on the cigar. I caught my breath, relieved and irritated at the same time as I approached him.

"You—you might have let me know you were there!" I said crossly.

"Did I frighten you?" he asked in a bored voice.

"I thought—I don't know what I thought! I didn't expect anyone to be there—"

"No need to be frightened, Mrs. Baker. Contrary to what your husband may have told you, I don't leap out of the darkness to strangle lone women whenever the moon is full."

"He said no such thing. Don't be absurd."

"I dare say he painted me black, though."

"How long have you been standing there?" I asked, ignoring his comment.

"Half an hour or so."

"Then you were there when—"

"When you came out. Yes. I was rather surprised to see you. I thought perhaps my wife had eaten you alive. You're going to be something of a trial to Vanessa, I'm afraid. She's not accustomed to competition."

"I have no intentions of competing with her."

"Your mere presence will be a challenge to her," he continued. "She'll feel threatened, outdo herself in order to compensate. No, Vanessa's not going to be easy to live with, I fear. Not that she ever was."

"I—this evening, before dinner—"

"Yes?"

"I wasn't eavesdropping. I was already sitting in the recess when you came into the gallery. I didn't know what to—"

"Forget it," he said.

"I wouldn't want you to think—" For some reason I didn't seem to be able to finish a sentence.

"What could it possibly matter to you what I think, Mrs. Baker?"

"It doesn't!" I snapped.

"Vanessa and I have no secrets from the world. Everyone knows about us. Feel free to eavesdrop anytime you like."

I bit back the scathing retort that sprang to mind. I said nothing. The man was insufferable, insufferably rude. My eyes had grown accustomed to the darkness now, and I could see his face, all shadowed planes, broad cheekbones prominent, eyes dark, half concealed by their heavy lids. Locks of raven hair fell in a fringe over his forehead, giving him the appearance of an evil monk. Even here, enclosed by darkness, I could sense the bull-like strength, the vitality. He was watching me, his mouth half curled in a mocking smile.

"You resent me," I said. "I know that. I know why, too."

"Resent you? No, Mrs. Baker, I pity you. You've no idea what you've let yourself in for."

"No?"

"When you first arrived, I thought perhaps you knew nothing of the situation existing at Mallyncourt. I thought perhaps you might be innocent of any complicity in Edward's plan. I see now that he must have told you everything. You couldn't have married him for love. Edward's incapable of love, and you quite plainly despise him."

"I've never heard anything so—"

"Surprised? I may be just a crude farmer, Mrs. Baker, but I'm not quite as dense as you may think. I observe things. When I saw the two of you together tonight, I knew it wasn't a love match on your part either. There was only one other explanation for your marrying him."

"How dare you say—"

Lyman Robb took a long drag on the cigar, then hurled it over the balustrade. It made a wide orange streak in the darkness, exploding on the ground in a shower of sparks.

"I'll say one more thing, Mrs. Baker, and I'd advise you to listen very carefully. I've worked all my adult life for my uncle's estate—it's *been* my life —and I don't intend to stand by and let it fall into Edward's hands. I'll crush anyone who stands in my way."

"Is—is that a threat, Mr. Robb?"

"You might say so—yes, you might say that. If you had any sense at all, you'd turn around and take the first coach back to London, but you won't, I fear. That being the case, I'd advise you to stay out of my way. You're much too attractive to be hurt."

"Do me a favor, Mr. Robb," I said quietly.

"Yes? What's that?"

"Go to Hades!"

He looked stunned, startled, and then he threw his head back and burst into gales of laughter. It rose and fell. It rumbled, loud, unrestrained, welling up from his chest with splendid richness. I stood there trembling with fury as he gave vent to that boisterous sound. He cut it off abruptly. He took a deep breath. When he spoke, his rough voice was strongly laced with mocking amusement.

"Ah, Jenny," he said, "it appears you're not

quite the grand, dignified lady I took you to be. No indeed. There's a bit of the fishwife in you, luv."

"I—I ought to slap your face!"

"I shouldn't," he said. "You see, I don't even *pretend* to be a gentleman. I'd slap you back, promptly, Probably hurl you over the balustrade as well."

"You—you—"

"Run along, luv. Get back in the house. It's much too chilly for you to be out here in that preposterous gown. I shouldn't be at all surprised if you caught your death of cold."

Although I was seething with rage, I moved down the veranda with cool, haughty dignity, followed by the sound of Lyman Robb's hearty chuckle. Once inside, I walked quickly down the long hall with its patched and faded tapestries and up the wide stone steps built for the horses. In the vast, shadowy gallery, I paused, taking a few moments to compose myself before going on to the west wing apartment.

Most of the candles had been extinguished in my bedroom, one burning in a silver holder beside the bed, another on the dressing table. The bedcovers had been turned back, the fire banked down, a mere heap of glowing red-orange coals. As I entered, I was momentarily dismayed to see a diminutive creature in black dress and white organdy apron climb up out of the large chair beside the fireplace. Her short blond curls were tousled. Her comic little face wore a timid, sleepy expression. She couldn't have been much over fourteen, I thought.

"I'm Susie, Ma'am," she said, "'n I'm to be your abigail. Jeffers, 'e told me to wait 'ere in your room 'n 'elp you get ready for bed. I've never *been* an abigail before, Ma'am. I 'ope you'll understand if I botch things up a bit till I get the 'ang of it.''

"Hello, Susie," I replied, warming to the child immediately. "You look sleepy."

"I *am*," she admitted frankly, "but at least I'm not workin' in the pantry any more. Most abigails 're tall 'n skinny, usually *French* and very grand, like Miss Vanessa's. 'You'll do in a pinch,' Jeffers told me, 'n 'e said I was to please you or *else*. Said I wasn't to chatter—oh dear, and here I am chatterin' away. I'm the one who unpacked all your things 'n put 'em away earlier on," she said proudly. "Shall I 'elp you undress now, Ma'am?"

"I think I can manage by myself, Susie. It's very late. Why don't you run along to your room and go to sleep."

She seemed crestfallen. With her enormous blue eyes, turned-up nose and wide pink mouth, she looked like a worried pixie. There was a scattering of light tan freckles across her cheeks, and she spoke with a decided Cockney accent.

"Oh dear, I 'ope I 'aven't displeased you! Jeffers'll be livid. 'E's a terrible bully, Jeffers. 'E'll send me back to the pantry—"

"I'm delighted with you," I told her. "Don't you worry about Jeffers. I won't let him bother you."

"Oh, Ma'am! You're an angel! You truly are. I was so *wor*ried, you see. I wouldn't be Miss Vanessa's abigail for the *world*. I'd rather sweep chim*neys*. I was afraid you might be like 'er. There I go—chatterin', chatterin'. If you don't require my services, then I shall retire," she added, striving for grandness with a most comic result.

"Good night Susie."

The girl dropped a quick curtsy, her blond curls bobbing, her wide pink mouth splitting into a pixie grin. Beaming with delight, she scurried out of the room, black taffeta skirt crackling stiffly. I smiled, enchanted with her, pleased to have discovered at least one friendly person at Mallyncourt.

Twenty minutes later, wearing only a low-cut petticoat with full ruffled skirt, I sat at the dressing table, brushing my hair. The long titian locks crackled and curled under the brush, redder than ever in the light of the candle. My green eyes were dark, my face composed, rather hard. My first night at Mallyncourt was over now, and I knew exactly what to expect in days to come. Lord Mallyn, Lyman, Vanessa: All were definitely going to present problems. No doubt I would earn every penny of that five hundred pounds before it was all over with, but I felt confident I could cope. Putting the brush aside, I stood up, weary, more than ready for some much needed sleep.

"Tired?" Edward asked.

I whirled around, startled. He was leaning in the doorway leading into the sitting room that connected our chambers, his shoulder propped casually against the door frame. Over his dark trousers and white shirt he wore a dressing robe, a splendid garment of heavy navy blue satin, tied loosely at the waist with a sash. One thick dark blond wave had fallen across his brow, and there was an odd expression in his eyes, one I hadn't seen there before. I wondered how long he had been standing there, watching me.

"I—I didn't hear you," I said.

He smiled. It was a lazy smile. That expression in his eyes was disturbing. His lids drooped down sleepily. The sumptuous robe gleamed darkly. He was incredibly handsome, and he looked relaxed for the first time, not nearly so remote as he had been earlier.

"Thought I'd drop in to say good night," he said.

"Oh?"

"You needn't look so alarmed, Jennifer."

"I—I'm not alarmed."

That wasn't true. This lazy, relaxed Edward was far more formidable than the aloof, distant stranger. I recognized that look in his eyes now, and I was acutely conscious of my half-clothed state. The petticoat left most of my bosom bare, and the waist was extremely snug, the full skirt aswirl with white cotton ruffles. Arms folded across his chest, his head tilted to one side, Edward gazed at me.

"There are one or two things I thought I should mention," he drawled. "About our sleeping arrangements. It's perfectly customary for us to have separate chambers, but—uh—be sure you muss up both sides of the bed, be sure you dent both pillows. A servant will awaken you in the morning. Servants gossip. We wouldn't want it to get around that we're not—"

"I quite understand," I said stiffly.

"You're blushing, Jennifer."

"I—that door. There's a lock on it, I trust?"

He nodded, amused. "Think you'll need one?"

"I—I'm not sure."

"No?"

"Mr. Baker—"

"Don't look so alarmed, Jenny," he said casually. "We made a bargain, remember? Part of it was that I wouldn't—uh—molest you. You needn't fear. I've no intentions of raping you."

"I think you'd better—"

"I'll leave in a minute or so. No, rape isn't my

style. If I wanted you, I'm sure it wouldn't be necessary.''

Slowly, nonchalantly, he strolled across the room toward me, the skirt of his robe rustling with a soft, silken whisper. I watched, appalled, unable to move, to speak. He stopped directly in front of me, standing so near I could feel the warmth of his body, smell the tart, masculine cologne he'd used after shaving. Although I met his languid gaze with level eyes, I was trembling inside. My knees felt weak, and my pulses raced. Edward curled his lips into a sardonic, mocking smile.

"Not necessary at all," he murmured.

He pulled me into his arms, lazily, indifferently. His mouth fastened over mine, and, as his arms tightened, he swung me around. Bending at the waist, I clung to his back, horrified by what was happening. The kiss was long, lazy, excruciatingly prolonged, and when he released me that mocking smile was still on his lips.

"Just thought I'd prove my point," he said. He yawned. "Good night, Jenny. You needn't bother about locking the door. Your maidenhood is quite safe—at least for the time being."

He sauntered out of the room, passed through the sittingroom and into his own chamber. I stood where he had left me, weak, shaken, unable to even think coherently. Soft candlelight washed over the white walls. A bit of wood snapped in the fireplace, sending a tiny shower of sparks onto the hearth. I could hear Edward moving about in his room, getting ready for bed. I don't know how many minutes passed before I moved to the door. I closed it firmly. I shoved the lock in place. I blew out the candles and climbed into bed, but I didn't close my eyes. It was a long, long time before I finally slept.

Six

HE RAIN poured as it had been pouring for three days, a pounding, swirling gray mass, lashing the windows, making its own monotonous music. Seemingly endless, it caused nerves to fray, tempers to grow short, and Mallyncourt was like a solitary brown island, cut off from the rest of the world, surrounded by the ceaseless, shimmering waves of water that broke against it with such constant fury. The house was cold, damper than ever. The chimneys wouldn't draw properly. The smell of smoke hung in the air. I sat at the side of Lord Mallyn's bed, examining my cards. He waited impatiently, tapping his fingers on the large wooden tray we used for a table. I smiled and placed my cards face up on the table.

"I win," I said.

Lord Mallyn looked at the cards, bristled, lowered his brows fiercely and then swept the tray off the bed in one mighty shove. It clattered to the floor. Cards rattled loudly, flew in the air and settled on the carpet like brittle leaves. He glared at me. I gazed at him calmly, totally unperturbed. We had been playing cards together every afternoon for over a week now, and he had won only two games. I refused to let him win merely in order to humor him, and when I caught him cheating I was quite adamant. Lord Mallyn was, I think, secretly delighted, but he was a sore loser nevertheless.

"It's a shame we're not playing for money," I remarked.

"Why's that!" he barked.

"If we were, I'd be a very wealthy woman."

"You think *so*, dearie?"

"My dear Lord Mallyn, I *know* so."

Brows lowered, eyes snapping furiously, mouth screwed up in disgust, he told me in no uncertain terms that I was a scheming minx, a female card sharp and a rotten sport to boot, adding that he rued the day I came to plague him with my detestable presence.

"I'm not particularly fond of cards," I said calmly. "I'm quite willing to end these games. I find them rather a bore, if you want to know the truth of the matter. I only play because you insist."

"Bore! You find me a *bore*!"

"I find the *games* a bore," I replied. "You, I find a thoroughly wretched scoundrel who can't abide to lose. Just because you're old and ill doesn't give you the right to—"

"Do you realize who you're *talking* to!"

"Quite," I said.

Flustered, irate, he continued to glare at me, but the dark brown eyes were twinkling with amusement now, and there was the faintest suggestion of a smile on those thin white lips. Cheeks a bright pink, tarnished silver hair unruly, he looked like an incredibly aged, incredibly spoiled child pretending to be a wicked old rake. His costume was as outlandish as his conduct. His fine white muslin nightshirt frothed with ruffles at the throat and

wrists, and the rich brown satin robe he wore over
it had wide golden stripes. An enormous ruby ring
sparkled on one finger, a great hunk of turquoise on
another. Ching, Zang and Blossom, the Pekes, were
three feathery balls of red-brown fur arranged
about him, breathing asthmatically, round black
eyes bored. Quite accustomed to their master's eccentricities, not one of them had so much as lifted
an inquiring gaze when he had tumbled the tray off
the bed.

"Well? Are you going to pick up the cards?" he
grumbled.

"I'm not a servant, Lord Mallyn. Furthermore,
I have no intentions of playing another game with
you this afternoon."

"No?"

"Nor tomorrow afternoon either if you're still
in this foul mood."

"You *do* test my patience, girl," Lord Mallyn
said crossly. "I don't know why I put up with you!"

"Perhaps because no one else will put up with
you," I suggested.

"You might at least keep a civil tongue in your
head," he pouted. "I don't allow anyone *else* to talk
to me like that."

"If you find my company so disturbing, perhaps
I'd better—"

"Don't go yet! I want to chat a while."

I glanced at the clock over the mantle. "It's
time for your medicine, anyway," I said. "I suppose
I'd better stay and see that you take it. The red bottle, isn't it?"

"Damn you!" he snapped. "I don't *want* to take
that dreadful stuff! I won't!"

"It's all the same to me," I said. "If you want to

remain ill, if you want to stay in bed for the rest of—"

"Oh, all *right!* Give it here!"

I handed him the bottle and a silver spoon. Lord Mallyn took his medicine, made a face, shook his head and then grimaced again. He was in a much better condition than he had been ten days ago, when I first saw him, and both doctors attending him were amazed. They predicted that, if he continued to improve, if he took his medicine, if he ate properly and gave up his daily bottle of port, he would be up and able to exercise a bit in another week or so. Lord Mallyn fretted and stormed, threw things at the servants, conducted himself in a shocking and thoroughly deplorable manner, but he gave up the port, he ate his vegetables and beef, he took his medicine. "I intend to get well just to spite those nephews of mine," he had confided to me, and it looked as though he was truly on the road to recovery. His growing strength pleased the doctors, but it failed to elate Edward or Lyman either one.

I was delighted with his improvement, delighted to see his strength returning, but I wondered what effect this would have on my bargain with Edward. When we made it, Edward had thought his uncle was on the verge of death, had hoped to convince him to draw up the will in his favor shortly before he died. Mallyncourt would belong to Edward then, and it wouldn't matter one way or another when people discovered we weren't really married. Now, however, it looked as though Lord Mallyn might indeed live for another ten years, and even if he *did* make Edward his heir, he would be certain to change the will when he learned the truth. I couldn't stay at Mallyncourt indefinitely . . . well, that was Edward's problem. I had agreed to carry on this masquerade for six weeks at the longest, and at the end of that time I intended to leave, five hundred pounds richer, no matter how things might stand with my 'husband.'

"Nasty, vile concoction," Lord Mallyn muttered, handing bottle and spoon back to me. "I think they're trying to poison me!"

"Nonsense. You look better already. Are you warm enough? Shall I have one of the servants heat some bricks and wrap them in flannel to put under the covers? Would you like—"

"Don't *fuss* over me, girl!"

"I merely want to see you get well, Lord Mallyn."

"Do you? Yes, I believe you actually do. I wonder why."

"Why? Because for all your temper tantrums, for all your outrageous conduct, I'm slightly fond of you. Slightly, I say. Don't think that means I'll let you push me around, though, because it doesn't."

Lord Mallyn grinned. I moved across the room to one of the tall windows and, holding aside the yellow silk drape, peered out at the world of silver-gray frenzy. The thick window panes had a faint bluish tint, gleaming with slipping, sliding webs of raindrops. I could barely see the trees beyond, tormented green giants huddling in anguish as the rain continued to lash them.

"What's wrong?" the old man asked.

"Wrong?" I turned, facing him. I forced a smile. "Nothing's wrong. Whatever put such an idea in your head?"

"I haven't lived for seventy years without picking up a bit of insight into human nature, girl! I've learned a thing or two about people. I know how to read 'em. You're unhappy."

"Fiddlesticks," I said, striving for lightness.

"Is it that nephew of mine? Edward's a cold one, no doubt about it. Incapable of showin' emotion. Marryin' him was a grave mistake, lass. I shouldn't think he'd be able to make anyone happy."

"That's preposterous."

"You've been married for—what? Just under a month now. A new bride should have a certain glow. You don't, girl. And Edward—when he comes to see me he's the same as ever—cold, cynical, perfectly groomed, perfectly composed. *He* doesn't look like a man who's just married a fascinating red-haired vixen. Me, I'd be burstin' at the seams, grinning all over the place, filled with pride—"

"Edward is—he just doesn't show things," I said nervously.

"Is everything all right between the two of you?"

"Of course it is. What a silly question."

"He mistreatin' you? If he is, you just let me know! You're too good for him, I've told you that before, and if he thinks—"

"*I* think you'd better try to sleep now, Lord Mallyn. You need plenty of rest. Cook is preparing a special meal for you tonight, and when the footman brings it, I want you to eat every bite. If I hear you've been acting up again, I won't play cards with you tomorrow."

Lord Mallyn scowled, but I could see that he was tired. He pulled the old patchwork quilt up over his chest, shoved Blossom out of the way and sank back against the cushions with a weary sigh. Those shrewd brown eyes were still regarding me with close scrutiny. I picked up one of the lovely jade ornaments, pretended to examine it, set it down, studied the collection of small ivory elephants herded on top of an ebony table inlaid with mother-of-pearl.

"It's been dreary for you, girl, I know that," Lord Mallyn remarked. "Somethin' of a strain as well—bein' brought to a strange house, full of people you don't know, playin' nursemaid to a sick old man. No music, no laughter, no gaity. Any bride would find that depressin', I imagine. Well, it's going to change, lass."

"Is it?"

"I've given Vanessa permission to go ahead with her plans for a ball. Invitations have already been sent out. It'll be held two weeks from now, and you know what? I'm going to bloody well put in an appearance myself. Just you wait!"

"You'd better go to sleep now," I said crisply. "I'll be back to see you again before I go down to dinner. Behave yourself, hear?"

"Ah, Jenny, you're the best thing that's happened to me in years. I envy that lad, I do. He doesn't *deserve* a wife like you! I've told him so repeatedly."

Rain slapped viciously against the windowpanes as I moved slowly down the hall. I paused to look down at the front gardens, a writhing mass of colors tossed in the wind, red, blue, violet, gold, yellow, half-veiled by the rain. I was restless, wondering what I was going to do with the rest of the day. The past ten days *had* been dreary. Edward was distant and polite, avoiding me except when it was necessary for us to be together, never once referring to that lazy, prolonged kiss our first night here, never once indicating that he had any desire for another. Lyman was gone all day, working, working harder than ever since the rain, afraid the fields might flood.

Vanessa was completely occupied with young Lyle Radcliff. He was a handsome youth, barely twenty, obviously head over heels in love with her. They had gone out riding every day, and when the rain made that impossible he came to visit her. They were down in her private sitting room now, amusing themselves. Lettice stayed shut up in the nursery with Miss Partridge most of the time. I had seen her only once or twice since that unpleasant little scene in the drawing room when she refused to play the piano.

I had been at Mallyncourt for ten days now, filling each day as best I could. I played cards with Lord Mallyn. I explored the house. I took books from the large, beautiful formal library and read them in my room. I wrote long letters to Laverne. I chatted with Susie, a lively sprite bursting with gossip and saucy, audacious observations. The girl worshipped me, fussing over me like a hen, keeping my things in perfect order, snubbing the other maids who, she felt, were now beneath her notice. I learned quite a lot about the household from Susie, and none of it made me feel any less insecure. Although the past ten days had been serene on the surface, there was an undercurrent of tension in the air. It seemed to hang over Mallyncourt like an invisible gas that would soon explode.

I wandered slowly down the long gallery, all dim and gray now with no candles burning, the rain pounding against the hundreds of panes in the recesses. The mat of woven rushes crackled under my feet. The majestic portraits, dark, almost devoid of color in this half light, seemed to stare down at me accusingly. What are you doing here? they seemed to ask. Long gray shadows spread across the floor, nestled in the corners. There was a strong odor of damp stone, of cold ashes. It was barely two o'clock. What should I do? I couldn't wander in the gardens. I didn't feel like reading. I had written a lengthy letter to Laverne only the day before. I was at a loss, depressed by the rain, lonely, wishing something, anything, would happen to break the monotony of the past ten days. I paused to gaze up at one of the Vandykes, studying it without really seeing it.

As I stood there, listening to the violent splatter of rain against glass and stone, I was gradually aware of other noises. There was a sound of scuffling, a smothered giggle, a shuffle of footsteps. I whirled around just in time to see Susie emerging from one of the recesses. The white organdy cap she wore atop her shiny gold curls had slipped to one side, and her organdy apron was crushed. Cheeks flushed a bright pink, she dropped a quick curtsy, black taffeta skirts crackling. Then she giggled again. Her expression was undeniably sheepish, and I wasn't at all surprised to see one of the footmen step out of the recess behind her. I recognized him immediately. He was George, a husky lad with shaggy blond hair and roguish brown eyes who, Susie had confided, was ever so masterful and excitin'. Cheeky, too, she added. Very. George looked rather worried now as he tugged at his dark blue tunic to straighten it.

"Afternoon, Miss Jenny," Susie said brightly.

"Susie, you—you startled me."

"Did I? Me 'n George, we was—uh—I was 'elpin' 'im—"

"Indeed?"

Susie grinned. George looked more worried than ever. I smiled, amused at the pair of them.

"You won't tell *Jeffers*, will you?" Susie asked.

"Of course not," I assured her.

George frowned, muttered something about getting back to his post and moved briskly toward the wide steps. Susie smiled, straightening her cap, sighing contentedly as he disappeared.

"Idn't he somethin'?" she said. "Tell me, Miss Jenny, 'ave you ever *seen* such 'andsome eyes, such broad shoulders? I go limp all over, just thinkin' about 'im."

"It appears, Susie, that you're not nearly as young and innocent as I first assumed."

"What a shockin' thing to say! I'm a *good* girl, Miss Jenny, but I'm pushin' seventeen now, and it's 'igh time I started thinkin' about gettin' myself a 'usband."

"You hope to get George?"

She nodded, grinning. "'E's a regular stallion, that 'un is. All the other maids, they *hurl* themselves at 'im, chase after 'im somethin' awful, but me, I use *strategy*. I ignore 'im. I pretend I wouldn't have nothin' to do with 'im on a *bet*. It aggravates 'im no end!"

"You weren't ignoring him a few minutes ago," I remarked.

"'E's such a brute! I finished ironin' your things, Miss Jenny, and I was walkin' along, mindin' my own business when he leaped out and *grabbed* me, pulled me into the recess. If you 'adn't come along when you did, Lord *knows* what might-a 'appened—" She sighed again, dreamy-eyed as she contemplated that delicious eventuality.

I knew I should scold the girl, but it was impossible. In just this short time Susie had already captivated me. She was rather bossy, telling me what I should wear, when, what jewelry should go with it, how I should arrange my hair and so on, taking the duties of an abigail quite seriously, feeling it her own personal responsibility to see that I was turned out in grand style. I indulged her, finding it both amusing and touching. If the girl wanted to spend her spare time setting traps for the footman, that was fine with me. In a way I rather envied her. Things were so simple and clear cut for a girl like Susie.

"I guess you've been playin' cards with the old terror—uh—with Lord Mallyn again," she said. "I admire you for it, Miss Jenny. Me, I wouldn't go *near* 'im! Once I 'ad to take 'is tray in to 'im, and you know what 'e *did?* 'E *pinched* me! I got out-a there quick, I don't mind tellin' you. A girl idn't *safe.*"

"He loves to tease the servants," I told her.

"Well, he can just tease someone else! What are you going to do for the rest of the day, Miss Jenny? I 'ope you're not goin' to sit around and *read*. It idn't 'ealthy, all that readin'."

"I don't know. I—I think I'll explore the east wing. It's the only part of the house I haven't—"

I cut myself short, puzzled by the sudden change in Susie's expression. Her cheeks had gone a bit pale, and her enormous blue eyes looked worried. A frown creased her brow.

"What's wrong?" I asked.

"I wouldn't, Miss Jenny," she said.

"Wouldn't what?"

"Go into th' east wing. It—it idn't—" She paused, the frown deepening. "Me, *I* don't believe in ghosts, I've got too much sense, but just the same —well, I've 'eard them noises my*self*."

"What are you talking about, Susie?"

"Cook, now, she claims it's 'aunted for sure, but then Cook's always readin' them Tarot cards and talkin' about spirits 'n things. None of the servants'll step foot in the east wing since Betty 'ad 'er fright. It's all closed up, you see, the furniture covered with long white sheets, dust 'n cobwebs all over th' place, and one night—"

"Yes?" I prompted.

"Well, the servants' quarters are up in the attic, you know—we 'ave rooms directly over the east wing, and for over a year we've been 'earin' these strange noises—footsteps in the middle of th' night, crazy laughter, real spooky noises, Miss Jenny. I'm not lyin'. One night, oh, it must-a been six months ago, Betty, one of th' parlor maids, she was comin' in late—she'd been out behind the stables with Bertie Rawlins, one of th' grooms—and, fearin' someone might see 'er, she decided to come up the back stairs in the east wing. Just as she reached the landin' on this story, she 'eard that laughter. She stopped, terrified. Then she 'eard them footsteps and *saw* somethin'—somethin' white and misty, floatin' down the 'all. She 'ad 'ysterics. Took 'er three days to get over it."

"And?"

"Mister Lyman, 'e was furious. 'E shook 'er, told 'er to stop babblin' like an idiot, said 'e'd sack 'er if she didn't come to 'er senses. Betty never said anything else, she was too scared, but—well, none of us care to go into the east wing."

"Do you still hear the noises?" I inquired.

"Now 'n then," she said, nodding. "They never occurred every night, you understand. Just—oh, maybe once or twice a week. Night before last Tillie swore she 'eard th' footsteps again, but none of th' rest of us did. I ain't sayin' the place *is* 'aunted, Miss Jenny, but—"

"I'll be careful," I assured her.

"You mean you're still *goin'*?"

I nodded, smiling. "If a ghost leaps out at me, Susie, I promise to give you a full report."

Susie looked aghast, blue eyes wide, hands clasped across her bosom. I was greatly amused by her tale of strange, spooky noises and misty white things that floated down halls. Every great house was supposed to have its own ghost, and I was pleased to find that Mallyncourt was no exception. I rather doubted that I'd run into it, though. Still smiling, I moved past the wide steps leading down to the back hall below and stepped over to the large door that opened from the long gallery into the east wing beyond. It was closed, and the hinges screeched as I shoved it open.

I had only gone a few steps when the door swung to, slamming behind me with an explosive bang. I jumped, startled, then laughed quietly and moved on down the hall. Susie might claim she didn't believe in ghosts, but she hadn't sounded very convincing about it. The servants all tended to be superstitious, and I was far too sensible to put any stock in their tales. Betty, no doubt, was an exceedingly high strung lass with a vivid imagination, and as for the noises—well, every old house had peculiar noises. I had heard them myself. The wind whistling down the chimneys sounded like querulous voices, the windows rattling in their frames like prowlers trying to break in. The old house creaked and groaned and settled. Mice scratched behind the paneling. Tapestries flapped. The house was like one vast echo chamber, and the noises were probably magnified by the time they rose up to the attics. It was fun to think a ghost might haunt the east wing, but it was, I knew, highly unlikely.

Leaving the hall, I passed through a large room

with a great chandelier dangling from the high ceiling. Rain lashed against the tall, curtainless windows. The parquet floor was dusty. The furniture was covered with grayish white sheets. The walls, no longer white, were stained with mildew, and the gold leaf panels were flaking. It must have been a drawing room at one time, I thought, watching the cobwebs billow. The room was extremely cold, and there was a sour, unpleasant smell. Shivering, I moved on through into yet another hall. There were no windows here. Everything was dim, gray, spread with shadows, and that sour smell was stronger than ever.

Doors on either side were closed tightly. I tried to open several of them, hoping to discover another Adam fireplace, another wooden paneling carved by Grinling Gibbons, but all the rooms were locked. They were probably guest rooms in those earlier, more colorful days when Mallyncourt was visited by Queen Elizabeth and her court. This hall must at one time have been filled with gaiety and laughter as ladies in farthingales and courtiers in velvet doublets and starched neck ruffs gossiped and flirted on their way to the long gallery. It was a shame the wing was closed off now, given over to dust and decay, but even a man as wealthy as Lord Mallyn couldn't keep all the rooms in a house this large open, not in this day and age.

Slowly, aimlessly, I moved on down the hall, engrossed in my thoughts, and I don't know when it was that I noticed the silence. I stopped. Everything was still. Far, far away I could hear the sound of the rain, muted by solid stone walls, a mere pattering whisper that only intensified the silence here in the hall. I shivered, suddenly uneasy without knowing why. The walls seemed to be watching me, pressing in, and the air was fetid. I was reminded of a tomb. It was as still, as silent as a tomb, and the atmosphere was suffocating. I stood very still, my heart beginning to beat rapidly, my nerves taut. I couldn't understand it. A moment or two ago I had been thinking about gallant Elizabethans, about the pageantry of times past, and now . . . now I was tense, alarmed. There was something malevolent in the air. I sensed it all around me.

When the door swung open, when the hinges creaked rustily, I felt the color draining out of my cheeks. I almost fainted. For a moment I half expected to see something white and misty drifting toward me, and I leaned against the wall, my heart in my throat. Nothing happened. The door to a room across the hall had simply swung open. For some reason or other, it hadn't been locked like the others. There was no ghost, no malevolent presence. It had all been in my mind. Susie's tale must have registered more deeply than I thought. Taking a deep breath, I stepped across the hall to pull the door shut again.

My hand on the knob, I paused, peering into the room. How strange, I thought. This room wasn't dusty like the others. No cobwebs billowed from the ceiling. There were no dingy sheets over the furniture. Puzzled, I stepped inside. Though the light was dim, I could see that it was a bedroom with rich old mahogany wainscoting on the lower walls, deep scarlet embossed silk above. The black marble fireplace was beautifully carved, a heap of charred logs inside, a fine sprinkling of ashes on the hearth. A deep crimson carpet covered the floor, and the huge mahogany bed had a canopy of deep scarlet matching the silk on the walls. On the mantelpiece and on the low ebony tables stood a collection of fine bronzes, decidedly erotic, depicting mighty centaurs wrestling with nude men, centaurs abducting nude women, each small piece magnificently wrought, worthy of Cellini. The candles in the wall sconces were half burned, waxy drippings caked on the brass holders.

Although the rest of the wing had an aura of desertion, of being left to crumble away, I sensed an impression of life here in this room. It was as though someone had just left, as though the air itself retained the vibrations of movement, activity. The room was bizarre, unpleasant. All that red, those erotic bronzes. There was a vaguely disturbing atmosphere, impossible to define, but I had the feeling that something evil had happened here, something furtive and perverse. Why should this room be open when the rest were locked? There had been a fire in the fireplace recently. A faint odor of smoke clung to the scarlet hangings. Moving over to one of the wall sconces, I touched the wax caked on the brass holder. Though hard, it was still malleable. The candles had been burning recently, too. Who lighted them? There was a mystery here, I thought, frowning.

I remembered those disturbing, enigmatic words Lord Mallyn had spoken that first day, just before I left his room. Although I had decided later that he had been playing a prank, deliberately trying to frighten me, I had been alarmed as I stepped into the hall. I had sensed that something was wrong. I had that same feeling now. The frown still creasing my brow, I took a final look at the room, and then I turned to leave. I let out a cry as I saw the man standing in the doorway, glaring at me. The shock was so great that it took me a moment to recognize him.

"What are you doing here!"

"Edward, you—you frightened me."

"Answer my question!"

"I—I was just—"

I cut myself short, staring at him. I had never seen him this way before. His high cheekbones were chalky white, his eyes hard, snapping with angry blue fire. His mouth, set in a grim line, twitched at the corners, and he looked murderous. He looked worried, too, the icy composure gone, as though he had received a great shock.

"What—what's wrong? Why—"

"I came upstairs. You weren't in your room. The girl said you'd come to the east wing. I couldn't believe it! Don't you know—" Overcome with anger, he broke off, his nostrils flaring.

"Edward, I don't understand why you should be so—"

"You shouldn't be here. It's not safe!"

"Not safe? But—"

"Don't ask questions!"

He seized my wrist, pulling me out of the room. Still seething, he moved briskly down the hall, half dragging me along beside him. Our footsteps echoed against the walls, his loud and firm, my own beating a rapid staccato. When we reached the large, shrouded drawing room, he stopped, releasing me. He took a deep breath, his chest swelling. I could see him fighting for composure. The rain swept against the windows in angry waves. I could hear it drumming on the rooftops.

"I'm sorry," he said. "I had no cause to explode like that."

"I—I merely wanted to explore. I'd explored the rest of the house. I saw no reason why I shouldn't—"

"Of course not," he replied. He was calm now, in complete control of himself. "It's my own fault. I should have warned you."

"Warned me? About *what?* Edward, is—"

"There's nothing to be alarmed about," he said smoothly. "You're quite unharmed. The east wing isn't safe, you see. It's half decayed. The walls aren't sturdy, they've collapsed in several of the rooms. There was an accident a couple of years ago. One of the footmen was injured. When I heard you'd come here, I—well, I was frantic, afraid you might get hurt."

He was lying. I knew that immediately. His explanation was glib, well delivered, but not a word of it rang true. He was concealing something, and I sensed it was somehow connected with that room. He had been livid, consumed with fury, and there had been alarm as well. Why should he have been alarmed? Why should he have been worried? Because he feared I might have an accident? No, I couldn't accept that.

"The door to this wing should have been locked," he remarked. "I'll see that it is in the future. One of the servants might wander in here. I wouldn't want another accident."

"The servants think the place is haunted," I said.

"Haunted? Nonsense."

"Susie says they've heard peculiar noises. She said one of the maids saw something moving down the hall—"

His lips curled in a thin, deprecating smile. "I remember the incident well. The girl—Betty, I believe she's called—is an illiterate, hysterical ninny who should have been sacked."

"Edward, that room—"

"What about it? It's just a room."

"It wasn't locked. It—there were no sheets over the furniture. The fire had been—"

"We'd better get back," he interrupted, ignoring my words. "It's icy cold here. You're shivering. Come along, Jenny, and don't ever let me catch you in this wing again."

I didn't pursue it. I saw it would be futile. Edward had no intentions of answering any of my questions. Gripping my elbow firmly, he led me down the narrow, shadowy hall and into the long gallery. He closed the door to the east wing behind him and snapped the lock in place. During the time I had been gone, a servant had lighted candles in the gallery. They glowed with a wavering golden light.

"You mentioned being in my room," I said. "Was there something you wished to see me about?"

Edward nodded. "Your gown was delivered," he replied. "I thought you might like to see it."

"My gown?"

"For the ball. As soon as I heard Vanessa talking about it, I realized you hadn't anything suitable to wear. I sent a special order off to Madame DuBois, telling her what was required. She already had your measurements, naturally and it was merely a matter of selecting a suitable garment and making a few alterations."

"I—that was very thoughtful of you, Edward."

He smiled again, as cold, as remote as he had ever been. "I can be quite thoughtful on occasion, Jennifer. I'm not entirely villainous, you know. There are one or two redeeming qualities."

"Are there?"

"I'm quite pleased with the way things are developing. I had an interesting talk with my uncle last night. I believe he's almost ready to write a letter summoning the lawyers to Mallyncourt."

"Indeed?"

"He's quite taken with you. I'm certain he'll make the will in my favor. We're almost there, Jenny."

"I wonder," I said.

"What do you mean by that?"

"When we made our bargain, Edward, you thought he was on the point of death. He's recovering rapidly now. Even if he does make the will in your favor, he's bound to change it when he discovers the truth. He's not going to die conveniently as soon as he's finished signing his name. He may live for years. His recovery—changes things."

"I've thought about that, too," he replied. "You needn't worry about it. We can remedy the situation easily enough."

"Oh?"

"If worse comes to worse, I can take you back to London and marry you for real. No one need ever know the ceremony was—uh—a bit belated."

I stepped back, amazed. "That wasn't—"

"That wasn't part of our bargain, I know. The situation has altered. You needn't look so horrified, Jennifer. It might not be necessary, but if it is—I think marrying me should suit you nicely."

"If you think I—"

"I sent the gown up to your room," he said coldly. "I know you'll want to examine it. There are a few more things I need to attend to downstairs. I'll see you at dinner."

Cool, perfectly poised, he left me standing there in the gallery and moved casually toward the steps. I stared at his back, watched him disappear down the well. I heard his footsteps ringing on the wide, flat stones for a moment or so, and then they were drowned out by the sound of the rain beating, pounding, lashing against the window panes with an ever-increasing fury.

Seven

THE SUNSHINE was dazzling, splattering the gardens with warmth and radiant yellow-white light that seemed to shimmer, gilding dark green leaves, making brilliant golden patterns among the shadows cast by tree limbs over the grassy lawns. The rain was over, at last, and everything was newly washed, colors brighter, richer, the air cool and crisp and invigorating. It was impossible to stay indoors on a day like this, and I had been out for over an hour, exploring the extensive gardens behind the back lawn, marveling at the ponds afloat with pink-white lillies, surrounded by Japanese rushes that rattled in the breeze, at the mossy grotto, at the charmingly rustic stone bridges spanning a dozen artificial streams.

Wearing an old, slightly faded tan cotton dress printed with delicate blue and green flowers, my hair tangled and mussed from low-hanging twigs that had caught at it, I must have looked a bit rustic myself, but I didn't care at all. This morning I wasn't Edward's elegant, dignified wife. I was carefree, exhuberant, reveling in the rich, loamy smell of damp soil and the fragrant scent of blossoms. Bees droned, filling the air with a buzzing music. Birds twittered merrily, as elated as I was that the rain no longer fell, and, in the gentle breeze, trees seemed to stretch and shake their boughs in glorious relief.

Leaving the watery gardens behind, I explored the walled gardens that extended in terraces on the west side of the grounds. The flat, brown stone steps were warm from the sun. Hollyhocks, red, purple, violet, grew in untidy heaps against the walls, alternating with vividly blue larkspurs. I passed under trellises heavily laden with honeysuckle, the bees a veritable orchestra here, and, finally, reached the small walled herb garden. There was a low stone bench outside the wall, shaded by a giant elm that spread enormous boughs overhead, and I sat down, leaning back against the wall, peering across the expanse of raked gravel at the maze of clipped yews that grew on this, the lowest level of terrace.

Perhaps it was the sense of release after almost a week of rain, but I was in a remarkably light-hearted mood. All problems seemed minor, and the "mystery" of the east wing seemed, this morning, an absurdity I had created in my own mind. Not even the argument I had had with Edward after breakfast could deflate my high spirits. I had been in the back hall, ready to go outside, when he stopped me, a stern, icy expression on his face. Without a word, he handed me a cheap, rather battered envelope with a postmark from London.

"What's this?" I inquired.

"Jeffers brought the mail to me in the study. It seems you've received a letter."

I examined it, surprised, and then I smiled.

"Why—it's from Laverne!" I exclaimed.

"Laverne?"

"One of the actresses from the company. I've

been writing to her. I wonder what she's doing in London—"

"You've been writing to her?"

"Of course. We were very close, you see, and—"

"I see that the letter is addressed to Mrs. Edward Baker," he said in a smooth, silken voice. "That would seem to indicate, Jenny dear, that this —Laverne person knows far more than she should."

"She knows everything," I replied. "Oh, don't worry, Edward. Laverne was like a mother to me. She'd never—"

"You told her about our arrangement?" he interrupted.

"Naturally. There's nothing to be—"

He was livid, his mouth tight, his blue eyes crackling with anger. For a moment, I thought he was going to seize me by the shoulders and shake me, but he managed to control his rage, growing more rigid and aloof, and when he spoke, his voice was as smooth, as silken as ever, far more chilling than heated exclamations would have been.

"You realize, of course, that you've jeopardized everything? What if your dear Laverne decided to take advantage of this knowledge? What if she decided to employ a little blackmail? If she knows about the situation, she must know how imperative it is that it be kept secret. You didn't think about that, did you, Jennifer?"

"Laverne would never do a thing like that!" I said angrily.

"Keep your voice down. I don't want the servants to hear."

"You think everyone is vile, don't you? Just because you—you have no scruples yourself, you think everyone else—"

Flinging an arm around the back of my neck, he

clapped his other hand over my mouth before I could say more. He held me like that, a thin smile on his lips as he peered down at me. I tried to break free. His grip tightened. Even though it was firmly controlled, I could feel his rage. I was furious myself as that palm crushed my lips.

"Listen to me, luv," he said tenderly, "and listen very carefully. You will write to this woman. You will tell her we're leaving for France, that we plan to spend several weeks there and will no longer be at Mallyncourt. If she has blackmail in mind, that should hold her off for a while. You will give the letter to me when you've finished writing it, and afterwards you will write no more. Do you understand?"

I glared up at him with blazing green eyes, stubbornly refusing to nod. The smile tightening on his lips, Edward pressed his palm brutally, forcing my head back against the curve of his arm. The muscles in my neck stretched painfully. I felt I was going to smother.

"Do you understand?" he repeated gently.

I nodded. He held me for a moment more, studying my eyes, and then he released me. My anger hadn't abated one jot. I wanted to slap him across the face. I wanted to drive the toe of my shoe into his shin with a savage kick. I didn't. I didn't dare. Edward seemed amused, as though it had delighted him to display such brutal mastery.

"I hate you!" I whispered fervently.

"I think not, my dear," he replied, relaxed now. "I could prove it to you if I cared to, but I really haven't the time this morning. I still have to check over some ledgers and make sure Lyman hasn't robbed us blind while I was out scouting for a wife."

"You—"

"Later, perhaps, I'll prove to you what your feelings toward me really are. It should be a—most pleasant task. In the meantime, think what you like, by all means. Don't forget about that letter, Jenny luv. I'll expect you to give it to me before we go down to dinner tonight."

Livid, I marched outside, slamming the door behind me in a most undignified manner, and, crossing the veranda, walked briskly to the white marble bench at the back of the lawn. I was so angry that I could hardly tear the letter open, but, curiously enough, the anger soon evaporated. The dazzling sunlight, the warbling birds, the heavenly scent of flowers: All cast their spell over me, and Laverne's cheerful, gossipy letter completed the job. Folding the letter, putting it in the pocket of my skirt, I began to explore the gardens, and now, an hour later, the quarrel with Edward seemed trivial.

He had been right, of course. Under the circumstances, I should never have written to Laverne. I took her letter out, rereading it as rays of mote-filled sunlight slanted through the boughs of the elm. I wasn't really surprised to learn that the Gerald Prince Touring Company was no more. The engagement following Brighton had been disastrous, the box office receipts practically nil, and, to top it off, a fire had broken out backstage, destroying half the scenery and most of the costumes. Putting what money there was in his own pocket, Gerry had taken a train to parts unknown leaving the company stranded and, for the most part, penniless. Laverne had been fortunate. Having saved a few pounds for a rainy day, she departed for London where, miraculously, she learned from an old theatrical crony that the Haymarket needed a wardrobe mistress. She had applied immediately, got the job with no trouble at all and was now happily sewing spangles and feathers on tattered costumes, ironing threadbare gowns and mending holes in worn silk tights. Her letter was full of chatty anecdotes, and she even hinted at a possible romance with the stage manager, a gruff, grizzled chap of forty-some-odd who found her most appealing.

Putting the letter away, I sighed, thinking about those four tumultuous, highly-colored years I had spent with the company. All that seemed so long ago now, a vague, distant memory, although it had been little over a month since I had departed from Brighton. I had been lucky to get away when I did. How like Gerry to leave the troupe stranded. It was a wonder the company hadn't fallen apart years ago, I thought, resting my back against the sun-warmed brown stone wall, watching the play of sun and shadow shifting over the gravel. In the elm, a thrush sang lustily, chest puffed up as he celebrated the radiant blue sky, the heady spring air. I was pleased with Laverne's good fortune. I was eager to write and tell her so. Oh, I would write the letter for Edward, just as he had ordered, but I would write another one secretly. I would explain that she wasn't to write to me again and tell her why, and then I would give the letter to George to mail for me. Ever since I had discovered him with Susie, he was eager to serve me in any way he could.

Idly brushing a twig from my skirt, I thought about the encounter with Edward this morning, no longer angry about it. In fact, it gave me a curious exhilaration to replay it now in memory. He had been vile, true, but at least he had shown *some* emotion. I hated him, I told myself, but, deep down, I knew that wasn't true. So did Edward. I wondered about my feelings toward him. He was a fascinating creature, I couldn't deny that. I remembered that kiss, remembered the sensations I had experienced in his arms. Was I merely an employee to him? If necessary, he was ready to marry me, but that was because of greed. He hadn't mentioned that possible marriage again, but I frequently found myself contemplating it, wondering if I would agree to it. Of course not! I told myself harshly. I wanted only to finish my part of the bargain and leave. I wanted to open my dress shop. I wanted independence. Edward Baker meant nothing to me but five hundred pounds, and I would be delighted to see the last of him.

I sat up with a start as I heard the voices.

"She's such a *drab* child," Vanessa said.

"She can't help it if she's not beautiful," Lyman growled.

"I simply fail to understand how *I* could be the mother of such an ugly little sparrow." Her voice sounded strange, a bit too high-pitched. "She has no wit, Lyman, no sparkle. Surely a gypsy must have switched babies on us."

"Maybe so," Lyman rumbled.

The voices were coming from the herb garden, immediately behind me. I was appalled, afraid they might discover me, afraid Lyman might think I was eavesdropping again. Then, as the conversation continued, I frowned, puzzled. Lyman's voice sounded peculiar, too, not nearly deep enough, and when Vanessa spoke again there was a tremulous quality, the sentence ending with a tight little squeak. I realized then that both voices were one, that both were exceptionally clever imitations. A third voice spoke. It was soft and crooning, incredibly tender.

"Don't you fret, precious. Mother loves you.

You're not beautiful either, but it doesn't matter, you see. I love you just the same—"

It was one of the most heartbreaking things I had ever heard. It hurt, hearing that voice, hearing those words, and I was unable to help myself. Rising, I moved to the wrought-iron gate that led into the herb garden. I opened it very quietly, closed it soundlessly behind me. A small, gnarled apple tree, frothy with pink and white blossoms, grew beside one of the uneven stone walls espaliered with neatly clipped green shrubs. The child sat beneath the tree, her legs folded under her, her simple yellow dress making a wide circle on the grass. In her arms she cradled a shabby, tattered rag doll, and beside her were several more dolls, far more splendid. One was male, black hair painted on china skull, wearing an elegant suit, and one was dressed in a golden gown, obviously the pair she had been using to represent her parents.

In the sunlight, her long straight brown hair gleamed with rich golden highlights. Her pale, thin face had a pinched look, an undeniably plain face, but the sour, belligerent expression was missing. Her gray eyes, ordinarily hostile, were filled with tenderness now as she gazed down at the rag doll, her lashes casting soft shadows over the sharp, angular cheekbones. It was a poignant sight. I felt a lump forming in my throat. Unaware of my presence, Lettice continued to croon, rocking the doll in her arms. Then, gently, she placed it in the doll carriage setting beneath the tree and, sighing, stood up.

She saw me. She bristled. The tenderness left her eyes. They snapped with hostility again. Her hands clenched into tight fists.

"Hello, Lettice," I said casually.

"What do you want here!"

"I—I don't want anything. I didn't mean to disturb you. I was exploring the gardens, and I smelled the herbs. I thought I'd come and look at them. What a lovely knot garden, all laid out in geometrical designs. I don't know that I've ever seen a prettier one—"

"Go away!"

"You don't want to be friendly?"

"I don't *need* friends. Besides, you're a grown up."

"Does that mean I can't be your friend?"

"You feel sorry for me. I can see it in your eyes. Poor little Lettice, you're thinking. She's so lonely. She needs someone to take an interest in her. Well, you can forget that. I'm a very *bright* child, and I don't want to be patronized."

"I see. Well, I suppose I'll just have to do without."

"Do without what?" she asked harshly, suspicious.

"A friend. You see, I'm lonely, too. Your mother —I might as well be frank, since you're so bright— your mother doesn't care for me, and my husband has been very busy, going over the estate books. I've had nothing to do, no one to talk to."

"You play cards with my great-uncle. You play several games with him, every afternoon. He used to play cards with *me*."

"And you resent that. I understand perfectly. Well, that's all right. I'd much prefer to have an *adult* friend anyway. Why should I want to be friends with a child? I've no idea."

Turning my back to her, I strolled over to the edge of the knot garden and peered at it. It was small, a patchwork of color, and beyond grew the beds of tangy-scented herbs. I could feel the child's eyes glaring at me as I bent to examine a sprig, touch a petal. When I turned, her face was like the face of a fiery young Amazon warrior.

"You still here?" I asked idly.

"I was here *first!*"

"My, you *are* a shrewish little thing."

"You don't like me, do you?"

"Of course not. No one likes a shrew."

"I don't *want* anyone to like me."

"I quite understand, dear. Do go on about your business. Don't let me bother you. Oh my, what lovely dolls—" I exclaimed, pretending to notice them for the first time.

"You're too old to be interested in dolls," she said scathingly.

"I know, dear. I gave them up *years* ago, but seeing them reminds me of Amanda."

"Amanda?"

"She was such a dear thing—I loved her deeply. When I was lonely, when I was sad, I'd talk to Amanda. It was—very comforting. She had big blue eyes. She looked up at me. She seemed to understand every word I was saying. Poor dear, she's stuck away in a trunk now."

"You still have her?"

"Naturally. I used to make clothes for her. I made the loveliest little gowns. Hats, too. I covered cardboard with silk, pasted tiny colored feathers on them, and—oh my, you probably think I'm patronizing you! I shouldn't have brought it up."

Lettice scowled, intrigued in spite of herself but determined not to show it.

"Amanda's a *stupid* name for a doll!"

"You think so? Perhaps you're right, but I was inordinately fond of her just the same. She was quite the best dressed doll you'd ever hope to see. I wonder if I can still make doll clothes? It's been such a long time since I've made any. Oh well, why should I *want* to?"

"I—" She hesitated, still scowling.

"Yes?"

"I don't believe you *have* a doll named Amanda! I believe you made it up. And even if you do, I'll bet you never made clothes for her."

"I beg to differ with you, dear. I might be out of practice *now*, but at one time I was the best doll seamstress in all of York. Why, I even made clothes for *other* girls' dolls. It was such fun—gathering up pieces of cloth, hunting for bits of bright ribbon. The other girls would bring their dolls over, and I'd sew for them, too. Of course, I *charged*—" That, I thought, was a very realistic touch. "A penny a hat, tuppence a dress. I made quite a lot of spending money that way."

Totally uninterested, or at least pretending to be, Lettice began to gather up the other dolls and place them in the carriage alongside the ugly rag doll. When they were all lined up, she pushed the small black hood in place, took hold of the handle and turned to me with a sour, derisive expression.

"If you *do* have a doll named Amanda, you may bring her up to the nursery to visit tomorrow morning at ten. I don't believe you do, though. I still think you made it all up."

Pointed chin at a haughty angle, long brown hair streaming down her back, she left the garden, the wheels of the doll carriage creaking noisily as she pushed it ahead of her. I was in rather a fix, I reflected. I had made the first tentative step toward breaking through Lettice's crusty shell and winning her friendship. However snippy her voice may have been, she *had* invited me to come to the nursery, but

I couldn't go without Amanda. Amanda, of course, had been created from whole cloth. As a child I had been interested in books, not dolls, and I had no earthly idea how I was going to obtain one before tomorrow.

Eight

I WORRIED about it the rest of the morning, and after lunch I sent word to Lord Mallyn that we wouldn't be able to have our regular card game that afternoon. Someway, somehow, I had to find a doll. When I explained my dilemma to her, Susie solved it promptly. Although she couldn't understand why I would want to make friends with a thorny, 'ateful brat like that Miss Lettice, a regular terror if ever there was one, she informed me that there was a small shop in the village that sold a few toys and said I could probably find a doll there. She would send George down to the stables immediately and have arrangements made to drive me there.

"It's such a lovely day—I'd rather walk," I told her.

"Walk!" Susie was horrified. "That idn't *thinka*-ble, Miss Jenny. Mr. Edward's wife can't *walk* to the village—unescorted, too! It'd cause a bloomin' scandal!"

"Don't be absurd. Besides, no one in the village knows who I am, and in this old dress I'm wearing they'd never guess."

"Mr. Edward wouldn't like it either. 'E'd be furious if—"

"No one need ever know," I said calmly. "I should be back by four at the latest, Susie."

Seeing that any further argument would be futile, Susie gave an exasperated sigh, told me where to locate the shop and added that if I'd walk through the woods and over the fields behind the tenant farms I could save a good half mile both ways. I set out, amused by Susie's sense of propriety. I supposed it *was* rather unconventional, but then I had spent four years in the theater and was quite accustomed to breaking conventions.

The walk was lovely, the woods thick and green and dark, filled with glorious smells and rustling noises. The fields I crossed, far from the road leading to Mallyncourt, were uncultivated, rather stark, going to waste. Lyman, I knew, wanted to buy this land and add it to the estate, claiming it could be made to yield a good profit, but Lord Mallyn refused to authorize such an expenditure. Pausing on a grassy knoll, the wind whipping my skirts about my legs and tearing at my hair, I looked down at the tenant farms almost half a mile from where I stood. They were lovely, lush, squares of gold, green, brown, all enclosed with their low gray stone walls. I saw a flock of sheep moving up a rolling green hill, fleecy white lambs gamboling after the ewes, and the sky was like a clear, incredibly blue canopy stretching overhead.

The village was busy and bustling, for it was market day, farm carts from all over the county pulled up around the square, the air filled with noisy bartering. I was enchanted by the rustic charm of the place. The cobblestone streets were steep and narrow, and the old stone shops, brown and gray-brown and mellow gold-brown, had painted wooden signs dangling over their doors. Tall trees spread soft violet-gray shade over the pavements, thick green leaves rustling overhead. There was an ancient church with a tarnished copper spire rising over the treetops, and from the blacksmith's shop came the monotonous clang of iron on iron. Although the village was crowded today, no one paid any attention to me as I moved past the market stalls and headed toward the shop Susie had told me about.

It was wonderful to feel so carefree, so alive, to be Jenny Randall again and forget about the role I had been playing for the past weeks. The strain of those weeks had been worse than I thought, but now I could revel in freedom, if only for a short while. I stopped to peer over the wall at the old, moss-covered marble tombstones in the churchyard, moved on up the street to see the loaves of freshly-baked bread in the baker's window. The shop I was looking for was located on the next corner, a dim, dusty place with a charm and character all its own. I found the doll immediately. It was very old-fashioned, a bit shopworn, but that suited my purpose nicely. I wouldn't want anything too grand. The shopkeeper wrapped it up in a neat parcel for me, and, my mission accomplished, I left the village just shortly after three o'clock.

Moving down a narrow, sandy lane with wild hawthorns, ablaze with red and pink blossoms, growing thickly on either side, I soon reached the wooden stile that led into the fields. I climbed over it and stood there for a moment, marveling at the sight unfolding before me. To my right, as far as the eye could see, were the cultivated tenant farms belonging to Mallyncourt, while the fields on the left were gray green, moorlike, making a striking contrast. In the distance, a mile and a half away, I could see the rooftops of the great house, just visible beyond the woods. Silhouetted against the sky, a darker blue now, gray clouds drifting and casting great rolling shadows over the land, it all made a magnificent panorama. Something inside of me responded to this land, unlike any I had known before. It was so vast, so lovely. I could see why Lyman loved it, why it meant so much to him. Unlike Edward, he *belonged* here. He was a part of all this, as his ancestors had been before him. It meant nothing to Edward besides a source of income.

I was in a thoughtful mood as I wandered slowly across the fields. How strange life was, I reflected, and how unpredictable. Five years ago I had been living in a genteel country house, surrounded by friends and two loving parents, a completely typical product of our age with a typical future in store: a husband, a home, children. That had changed so quickly, so abruptly, and now, after four years in the gaudy, flamboyant world of a ramshackle theatrical company here I was, strolling across a rough, grassy field with a doll under my arm. Six weeks ago I had never heard of Mallyncourt, yet now my whole life was centered around the house and the people who lived there. What did the future hold in store for me next? Would there be another abrupt, dramatic change? I wondered what I would be doing a year from now.

Not paying much attention where I was going, I stumbled down a grassy slope covered with gay yellow buttercups and tiny, delicate pink flowers I didn't recognize. The fragrance was delicious. I stopped to gather a handful, holding them up to my nostrils. A shadow fell over the land as another cloud passed over the sun, and everything was dark for a moment, gradually lightening again as the cloud rolled on. The sunlight was dimmer now, a pale, misty white, and the sky an even darker blue, blue gray. Moving on across the fields, I saw an old, deserted barn ahead, a weather-beaten relic of more prosperous days. The great doors sagged open, revealing the darkness within, and damp, ancient hay spilled from the loft. Absorbed in my thoughts, I drew nearer and nearer the barn, the ground rough and soggy underfoot.

" 'Ey, lassie, what's your 'urry?"

The voice startled me. I dropped my parcel. The wildflowers scattered over the ground at my feet.

"She's a ripe 'un, ain't she, Burt? Ain't never seen *'er* around these parts before."

"I ain't either. Maybe she's a new maid at th' big 'ouse. Yeah, that's it. I 'ear th' dandy nephew got 'im a new wife. This 'un's probably 'er maid."

Completely lost in thought, I hadn't heard them approaching, and now it was too late. There were two of them. The blond was tall and muscular, a leather jerkin hanging open over his coarse white linen shirt, his faded tan breeches tucked into the tops of tall, muddy-brown boots. He looked at me with good-natured blue eyes, but there was a smile of anticipation on his sensual pink lips. His companion, similarly dressed, was thin and wiry with a pale, ugly face pitted with pock marks. A fringe of thick black hair fell over his brow, and his black eyes were sullen. They were yokels, obviously illiterate, and I blanched as I remembered the tales Susie had told me about their like. Rowdy, usually out of work, they roamed the countryside getting into fights, stirring up trouble, and any girl who fell into their hands was considered fair game.

"What's your name, lassie?" the blond asked.

I tried to speak. I couldn't. My throat was dry. My heart began to pound.

"She's shy, Burt," the other replied. "My name's Charlie, lass, 'n this 'ere's Burt. We're a couple-a sparks, we are, always lookin' for a bit of fun. You like a bit of fun?"

"Don't pay no 'tention to *'im*, lass," Burt said, grinning. " 'E's full of talk, nothin' but talk. Me, I'm a man of action. 'Ow's about a friendly little kiss? Hunh? The girls 'round 'ere, they say there ain't no one can plant-a kiss like Burt Brown, 'n that's me!"

"Don't—don't come near me," I stammered.

" 'Ey, Charlie, she don't wanna be friendly."

"That don't matter to me. It don't matter at all. She's a beauty, she is. I ain't waitin' for no invitation."

I was terrified, positively terrified. During the past four years I had grown very adept at dealing with men—rowdy students, fresh salesmen, pseudogentlemen who had had too much to drink— but I had never been confronted with this sort. Burt was like a great, overgrown puppy who could turn vicious at a moment's notice, and the other, Charlie, had a sharp, mean look. Rape would be second nature to either of them, a bit of frolic all in a day's fun. I tried to still my pounding heart. I tried to think. Burt grinned. Charlie glared at me with smouldering black eyes.

"You—you're making a big mistake," I said. There was a tremor in my voice. I fought to control it. "You—you'd better go on about your business. You don't know who I am."

"Yeah? Just who are ya?" Charlie asked in a mocking voice.

"I'm Edward Baker's wife. You know who *he* is, surely?"

"Yeah, I know. A regular bastard. 'N I know about 'is wife, too. She's a fine lady, I 'ear, all elegant 'n swell. She don't go traipsin' across th' fields in no grass-stained cotton dress."

"I am Jennifer Baker," I said coldly. The tremor was gone now.

"Yeah, 'n me, I'm th' Prince-a Wales."

"Charlie—" Burt's voice sounded rather nervous. "I 'eard she 'as red 'air. Angus Crow, 'e saw Baker 'n 'is wife gettin' off th' train. 'E said she 'ad red 'air."

"So?"

"Maybe—"

"You gonna let some lyin' wench cheat-ya outta a bit of fun? She ain't no swell Edward Baker's grand wife. Look at 'er! You're a maid, ain't-ya, lass? You work at th' big 'ouse. Come on, Burt, we're wastin' time standin' 'ere talkin'."

"Look, if she works at th' big 'ouse, maybe we'd better lay off. Them footmen, they're a rough bunch. One of 'em's bound to 'ave 'propriated 'er for 'imself already. That George—I tangled with 'im last month at th' pub. I ain't lookin' forward to no rematch."

"Go on, then. Run 'ome to your mother. I can 'andle this 'un all by myself."

"'Ey," Burt growled. "You sayin' I'm scared?"

"I ain't sayin' nothin'. You wanna stand there gawkin', it's fine with me. I got better things to do. Yeah, I'm feelin' real randy. Come on, lass, you 'n me 're goin' in that barn."

Frantic, I backed away. Charlie advanced, his eyes glowing like angry black coals. He seized my arm, but I managed to pull away. That made him even angrier. His mouth turned down at the corners. He lunged at me, flinging his arms around me, and both of us tumbled to the ground, Charlie on top. The impact of the fall knocked my breath away, but I was possessed with fury and a strength born of desperation. I fought. I pushed. I shoved. I caught my nails against his cheek, raked them down the length of it, and Charlie rolled off of me, yowling like a madman as blood poured from those four long gashes on his face. Burt was delighted. He stood there with his legs spread wide apart, balled fists planted on his thighs. Deep laughter rumbled from his chest as I climbed to my feet, panting. Charlie grabbed at my ankle and missed. I kicked him squarely in the face, putting all the strength I possessed into that kick.

Burt stopped laughing. He scowled.

" 'Ey now, you play rough, little lady. That ain't no way to treat my friend Charlie. Looks like I'm gonna hafta teach you a lesson—"

"You—you'll be sorry. My husband—"

"You ain't gotta 'usband, lassie. Charlie was right. You're just a maid. A lady, she would-a swooned. You're a regular wildcat. I don't care if you *do* work at th' big 'ouse, I'm gonna teach you a lesson. Poor Charlie—he's plumb out cold."

"Stay away from me!"

"I ain't scared, little lady. Me, I like 'em to fight a bit. Makes it more interestin' like."

Slowly, heavily, he moved toward me. Half veiled by drooping lids, his blue eyes were filled with lazy anticipation. An amused smile played on the sensual pink mouth. As he reached for me, I swung my hand back and sent it forward in a vicious slap. Burt caught my wrist in midair, giving it a savage twist that caused me to cry out in pain. Chuckling now, he pulled me into his arms. He was much larger than Charlie, and much stronger, too, those muscular arms like steel bands wrapping

around me. I tried to hit. I tried to kick. It was futile.
Swinging me around, Burt seized me by the hair,
curling his other arm around my waist in a crushing
hold. Chuckling with lusty glee, he started toward
the gaping barn doors, half dragging, half carrying
me along with him.

There was a great pile of moldy hay just inside.
He set me down. I was so weak and frightened I
could hardly stand, but, nevertheless, I tried to push
past him and run back out into the sunlight. Burt
scowled and then slapped me across the cheek with
such vindictive force that my head snapped back
and I fell hurtling into the hay. Stunned, my head
whirling, I sank against the hay, half-conscious. Everything seemed to shimmer and blur before my
eyes. The barn was dim, filled with shadows beyond
the patch of sunlight slanting through the doors. I
saw rotten wooden rafters, cobwebs, huge sacks of
spoiled grain spilling onto the hard earth floor. This
wasn't happening. It wasn't real. It was a nightmare, a horrible nightmare, and I would surely
wake up.

My heart was pounding, pounding, like horse
hooves, it sounded like horse hooves pounding on
the turf, and the barn was spinning around me and
the damp, ancient hay clung to me, claiming me,
and I tried to wake up, tried to end this tormenting
nightmare, but it was real, no dream, real, the barn,
the terrible odor of sweat and manure and molder-
ing hay, and the man was real, too, standing there
with those strong legs spread apart, his chest heaving, hands fumbling awkwardly as he tugged at his
jerkin to pull it off. Someone was sobbing, low, frantic sobs that were hoarse tormented gasps, and I
realized I was making those sounds. I tried to get to

my feet. His arm shot out. His palm hit my shoulder, shoving me back, deeper into the hay.

"Please—" I whispered hoarsely. "You can't—"

"Shut up!" he snarled.

"You can't. You mustn't—"

"Stop whinin'. You're gonna luv it, lass. All th' girls do. There ain't no better man than Burt Brown, not in th' whole bloomin' county. Me, I know 'ow to make a lass feel real—"

He broke off abruptly, an incredulous expression on his face. The haze before my eyes was thicker than ever now, shimmering like bright mist, but I saw him tense, saw the muscles in his face tighten. Struggling into a sitting position, fighting the hay, I heard the horse hooves pounding and through the door I saw the great black beast racing toward the barn, clods of earth splattering beneath its hooves. With a mighty jerk of the reins the rider brought it to a sudden halt a few yards away from the door, flew off its back, came hurtling into the barn like one possessed. Burt gave a yell as that body ploughed into his, sending them both crashing to the floor with a deafening thud. I heard painful grunts, the sound of breaths knocked out of bodies, the sound of bones crushing against bones.

My heart was beating furiously, my head whirling, and I felt sore and bruised all over, too weak to move, yet I climbed to my feet, showers of hay falling around me, clinging to my skirt, my hair. I backed up against the wall, flattening myself against it. Panting, my bosom rising and falling, I fought back the fluttering black wings that seemed to beat inside my head, threatening a total eclipse. I couldn't faint. Not now. Dazed, tears streaking down my cheeks, I watched the two men groping and grappling and rolling over the floor, a tangle of thrashing limbs.

Burt was stretched out on the floor now, and Lyman was on top of him, sitting on his chest, a knee on either side of his opponent, his fingers caught up in Burt's tawny hair. Yes, it was Lyman, his white linen shirt damp with sweat, his lips drawn back over his teeth, his dark brown eyes crackling with murderous rage as he jerked Burt's head up, pounded it back against the floor, again, again, raven locks spilling over his eyes as he dealt those punishing blows. Burt heaved, thrashed, arms flailing, and he threw Lyman off, sent him rolling against the sacks of grain. Both men scrambled to their feet, panting. Burt's fist swung through the air like a mighty hammer, catching Lyman across the jaw. I heard the crushing impact of that blow, saw Lyman's body banging against the opposite wall, his arms flung out.

I cried out, horrified. Neither man heard me.

Staggering, his knees seeming to give way beneath him, Burt almost crumpled to the floor, managing to catch himself just in time. Like some great, crazed animal, he shook his head, then reeled toward Lyman, fist drawn back to deliver another powerful blow. I saw the fist swing again, flying toward Lyman's jaw, saw Lyman throw himself to one side. Burt let out an anguished scream as his fist crashed against the wall, wood splintering beneath his knuckles. Leaping up, Lyman threw his arm out, slung it around Burt's throat, jerking upwards and back. Burt gurgled and gasped as the arm wrapped tighter and tighter in a crushing stranglehold. His face turned red, redder and Lyman was almost bent over backwards now, putting more and more pressure on that throat caught between his bicep and forearm. Burt threw his feet against the wall pushing violently, and they both fell to the ground again, Lyman losing his hold.

It was over very quickly then. Half choked, his strength gone, Burt was no match for the other man now. Eyes closed, blond hair plastered over his forehead, he held Lyman in a loose grip, but Lyman broke away quickly, springing to his feet. On his knees now, reeling from side to side, Burt managed to stand, only to fall again as Lyman delivered a knuckle-bruising right. Burt toppled against the sacks of grain like a giant rag doll, limp, sliding slowly to the hard packed earth floor in a crumpled heap, completely unconscious. Lyman stood over him, his chest heaving, fists hanging at his sides, trying to catch his breath.

Several long moments passed. Burt didn't stir. Lyman breathed deeply and stood up straight, shoving the damp raven locks from his forehead. His shirt, half-pulled out, clung to his chest in wet patches. His black doeskin breeches were streaked with dirt. I was still leaning flat against the wall. I stood up, brushing the hay from my skirt. Lyman looked at me, his dark brown eyes expressionless, his mouth set in a tight line. There was a deepening violet bruise on one broad cheekbone.

"Are—are you all right?" I whispered.

He nodded brusquely.

"There's another one—outside."

"I saw him. He was on his knees, moaning, holding his jaw. It looked broken. How did that happen? They fight over you?"

"I—I kicked him in the face. They were going to —it was—"

"Don't," he said gruffly.

"I didn't hear them. I turned around and there they were. I—if you hadn't—"

"I was working in one of the fields. I happened to look up and see you walking along the horizon. A couple of minutes later I saw the two of them following you. I ran for my horse, got here as fast as I could. Did anything happen? Did he—"

"No," I said.

I was calm, perfectly calm, and my voice was level. I looked at him, so calm, and then the haze was there again, shimmering in front of my eyes, and I was trembling, shivering, my body icy cold. I felt the wetness on my cheeks, and things were blurring. I seemed to be crying. Why should I be crying? It was over now. I was perfectly calm. I felt his warmth, the hard solid strength of his body. My cheek was buried against his damp shirt and he was holding me, supporting me. My knees were like water, and I would have fallen if those arms hadn't been fastened around me so securely. Sobs wracked my body. I continued to shiver, and everything seemed to hang suspended in a vague, hazy darkness. I could hear his heartbeats, smell his sweat and the pungent male odor of his body, and that strength was there, protecting me. One large hand was stroking my hair, brushing away the bits of hay.

"Don't," he said. His rough, husky voice was tender and incredibly soothing. "You're all right. Don't, Jenny, don't cry. It's over. I'm here. Hush now. Do you hear me? Don't cry—"

Time passed. I stopped sobbing. The shivering ceased. Lyman held me against him, and I moved in his arms. He released me, stepping back. I couldn't bring myself to look in his eyes.

"You all right now?" he asked. His voice was flat.

"Yes. I—I don't know what came over me."

"Shock. It was a perfectly natural reaction."

I looked up at him. His face was impassive, his features granitelike. I might have imagined that tenderness in his voice.

"Come on," he said tersely. "We'd better get you back to Mallyncourt now."

We stepped out into the sunlight. Charlie was gone. Back in the barn, Burt was beginning to stir. I could hear him moaning. Lyman's horse was a few yards away, grazing on the short, stiff grass. Lyman stepped over to it and gave it a swift slap on the buttocks. The horse snorted indignantly and then galloped off down the slope, disappearing from sight.

"Why did you do that?" I asked, puzzled.

"He'll go back to the stables by himself. We'll walk. You need some more time to compose yourself, Mrs. Baker."

It had been Jenny a few minutes ago, I thought ruefully. Lyman tucked his shirt more securely into the waistband of his tight doeskin breeches, brushed a few stray locks from his forehead. He was calm, unperturbed, his manner coldly severe. He exuded strength and self-confidence. It was difficult to believe he had half murdered a man less than ten minutes ago. Had I imagined that tenderness when he was holding me? Had that soft, crooning voice, those gentle hands been an hallucination? It seemed incongruous now. Now he was the terse, rude Lyman of old.

I stepped over to pick up my parcel. The wildflowers were still scattered on the ground where I had dropped them. Arms folded across his chest, Lyman waited for me to join him, and together we set off across the fields, both silent. Clouds continued to drift across the sun, casting large shadows that floated over the fields like misty gray veils. The barn was soon far behind us, out of sight behind a knoll, the woods ahead, dark green and shadowy under the deepening blue sky. The wind whipped at my skirts, causing them to billow behind me. Strands of hair blew across my face. Lyman restrained his normal brisk stride, keeping pace with me, yet he might have been alone, immersed in thought, a grim expression on his face. Once I stumbled over a rock, tottered. He grabbed my arm, supporting me, but still he didn't speak.

He loathed me. That much was obvious. He had disapproved of me ever since I arrived at Mallyncourt, resenting my presence, and I could understand that under the circumstances. I was in league with Edward, and Edward was his arch rival. He had come charging to the rescue back there, true, but that was no more than any man would have done, and he had comforted me, because I was in a state of shock, holding me in his arms, murmuring quiet words of reassurance, but it had meant nothing at all. It had been an act of charity, and he probably despised me all the more for my weakness.

Reaching the woods, we walked down the shadowy green tunnels, thick black-brown trunks on either side of the pathway, spreading branches making a leafy canopy above through which only a few rays of sunlight slanted like hazy yellow-white fingers. When the woods began to thin, when through the trees we could see the stables on the east side of the house, Lyman stopped and turned to me. His rough-hewn features were still like granite, his dark eyes expressionless.

"What happened back there isn't the sort of thing you'd want to have bandied about," he said sternly. "We'll say nothing about it to anyone. You were badly frightened and shaken up a bit, but you're unharmed. I have a couple of bruises, but I'll live. None of it ever happened, all right? No one else need ever know about it."

I nodded meekly. "I—I never thanked you, Lyman."

"That was a damn fool thing you did, going off alone like that. Ladies in this part of the country don't go out unescorted, Mrs. Baker. You're lucky I happened to see you. Maybe this taught you a lesson. Maybe you'll conduct yourself with a little more propriety from now on."

I didn't answer him. There was nothing I could say that wouldn't have made matters worse. We moved on toward the stables, leaving the woods behind us. As we drew near the buildings, a fine gray stallion pranced down the drive leading around to the front of the house, young Lyle Radcliff in the saddle. Lyman watched horse and rider disappear, expressionless, but when his wife came strolling around the corner of one of the buildings he tensed slightly. Seeing us, Vanessa stopped. A mocking smile began to form on her lips. She was dressed in an elegant riding habit, the red jacket beautifully tailored, the gray skirt full gathered. Her dainty black boots gleamed with polish, and a hat with curling white plumes slanted atop her sculptured ebony waves.

"How *charm*ing," she remarked. "The pair of you look delightfully disheveled, Lyman. Have you been amusing yourselves in the woods?"

"Shut up, Vanessa," he growled warningly.

"Oh, but I think it's divine, darling. Everyone's entitled to a tumble now and then. I'm glad you found someone to amuse yourself with, pet, truly, though I wonder if Edward will be quite so broad-minded about it."

"Mrs. Baker walked to the village to make a purchase," Lyman said in a flat voice. "On the way back she stumbled and twisted her ankle slightly. I happened to see her, escorted her back."

"How gallant of you, pet. Not that I be*lieve* it, mind you."

"Has my horse returned?" he asked gruffly.

"He came galloping back to his stall a few minutes ago. I wondered if you'd had an *ac*cident or something, pet. I must say I'm relieved to see that wasn't the case.

Lyman moved briskly on toward the stall where his horse was kept. Vanessa turned to watch him, that mocking smile still playing on her lips, and when she turned back to me her violet-blue eyes sparkled with amusement.

"I think it's divine you're getting on so *well*, Jenny. My husband is an extraordinary man, extremely virile, smouldering with banked-up passion. You needn't be upset, luv. I shan't breathe a word about it. What Edward doesn't know certainly can't hurt him."

Then, before I could make a rejoinder, she turned and sauntered back toward the stables, her step light and graceful, the long white plumes on her hat bobbing merrily. She had been deliberately baiting me. I knew that. She had hoped to upset me. Well, it wasn't quite that easy. Sooner or later I was going to cross swords with Vanessa, and that occasion would be spectacular to behold, but now wasn't the time for it. Clutching the parcel under my arm, thoroughly exhausted, I crossed the drive and moved slowly over the lawn to Mallyncourt.

Nine

LORD MALLYN stoutly declared that he would be on his feet and downstairs to greet each and every guest when they arrived for the ball. I had no doubt he would. There was absolutely no question about his recovery now. It was merely a matter of his regaining the strength that had been drained out of him during those months of severe illness. The night of the ball was just six days away now, and the old man was looking forward to it with the eager anticipation of a child. He had given orders to have the ballroom completely overhauled, the floor waxed, the chandeliers taken down and cleaned, the gold leaf panels touched up by a crew of artisans who had come all the way from London to do the job. He held conferences with Vanessa about the food and wine, the flowers, the special musicians to be hired for the occasion, and, vain old peacock that he was, had ordered a new suit and waistcoat from his tailor in London, sending minute instructions about each detail of cut and color.

Rapidly recovering his strength now, the old man was more querulous, more dictatorial than ever. This morning he had insisted on going outside to enjoy the sunlight, waving aside all protests, ordering the footmen to fetch a chair. Wearing a dark satin robe and half a dozen rings, snapping orders and making peevish comments every step of the way, he sat enthroned like some Eastern monarch as George and another footman bore the chair down the wide steps and out onto the back lawn. I had accompanied them, and for the next hour and a half kept Lord Mallyn company as he cursed the twittering birds, made insulting remarks about the gardener and, holding my arm, tottered slowly about the lawn, finally saying he was ready to go back up to his room. The return journey had been even more perilous as he refused to sit still. George and his partner almost dropped the chair on two different occasions, and both men were in a state of nervous exhaustion when they finally deposited their ungrateful charge on his bed.

Fortunately, he was too exhausted to have our customary game of cards after lunch, and I was able to fetch my sewing basket and go upstairs to the nursery, a large, rather drab apartment with low ceilings and windows looking down over the front gardens. Seeing me enter, Miss Partridge gave a sigh of relief and went on to her room to read a romantic novel. Lettice was sitting at the large table, a suspicious look on her face. A strong wind caused the windows to rattle in their frames. A fire crackled noisily in the fireplace.

"I didn't think you'd come," she said snappishly.

"You didn't? I promised, dear. Haven't I come every afternoon for the past week?"

"That doesn't mean anything."

"Well, dear, if you're going to sulk I can leave. There are dozens of other things I could be doing—"

"N-no," she said. "I—I'm *glad* you came."

I smiled. Lettice looked at me with grave eyes. She was beginning to trust me. She was beginning to respond. Yesterday, while I made a bright silk dress for one of her dolls, she had been her usual solemn self, but there had been a timid, tremulous note in her voice as she thanked me, and she had answered my frivolous inquiries with less stiffness than before. I was making considerable progress, I knew, and it was a joy to watch the thorny, prickly child begin to blossom.

"Did you practice the stitches I showed you?" I asked.

She nodded. "I—I'm still not very good at it."

"It takes practice, Lettice. Took me *weeks* to learn, but then I didn't have a teacher. Let me see—" I took the piece of cloth she held up. "Why, you're making wonderful progress. Your stitches are a bit *large*, true, but they're so *even*. That's the important thing. Today I thought we'd make a dress for Amanda, poor thing. Red silk, perhaps, or perhaps purple velvet. I've brought a whole basket full of scraps and ribbons. Now, let's put on our thimbles and begin—"

The table was soon littered with vividly colored scraps of cloth, bits of ribbon, scissors, dolls, spools of thread, a magpie's nest that added a bright warmth to the drab room. I sewed, I chattered, I insisted that Lettice help, gave her instructions, corrected her errors, praised her accomplishments. The child was quiet, that plain, pale face still solemn, but there was a pensive look in her eyes, and, in the light that slanted through the windows, her long brown hair was the color of ripening wheat. Amanda, whom she had adopted, who now lived with the other dolls, was soon wearing a splendid new dress, and, with cardboard, glue and feathers, I was making her a new hat. Lettice watched, silent, chin in hand, elbow on tabletop.

"I'll have to give them up soon," she said after a while.

"Give what up?"

"My dolls," she replied. "I'm too old for dolls. I know that. I'll have to give them up. It's sad."

"I know, dear."

"You can love them, you see, and you can pretend they love back. You don't have to be afraid. They don't expect you to be something you're not. They don't care if you're not pretty."

"Being pretty isn't—isn't all that important, Lettice."

"You're beautiful," the child said, "and you must have been beautiful when you were my age. It's easy for you to say it isn't important."

"Beauty—well, dear, beauty is a—a special quality. It doesn't have anything to do with how one looks. There was a writer, a woman, her name was Mary Ann Evans, but her books were written under the name of George Eliot—you're too young to have read any of them yet. Anyway, she was a very plain woman, ugly, in fact, as far as her physical appearance was concerned, but after they'd been with her a few minutes, people never noticed that. They went away with the impression that she was one of the most beautiful women in England, because of that quality she had."

Lettice made no comment. A bitter, disbelieving smile played on her lips, and I could see that she thought I was merely trying to humor her. I fastened a tiny black feather on the circle of cardboard covered with green silk, hunted for a bit of black ribbon to fasten the hat to Amanda's head. When I continued, my voice was extremely casual.

"In her last years, she was widowed. She had known great love with her husband, and she never thought she'd be happy again. But she still had that quality. It glowed inside of her. It made her beautiful. There was a young man named John Cross. He was golden haired, dashing, handsome, pursued by some of the most attractive women in society, but he ignored them. He fell in love with Mary Ann. People laughed, because he was young and she was old, because he looked like a Greek god and she looked like a sack of potatoes, but he didn't care. He was determined to marry her, and he finally persuaded her to accept him."

"What happened?" she asked in a bored voice.

"Mary Ann died—that was two years ago. She and John Cross only had a year together, but he told the newspapers it was the happiest year of his life. At the funeral he stood at her graveside, tears streaming down his cheeks. I think it's a great love story, and Mary Ann Evans was one of the plainest women who ever drew breath."

"You made it up," she said sullenly.

"No, dear. It's all quite true. I'm sure there are some of her books in the library here—*Silas Marner, Adam Bede, The Mill on the Floss*. Perhaps one of them has her picture in the front. You can see for yourself. There, the hat's finished. Amanda looks terribly stylish—"

We continued to sew, Lettice as grave and unresponsive as ever. I was relaxed, curiously content. It was satisfying to be here with the child, to be doing something constructive. I felt that I was serving some purpose, and, while I was in the nursery, Mallyncourt didn't seem nearly so brooding, so tension

filled. It was as beneficial to me as it was to Lettice.
She needed a friend. I needed an outlet. There was
something touching about the thin, pale, hostile
child, and the hours I spent with her were the most
peaceful I had spent in the house. I was surprised
when there was a knock on the door and a maid
came in with the afternoon tea tray. I hadn't realized it was so late.

Book clasped to her bosom, a dreamy expression on her plump face, Miss Partridge peeked out
of her room and, seeing that I was still with Lettice,
declared that she was far more interested in the fate
of Jane Eyre than in cakes, crumpets or tongue
sandwiches and asked to be excused. Lettice and I
had our tea together, sitting in front of the fire. The
child was uncommunicative, deep in thought, staring at the heap of glowing orange-black logs, barely
touching her food. When the maid returned to fetch
the tray, she still hadn't said anything.

I stood up, brushing my skirts.

"I'd better go now," I said. "I'll leave all the
sewing things here, Lettice."

"You'll be back tomorrow?"

"I promise."

"Jenny—"

I was at the door. I turned. It was the first time
she had called me by my first name.

"Yes?"

"Was there *really* a Mary Ann Evans?"

"There really was. Miss Partridge seems quite
literary. She's probably read some of her books. You
can ask her if you refuse to believe me."

"I—I believe you," the child said. "If—" she
hesitated, a deep frown creasing her brow, and
when she continued she spoke rapidly, crossly. "I
just wanted to say that if *you* were plain, if *you*

looked like a sack of potatoes, you'd still be beautiful, too, just like that writer."

"Why—" My voice trembled. I couldn't help myself. "That—that's the nicest thing anyone has ever said to me."

"It's true," she snapped.

Lettice glared at me, looking even crosser than before, and then, suddenly, she ran across the room and threw her arms around my waist, holding me tightly. I folded that thin, brittle little body against me. I stroked the long, wheat-colored hair. Several moments passed, and Lettice finally pulled away.

"I'm sorry," she said.

"Lettice, you needn't apologize for showing affection, ever."

Lettice looked up at me with grave eyes, her pinched face heartbreakingly serious. "You're the first real friend I've ever had."

"That's a wonderful honor, dear."

"I'm going to be beautiful, too," she said in a severe voice. "I'll never be *pretty*, but—I can be beautiful."

"Of course you can."

"I don't imagine it'll be easy," she said, frowning. "I have a very sour disposition, everyone says so, and I can never be one of those sweet, sunny children, but—I'm going to try."

She scowled, squaring her shoulders. Miraculous transformations never occur in real life, and Lettice seemed embarrassed now, slightly resentful, but the barrier had finally broken down. She looked much, much older than her ten years, and, paradoxically, much younger, too, tough and vulnerable. How would that young-old face look wearing a smile? I hoped to find out very soon.

"I'd better go color my geography maps now,"

she said stiffly. "I told Miss Partridge I'd done them already, and she'd be distressed if she finds I told a story. I'm *always* kind to Partridge, because she's an outsider, too, like me, and she needs kindness. I'll see you tomorrow."

"Good-bye, dear."

I left the nursery, deeply touched by what had happened. Lettice was a peculiar child, but it wasn't difficult to understand her, nor was it difficult to understand what had made her the way she was. Unwanted in the first place, unloved, ignored and neglected, she was the product of her environment, independent, hostile, inverted, but with the proper nourishment she could bloom like those thorny plants that grew in the desert. Inside, beneath that prickly façade, there was a wealth of tenderness and affection that, fearing rebuff, she had revealed heretofore only when she was alone with her dolls. Her parents were to blame. Vanessa was openly derisive about her daughter, not even pretending to care for her, but I wondered about Lyman. He took up for the child when his wife made slighting remarks about her, and he refused to send her away to school, but was he genuinely concerned about her welfare? I doubted it. Lyman's ruthless obsession with Mallyncourt left little room for anything else.

Having nothing in particular to do the rest of the afternoon, I went to my room, fetched the book I had recently finished and took it back down to the library, an enormous room, dim, musty, with dark garnet drapes at the windows, a vast marble fireplace and towering walls of books. Putting the novel back on its shelf, I spent half an hour browsing, finally selecting a book on Roman ruins in this part of England. As I left the library I could hear the bustle of servants in the ballroom at the end of the hall.

The great night would be upon us soon. I wasn't looking forward to it. Moving up the wide, flat stone steps, I crossed the long gallery and stepped into one of the sunfilled window recesses, curling up on the dusty velvet window seat with the book.

I read for some time, pausing to examine the stiff, lavishly detailed plates of various ruins, but after a while I found my mind wandering. The light was dimmer now, a faint yellow-gold. The back lawn was a dark green expanse, the battered white marble statues casting long black shadows over the grass, and the sky was a deep gray, streaked with faint brush strokes of rose and orange on the horizon. There really wasn't enough light left to read by now, and the history of Hadrian's Wall no longer held my interest. Legs curled under me, the book in my lap, I gazed out at the lawn without really seeing it, my mind wandering.

"You'll strain your eyes," Edward said.

I turned, startled by the sound of his voice. "Edward, I—I didn't hear you approaching."

"You seemed far away, lost in thought. Thinking of me?"

"Of course not," I said stiffly.

"No? I'm disappointed."

He folded his arms over his chest and stood there looking at me with a thin smile on his lips. He wore tall black boots, clinging gray breeches and a loose white silk shirt with billowing sleeves gathered at the wrist. A heavy blond wave had tumbled over his brow. With his harsh, handsome features and arrogant stance, he looked like the hero of some demonic romance, a cold and unscrupulous young nobleman who reveled in cruel delights. I was disturbed by the thought, irritated with myself for thinking it.

"What are you reading?" he inquired.

"It's a book on Roman ruins."

"You interested in them?"

"I think they're fascinating."

"Indeed? There's an old Roman fort five miles or so from here. I'll have to take you to see it. We'll carry a picnic basket, make a regular holiday of it."

I closed the book and placed it on the window seat, avoiding his eyes. I stood up, still not looking at him.

"You wouldn't enjoy that?" he asked.

"I don't know."

"Spending a day with me would be an ordeal?"

"I couldn't say. I've hardly seen you since we arrived."

"I know. That's my fault. I finished with the books this afternoon. My cousin, as usual, has been scrupulously honest. Not a single discrepancy to be found. But tell me, has my—uh—preoccupation with other matters bothered you?"

"Not in the least," I said coldly.

"I've hardly been a model husband, true. That's going to change now. Now I'm going to smother you with attention."

"I think I would prefer your indifference."

"Indifference? But I've never been *indifferent* to you, Jenny. Auditing the books simply took precedence. Now I intend to make amends. I plan to be a proper husband."

"What do you mean?"

"I thought I made myself quite clear."

"I don't want 'a proper husband.' We made a bargain, and—"

"My uncle has been bedridden these past weeks. He's been too ill, too confined to pay much attention to what was going on around him. Now he appears to be improving at a shocking rate. He's getting up and about, taking an interest in things. I think the front we present should be—uh—a bit more unified."

"I see."

"You've performed your role adequately. I've been lax in mine. What the others think doesn't matter, but now that my uncle is improving so rapidly he's bound to observe the two of us together. It's important that he believe we—"

"I understand," I said.

The light was almost gone now, the recess gray with only the faintest haze of light, the gallery beyond in darkness. Edward stood in front of me, arms still folded over his chest. There was a thoughtful look in his eyes now, and the thin smile lingered on his lips. I was extremely uncomfortable, wishing he would go, wishing he wouldn't look at me that way.

"I've been doing a lot of thinking about us," he remarked idly.

"Have you?"

"I find myself in a rather awkward position. When I brought you here, I thought my uncle was a dying man, and I hoped your presence would influence him to draw up his will in my favor. As I say, you've performed your role adequately—more than adequately. You've won the old man over. He actually depends on you. Were he a dying man, there'd be no problem. You might have to extend your—uh—engagement for a few weeks, but in the end everything would work out just as I planned. However, he isn't going to die. The doctors tell me he's going to make a complete recovery."

"And?"

"That alters things considerably. Were you to

leave, everything would be lost. I can't let you leave Mallyncourt, Jenny. You realize that."

"I agreed to stay for six weeks. They'll soon be up."

"I'm aware of that. It looks as if we're going to have to make other arrangements. It looks as if I'm going to have to take you back to London and marry you."

I didn't say anything. I stared at him with a cool, level gaze, not trusting myself to speak. The thin smile flickered on his lips. His eyes were filled with a wry amusement as he watched me, waiting for my reaction to his words. Cynical, superior, blond and lordly and incredibly handsome in those tight gray breeches and the flowing white silk shirt, he thought he was offering me a great opportunity, one any woman would eagerly seize. It never entered his mind that I might refuse. I hated him at that moment more than I ever had before. No, I didn't hate him. I despised him. I despised him for thinking I could be as venal and calculating as he. Yet even as those vivid blue eyes regarded me, I knew that he had every reason to think that. After all, I had willingly agreed to this deception. Coldly, and with my eyes wide open, I had come to Mallyncourt in order to deceive a rich old man. What else should he think? At the moment I didn't have too much respect for myself either.

"You hardly seem overjoyed," he remarked.

"I made a bargain with you, Edward," I said. "I agreed to pretend to be your wife for six weeks. For the remainder of that time I'll perform my role to the best of my ability, just as I agreed."

"And then?"

"And then I intend to leave."

He didn't seem at all disturbed. The smile still

flickered at the corners of his mouth. The wry amusement was still in his eyes. He didn't believe I could turn down the opportunity to be mistress of Mallyncourt, turn down the riches, the security that position entailed. And there was more. Spoiled over the years by countless women who had undoubtedly found him irresistible, his male ego wouldn't allow him to believe I could turn down the opportunity to be his wife in the true sense of the word.

"It looks as if I'll have to use some—persuasion," he said.

"Persuasion?"

"I think you might enjoy it."

"You'd be wasting your time, Edward."

"I think not," he said huskily.

I remembered that prolonged kiss in the bedroom, and I remembered my own physical response to it. I could tell that he was thinking about that, too. He stood with legs spread wide apart, black boots gleaming with a high gloss, tight gray breeches moulding calf and thigh. The white silk shirt billowed softly. His heavy eyelids drooped, half concealing his eyes, and he exuded a potent sensuality. I felt cold, terribly cold, and afraid. Edward moved toward me. He stopped. The noisy footsteps startled both of us. Whistling to himself, unaware of our presence, the footman began to light the candles. Golden blossoms bloomed in the long gallery. I took a deep breath, relieved. Or disappointed? Edward scowled, all sensuality vanishing abruptly.

"We'll continue this discussion later," he said coldly. "Now I suggest we dress for dinner. It's growing late."

What would have happened if the footman hadn't arrived when he did? I didn't know. I didn't want to think about it. Later, as he stood waiting in the hall to accompany me downstairs, Edward was as cool and remote as he had ever been. I was completely composed, all icy dignity as we joined the others in the drawing room. Dinner was an ordeal. Vanessa chattered brightly about the ball, telling us about the musicians who had been hired, describing the gown she intended to wear, gossiping about various guests who would attend. Lyman was surly, paying no attention to her. Edward was rigidly polite. I was relieved when it was finally over with and I could escape back to my room.

I went to bed shortly after ten, but I was unable to sleep. Restless, I tossed and turned, watching the velvety blackness melt into gray-black as my eyes grew accustomed to the darkness. Out of the shadows furniture began to take on shape and substance, and shadows dissolved until I could see my reflection in the mirror across the room. Edward hadn't come upstairs yet. I found myself listening for his footsteps. The door between my bedroom and the sitting room adjoining it was locked. Would he try it? Would he attempt to pick up where he had left off in the recess?

Time passed, slowly, so slowly, the ormolu clock over the mantle marking each minute with a barely audible metallic click, ten thirty, eleven, eleven fifteen, and still sleep evaded me. I thought about Edward, about Lord Mallyn, about Lettice and her parents, about the weeks I had spent here at Mallyncourt, and it all seemed terribly confused and unreal. What was I *doing* here? What was Jenny Randall, cool, sensible Jenny Randall doing in this house, a prey to conflicting emotions, inextricably involved with all these people? And what was going *on*? Although I had been distracted by Lord Mallyn's demands, by my involvement with Lettice, I had never lost sight of that mystery that seemed to shroud the walls, that crackling tension that filled the air.

Sleep was impossible. I realized that. The clock made another short, muted click. It was ten minutes till twelve, almost midnight, and still I was wide awake. I pushed the covers back and got out of bed. It was foolish to try and sleep when my mind was abuzz with so many questions, so many doubts. I might as well read for a while. Reading always soothed me. I had left the book on Roman ruins in the window recess. I would fetch it. Perhaps the descriptions of early garrisons and altars to Mithras crumbling in the middle of deserted fields would act as a sedative, sooth me into drowsiness. I didn't bother to light a candle. If I was going to prowl about in the middle of the night, I certainly didn't want anyone to see me. Moving quietly across the room in my bare feet, wearing only my thin cambric petticoat, I opened the bedroom door and stepped into the darkness of the hall outside.

My eyes were completely accustomed to the dark, and the hallways held no terror for me. A candle would only have intensified the darkness, and, besides, I was just going to fetch the book and come straight back to my room. Bare feet padding on the floor, my full, ruffled petticoat billowing, I moved confidently down the hall and turned into the shorter one that led into the long gallery. The house was full of rustling, flapping, creaking noises, soft groans, muted rattles, displaying a personality it didn't have during the day, as though now, now that its human inhabitants were asleep, it could assert its own force. It was a curiously exhilarating sensation to know I was the only one awake, the sole possessor of this world of shadow and sound. Shadows, black, gray-black and deep blue-black cascaded down the walls as I moved toward the gallery, and everything was brushed softly with silver, a dazzle of silver ahead as moonlight streamed through the many panes of the gallery recesses.

As I entered the gallery, the mat of woven rushes crackled underfoot. The room seemed larger than ever, like some great, vast cavern, long rays of pale silver light slanting through the windows, wavering, gilding the floor, magnifying the shadows beyond. The room was icy cold, and there was a chilly draft that caused the long velvet draperies to stir. Had someone left one of the windows open? I shivered. The bodice of my petticoat was formfitting, cut extremely low, leaving half my bosom exposed. I should have put on a wrap, I thought, moving on toward the recess. The book was where I had left it on the window seat. I picked it up, stood for a moment peering out at the dark, silvered lawn, then stepped out of the recess and started back across the room. The two marble fireplaces were large, yawning holes, and the portraits, barely visible in the faint light, seemed to look down at me with stern disapproval. The cold air stroked my naked arms and shoulders. A sudden draft of cold air made my skirt bell out, ruffles trembling. I moved quickly across the floor.

I stopped, abruptly, paralyzed.

The laughter was muted, coming from the distance, but it shattered the silence with explosive force. Muted as it was, it seemed to fill the whole house, harsh, demonic, reverberating in the air, and I didn't know if I was hearing the laughter itself or some distorted echo. My blood seemed to freeze, my flesh crawled, and I was a victim of sheer, stark terror, unable to move, unable to think. The laughter

rose, splintered, died away as suddenly as it had
appeared, and the silence that followed was somehow even more alarming. I stared across the room,
beyond the wide steps, and I saw the door to the
east wing, the door Edward had locked behind him.

It stood open. The laughter had come from the
east wing.

I tried not to think of the tales Susie had told
me, but, naturally, I remembered every word she
had told me, vividly. The servants heard noises at
night. They refused to go in the east wing. They believed it was haunted. The maid Betty had seen
something white and misty moving down the hall
toward her. I remembered the bizarre room with
the red walls, remembered Edward's alarm when
he had discovered me there. Standing perfectly still,
my heart pounding, shadows spreading thickly all
around, I stared at that opened door, waiting. For
what? I didn't know. Tapestries flapped against
the walls. Floorboards groaned. There were soft,
scratching noises behind the panels. Long moments
passed, each like an eternity, and nothing happened, nothing at all.

You're not Jane Eyre, I told myself. Mad Mrs.
Rochester isn't going to come rushing out to set the
place on fire. There is absolutely no reason to be
alarmed. It sounded like laughter, yes, but it could
just as easily have been the wind sweeping down
a chimney. Gradually, by slow degrees, calm returned. I took a deep breath, convinced now that
the noise *had* been caused by the wind, a freak dis-
tortion, nothing more. Edward had locked the door,
true, but the lock was old, probably not at all secure.
There was a strong draught coming down the hall in
the east wing. It had undoubtedly blown the door

open. I sighed, sensible once more, and walked across the room to shut the door.

Fright forgotten, I was almost amused at myself now. Susie and the other servants might babble of ghosts and such, but I had far too much good sense. My hand on the doorknob, I peered down the long hall leading into the east wing. No misty white figure moved toward me. The shadows fell in thick clusters, dense, not stirring. I started to close the door . . . and then I saw him.

I felt as though some piercing shaft had been driven through me. The shock was so great, so intense, that it immobilized me. He was leaning against the wall, just inside the hall, concealed by the shadows, just his forehead and those dark, hypnotic eyes visible. A split second passed, and I could feel the scream forming in my throat. Quickly, before I knew what was happening, he seized my wrist, pulled me against him with brutal force and clamped a large hand over my mouth. I didn't struggle. I was stunned, too stunned to do anything but pray this was a nightmare, pray it wasn't really happening to me. Holding me in front of him, one arm wrapped around my waist, that hand crushing my lips, he moved out of the hall and across the gallery, past the wide steps, forcing me ahead of him, finally stopping in front of one of the fireplaces, far away from that open door.

It was a nightmare, it had to be. I would awaken, I would be in my bedroom, this would dissolve, disappear, shredding like a mist and going the way of all nightmares, vaguely remembered, unreal, but it wasn't a nightmare, no, that arm held me tightly against a large, solid body, and that brutal hand was clamped savagely over my mouth, forcing my head back, and I closed my eyes, willing it to dissolve, disappear, knowing even as the hysteria swept over me in shattering waves that he was a madman and I was going to die, here, in the gallery, black brushed with silver, in front of the fireplace. My head whirled, mind spinning crazily, and then his lips were almost touching my ear.

"I'll let you go, but you mustn't scream. Do you understand? Do you promise not to scream?"

I managed to nod. He released me. I turned around to face him. My knees were weak. I almost fell. He caught my shoulders, supporting me. I was still holding the book in my hand, clutching it as though it were a spar and I drowning in tumultuous waves. A great shudder went through me. I closed my eyes again, whirling, and when I opened them I looked up at him and tried to speak. I couldn't. Although we stood in the shadows, he was perfectly visible, wearing a robe of dark, gleaming satin over trousers and shirt. His handsome, rugged face was a mask of anger, mouth stretched tight over his teeth, eyes dark with fury, raven locks spilling untidily over his forehead. His hands gripped my shoulders savagely, and he looked as though he wished they were gripping my throat.

Downstairs, a clock struck the hour. The sound spiraled up the stairwell. There were twelve brassy, muted bongs, and as the last one died away I found it impossible to believe that only ten minutes had passed since I left my bedroom. It seemed a lifetime ago.

"What the *hell* are you doing here!" His voice was low, but it seethed with rage.

"I—I came to fetch a book—"

"In the middle of the night! Without a candle!"

"I had left it in the window recess, you see, and I couldn't sleep and I remembered the book and I thought—I was only going to be gone a minute and I'm not afraid of the dark and—"

My voice broke. I couldn't go on. The shock hadn't all worn off yet. Seeing the book in my hand, Lyman knew I had been telling the truth. He let go of my shoulders, scowled, jammed his hands into the pockets of his robe. In the misty light his face seemed hewn from granite, sternly chiseled. I felt the last vestiges of shock leaving me, and some semblance of calm returned. I shivered, but from the cold now. My shoulders ached where he had gripped them. Brows lowered, Lyman stared at me, and there was a moment of prolonged silence. I was painfully aware of my scanty attire, the frail cloth barely concealing my bosom. I folded my arms around my waist, shivering. A gentleman would have offered me his robe, but then Lyman was no gentleman.

"I'm sorry if I frightened you," he muttered sullenly.

"I'm quite all right now."

"You had no business traipsing through the night like that, without a candle."

"At least I had a reason to be traipsing through the night. What *you* doing there?"

Lyman looked at me sharply. He didn't answer my question.

"I heard something coming from the east wing," I said. "It sounded like laughter."

"You must have imagined it."

"I didn't imagine it. What *were* you doing there?"

"Don't ask questions, Mrs. Baker."

"There's something wrong—the east wing. The servants claim they hear peculiar noises. They say it's haunted. That's absurd. There's—it has something to do with that room with the red walls."

"What do you know about that room?" he demanded, tense.

"I—nothing. I merely saw it. It wasn't like the others. There were no dust sheets, no cobwebs. Edward found me there. He—he was very angry with me. He told me never to—"

"It's just a room," he said tersely. "Forget about it!"

"But—"

"Come along. I'll take you back to your bedroom."

"You haven't answered my question. You—"

Seizing my wrist, he marched toward the hall, dragging me along behind him. I cried out in protest, but Lyman Robb paid no heed, moving briskly down the hall with long, angry strides, the skirt of his robe swinging with a loud silken rustle, his hand gripping my wrist firmly, tugging me along. I tottered, stumbled, my petticoat billowing in a flutter of ruffles. He turned the corner, briskly. I almost crashed against the wall. He didn't even notice. When we finally reached the door to my bedroom, he came to an abrupt halt. The door was closed. Grabbing my shoulders, he thrust me back against it. I gasped. He spread his palms against the door on either side of my shoulders, holding me there, his arms making a prison. I looked up at him, amazed, outraged, horrified. It was much darker here. I could barely make out his face: broad, flat cheekbones white, eyes dark and glowing, forehead half-concealed by the thick fringe of hair.

"How dare you!" My voice trembled with anger. "How dare you treat me like—"

"Listen," he barked, "*care*fully! Forget about tonight. Forget you heard anything. Forget you saw me."

"I didn't do *any*thing! I merely went to fetch my book, and you leap out of the darkness and grab me and—"

"Jenny! Damn you, listen! It never happened, none of it! You never left your room. Do you understand?"

"No! No, I don't understand. You can't—"

"You're not to tell anyone, not Edward, not anyone. You're not to say a word. For your own good. It's imperative! You've got to trust me."

"Why? Why should I trust you?"

"Because I'm asking you to," Lyman said. There was weariness in his voice now, all anger spent.

He moved his arms away from me and stood up straight. He brushed back the fringe of thick locks, sighing heavily. In the hazy semidarkness his face looked strangely vulnerable, all shadowed planes. His robe, wrapped loosely around his body, gleamed with a dark, rich sheen. He stood there in front of me, powerful, robustly male, and somehow or other I sensed that what he had done had been done to protect me. My own anger ebbed. I felt weak and bruised.

"Very well, Lyman. I—I won't say anything."

He looked at me for a long moment as though to determine my sincerity, and then, abruptly, he gave me a curt nod and padded away into the darkness. I went into my room, put the book down, climbed into bed, and, surprisingly, I fell asleep almost at once. I had no time to think about anything the next morning. A maid brought in my morning tea, and I had barely finished drinking it when one of the footmen knocked on the door and informed me that Edward wished to see me in the drawing room immediately. I dressed quickly, puzzled, and, giving a final pat to my hair, went down to see what he wanted. Edward was standing in front of the fireplace, his features impassive, telling me nothing. As I entered the room a man got up from one of the chairs, made a gallant, mocking bow and regarded me with dark, dancing brown eyes.

"My *dear* cousin Jenny," he said. "Isn't this nice? Your poor cousin Gerry finds himself in—uh—rather distressing circumstances. He's come to stay with you and your fine, wealthy husband."

Ten

HE LAST time I had seen him he had been wearing the resplendent costume of Cesare Borgia, his hair a cap of tight gold curls, the Borgia goatee adding a devilish touch, but now he wore tight tan breeches and elegant tan frock coat, his brown knee boots gleaming, his plum colored waistcoat decidedly flamboyant. His hair was its natural shade, a glossy brown, a bit too long, a bit too studiedly tousled. Though leaning to stoutness, Gerald Prince was still very much the matinee idol, undeniably striking, floridly handsome. I stared at him, stunned, at a loss for words. His mobile, sensual mouth curved into a smile. His magnetic brown eyes danced with amusement.

"You seem surprised, luv," he said.

"What—what are you doing here?"

"I've come to *stay* with you, Jenny dear. Surely you don't object? It's such a large house, and you wouldn't want your poor cousin to put up at an inn, would you?"

" 'Cousin?' I don't understand—"

I looked at Edward as though for an answer. He was calm and composed, totally unperturbed.

"It should be fairly obvious," he commented idly. "He's come here to blackmail me."

"That's such an *ugly* word, old chap," Gerald Prince remarked. "Let's just say I'm giving you an opportunity to make a cultural investment. Ten thousand pounds will enable me to form a new company, and you, Sir, will be our patron."

Edward made no comment. I found his calm far more alarming than anger would have been. Elegantly dressed in pearl-gray suit and black and green striped waistcoat, his blond hair sleekly combed, he stood in front of the fireplace as though he hadn't a care in the world, his arms folded loosely across his chest.

"We must be reasonable about things," Gerry said amiably. "The sum isn't all that great—you could raise it without the least effort, and it means life or death to me. Do try to see it my way, old chap, and try to remember that—as the saying goes —I've got you by the throat."

"That's putting it rather strongly," Edward remarked.

"But aptly," Gerry told him.

"Do you really imagine you can get away with this, Prince?" Edward inquired.

"But of course. You, Sir, have been getting away with your little deception for well over a month now. An admirable endeavor—I fully appreciate it. My own is far more direct, and not a bit more treacherous. Cousin Gerald has come to visit his dear, dear Jenny, and he will remain until the money is in his hands."

"And if you don't get the money?"

"Then, Sir, I squeeze."

"Meaning you'll inform my uncle of our little charade."

"Precisely."

"You'll regret this, Prince," Edward said lightly.

"I think not. I stand to lose nothing but ten thousand pounds, while you, Sir, stand to lose everything. Come now, no need for gloom. Once I have the money I'll be on my way, never to bother you again. Think of it as an investment."

Edward made no reply. The faintest suggestion of a smile began to play at the corner of his lips, as though he found the situation rather amusing. Gerald Prince stepped over to study one of the engravings on the wall, and I looked up at Edward. He didn't seem at all angry. That worried me. What was he thinking? What was he planning to do?

"Your letters," he informed me.

"I—I'm sorry."

"Your friend Laverne left them in her dressing room. He saw them."

"Quite so," Gerry remarked, turning to face me. "Careless of Laverne to leave them laying about like that. I chanced to step into her dressing room when she was out, spotted the letters immediately. They made most interesting reading. I was rather surprised—this sort of thing isn't your style at all, Jenny—but I didn't think too much about it at first. It was only after a series of—uh—most distressing circumstances that I began to formulate a plan."

"Laverne wrote me about those 'circumstances.' You left the company stranded. You absconded with the money, and—"

"Past history, luv. We needn't be concerned with that."

"And when the money ran out, you decided to employ a bit of blackmail. You came here, thinking you could get by with—"

"*Knowing* I could get by with it," he corrected. "Your—uh—husband can't afford to refuse me. I have the upper hand, and he knows it. Right, Sir?"

"So it would seem," Edward replied.

"I find your attitude most sensible—I half expected violent threats, smouldering rage, melodramatics. It's plain to see you're an extremely intelligent man, quite civilized."

Edward acknowledged the remark with a slight nod.

"You'll pay?"

"I can't raise a sum like that overnight," Edward told him. "I'll have to write my solicitor in London. It'll take at least a week for me to get the money."

"No hurry," Gerry said generously, "no hurry at all. I rather fancy spending a few days anyway. I've always been curious about how the other half lives—historic old house, servants at every turn, private stables and all. It should be pleasant."

Edward smiled his thin smile. I found it frightening, but Gerry was quite sure of himself now, and he found nothing at all extraordinary about Edward's attitude. But then he didn't know the man. I did.

"You brought bags?" Edward asked.

"I left 'em on the front steps," Gerry said.

Edward pulled a bell cord by the fireplace. A footman appeared at the door a moment later. Edward informed him in a calm voice that Mrs. Baker's cousin would be staying at Mallyncourt for a few days and gave instructions to have Gerry's bags taken up to the blue room.

"Glad to see you're being so reasonable about things," Gerry remarked after the footman had gone. "There's no reason why we can't keep things on a friendly basis."

"No reason at all," Edward replied. His voice was almost amiable. "My wife's cousin shall have every courtesy. I assume you intend to call yourself Randall?"

"Randall? Oh, yes, I hadn't thought of that. Clive, I think. I've always fancied that name. Clive Randall, the son of Jenny's dear Uncle Reginald."

To my surprise, Edward offered Gerry a glass of brandy, and, when he accepted, poured two glasses from the decanter. I watched them, fascinated. Edward was the exquisitely polite host, Gerry the convivial guest, both men playing their roles to the hilt. Flushed with success, visibly pleased with himself, Gerry was completely relaxed, sipping his brandy and chatting with total aplomb. There was a flicker of sardonic amusement in Edward's eyes. Gerry had quite plainly underestimated his man, but he wasn't aware of it. Seeing the look in Edward's eyes, I almost felt sorry for the man who had come to blackmail him.

Both men looked up when Vanessa stepped into the door. She appeared to be startled to find a guest, but her surprise was a bit too studied, and I could tell that she had known she would find a stranger in the room. Ebony hair spilling to her shoulders in luxuriant waves, her coral lips parted in surprise, she was radiantly beautiful, wearing a low-cut violet silk frock much too elaborate for this hour of the morning. Pausing in the doorway, she gazed at the men with attractive confusion.

"Oh dear, I hope I'm not inter*rupt*ing anything."

"Not at all," Edward replied. "Good morning, Vanessa. You're just in time to meet Jennifer's cousin, Clive Randall. Clive, Vanessa Robb, my cousin Lyman's wife."

Gerry stared at her, dazzled, taken aback by her beauty. Vanessa smiled, fully aware of her effect on him.

"How do you do?" she said. "Jenny," she scolded, "you never *told* me you had such a handsome cousin."

"Clive is going to spend a few days with us," Edward said.

"Oh? How en*chant*ing. Just in time for the ball, too. Do you dance, Mr. Randall?"

"Clive," he said, "please."

"Clive," she repeated, smiling.

"I adore dancing," he told her.

"I'm sure you dance divinely."

"Well—"

"I can *sense* it," she said.

They might have been alone together, Edward and I both forgotten for the moment. The chemistry between them was powerful, and immediate. Gerald Prince was even more susceptible to beautiful women than most men, and his response to Vanessa was plainly visible. Sensual mouth parted in a curling half smile, he looked at her with masculine appreciation in his eyes, and there was speculation as well. Although less obvious about it than he, Vanessa was just as taken as he was.

"It's nice to have you here," she said.

"Nice to be here."

"Are you interested in old houses?"

"Fascinated by them."

"You must let me show you around."

"That would be—smashing."

"I had Peters take his bags up to the blue room," Edward remarked.

"Oh? I'll show you the way, Clive. This house is so vast—quite easy for a stranger to lose his way."

"Thoughtful of you."

Her vivid blue eyes deep and shining, she gave a gay, tinkling little laugh and wrapped her arm around his.

"Come," she said. "You must tell me *all* about yourself—and our dear Jenny. Did you two grow up together? She's rather a mystery, you see. No one knows a *thing* about her—"

They left, her violet silk skirt rustling. I could hear her chattering in a bright, vivacious voice as they moved down the hall. I stood up, more worried than ever. Vanessa was definitely the enemy. She would do anything possible to hurt Edward's cause. Gerald Prince was not to be trusted with a woman. What if he was indiscreet? What if he let slip something he shouldn't? I looked at Edward. He seemed totally unconcerned.

"It's all my fault—" I began.

"Quite true."

"I should never have sent those letters."

"You should never have sent them," he agreed.

"I—I don't know what to say—"

"Then I suggest you say nothing."

"What are you going to do?"

Edward regarded me with frosty blue eyes, one brow arched, the other a straight line. "That needn't concern you," he said.

"You'll have to pay him."

"You think so?"

"He—he meant what he said."

"I'm sure he did."

"He'll tell Lord Mallyn—"

His lips curled into that thin smile, and once again I detected a hint of sardonic amusement in his eyes. "My dear Jenny," he said, "you brought this about through your own stupidity. I suggest you leave everything to me now."

"Vanessa is bound to question him, Edward."

"I feel certain she will."

"What if—"

Edward glanced at the clock. "I have business to attend to," he said impatiently, "and I believe it's almost time for you to accompany my uncle on his turn in the sunshine. Keep calm, Jennifer. I'll handle Mr. Gerald Prince, I assure you."

With those words he strolled out of the room, leaving me filled with a mounting alarm. What was he planning? What was he going to do? He *had* to meet Gerry's demands. Surely he realized that. There was nothing else he could do. He was altogether too calm, almost nonchalant about it, and that worried me. Anger I could have understood, but this. . . . I shook my head, wishing I were far, far away from this place.

Vanessa brought "Clive Randall" out to the back lawn to meet Lord Mallyn an hour or so later. Ensconced in his chair, wearing a vivid robe and wrapped in a number of shawls, Lord Mallyn was in a testy mood, complaining that the sunlight was too strong, the birds too blasted loud, and he gave a snort when he saw the two of them approaching. Standing behind his chair, I frowned. I had been meaning to tell him about Gerry's "visit" ever since we came outside, but his constant complaints had made it impossible to get a word in edgewise.

"Who's this?" he grumbled as they approached. "Another of Vanessa's squires? Don't like the looks of the fellow, too smooth—don't like the cut of him at all. That preposterous waistcoat—"

"He's my cousin," I said nervously.

"Your cousin! You're *related* to that stout popin-
jay?"

"He—he's come to visit. I invited him."

"You *invited* him! Must-a taken leave of your
senses!"

They reached us before I could reply. Vanessa
performed the introductions gracefully. Gerry was
impeccable, nodding politely, expressing his delight
at meeting such an esteemed personage. Lord Mallyn snorted again and extended a beringed hand.
Gerry squeezed it a bit too heartily, causing the
rings to crush against bone, causing its owner to let
out an anguished roar. Gerry dropped the hand
promptly, dismayed. Lord Mallyn glared at him
fiercely. Vanessa smiled prettily, called Lord Mallyn
a naughty old rogue and, saying they wouldn't
bother us any longer, led Gerry back toward the veranda.

"Just when I'm beginning to feel my oats, I'm
invaded by overdressed hooligans!" Lord Mallyn
said hotly. "The oaf damned near broke my hand! I
suppose he intends to *stay* here! Well, I don't mind
telling you, Jenny, if he weren't *your* cousin, I'd
have the footmen throw him off the premises! Most
unreasonable of you to invite him here in the first
place. Everyone's in league against me—"

Vanessa and Gerry went out riding that afternoon, causing young Lyle Radcliff considerable con-
sternation when he arrived shortly after their departure. I felt rather sorry for the youth. It was obvious,
already, that he had been supplanted. Heavy, sensual, undeniably handsome, Gerald Prince would
naturally be fascinating to a woman like Vanessa,
and she had wasted no time in appropriating him.
Edward might not be concerned, but it made me
extremely uneasy. I was in a distracted mood as I

sewed with Lettice in the nursery, unable to concentrate on the task at hand, and later on, as I dressed for dinner, my mood hadn't improved a bit.

Susie had arranged my hair on top of my head in smooth, sculptured auburn waves, leaving three long ringlets dangling to touch my bare shoulder. The girl was an artist, quite true, but she was also an incorrigible chatterbox, hardly pausing for breath. Ordinarily I found her chatter amusing, but tonight it was merely irritating. While she did my hair I learned that Cook had used her tarot cards this mornin' and 'ad a fright, a real fright, said somethin' dreadful was goin' to 'appen at Mallyncourt soon, death an' disaster bound to 'appen, it was in th' cards. I also learned that Betty 'ad a new dress, red, it was, most improper, and 'ow, Susie wanted to know, just 'ow could an *'onest* girl afford such a dress? Taking my gown from the wardrobe, she regaled me with an account of George's cheekiness. This mornin' 'e pulled 'er into the linen closet and gave her *such* a sound kiss and Lord knows what would-a 'appened if Jeffers 'adn't come saunterin' down th' 'all when 'e did. Susie slipped the gown over my head, smoothing the skirt down over the full petticoats.

"This golden brown satin," she said, "so fetchin', so pretty with your 'air. 'Ere, Miss Jenny, let me 'elp you fasten it up—there! You *do* look a picture, no mistake."

"Thank you, Susie."

" 'E's gettin' impossible, 'e is, George, I mean. I told 'im I wanted a *ring*, and 'e looked 'orrified, said there were lots-a girls who wouldn't mind sparkin' with 'im without expectin' to marry 'im, and you know what I told 'im? I told 'im to *find* one of those girls an' leave me alone. 'E's almost in th' bag now —I say, did you 'ear about the row?''

"What row?" I inquired, gazing into the mirror, not really paying attention to her babbling.

"Mister Lyman—'e was *furi*ous! Near murdered Anderson, 'e did. Anderson's th' gardener, you know, been at Mallyncourt forever 'n ever. 'E was almost sacked this afternoon.''

I reached up to pat one of the long auburn ringlets. "Indeed?"

"It was about th' well," Susie continued, heedless of her inattentive audience. "It's at th' back of th' property, beyond them water gardens, an old well what 'adn't been used for years—Mister Lyman put in a new water system some time ago with pipes 'n things, and this old well was abandoned. Dry as a bone, it is, an' several 'undred feet deep. A few years back one of th' farm children was nosin' about where 'e didn't 'ave no business bein' and tumbled into th' well—broke both 'is legs, 'e did, almost died before they were able to rescue 'im.''

"How dreadful—" I exclaimed, giving her my full attention.

"Awful, it was, just awful. They 'eard the boy yellin'—'e'd been down there for '*ours*—and Mister Lyman was marvelous. 'E got 'im a rope and went down after 'im 'imself, riskin' 'is life. George told me all about it. Anyway, 'e 'ad a cover built and nailed it over th' top of th' well so no one else'd 'ave an accident. That's what th' row was about—Mister Lyman discovered that a 'igh wind'd blown th' cover off th' well 'n Anderson 'adn't nailed it back on, 'adn't reported it either. Mister Lyman tore into 'im somethin' fierce, said there wudn't no excuse for such negli—" She stumbled over the word, frowning, "said 'e oughta 'ave 'is bloody 'ide for not re-portin' it immediately."

"I don't blame him," I remarked.

"Anderson was shook up mightily, and George says Mister Lyman was fit to be tied when 'e came back to the 'ouse. 'E 'ammered th' cover back on th' well 'imself, said 'e was surrounded by bloody in-competents and was goin' to sack th' whole bloody lot one fine day. Mister Lyman *does* 'ave a temper, though 'e's fair. Everyone says 'e's fair."

"I'm sure he is."

Susie shook her head and stepped back to ex-amine her handiwork, satisfied that my appearance met her high standards. A string of pearls might be nice, she said, but then with my high coloring I didn't really need any ornaments. She adjusted the hang of the rich golden brown skirt, wondered aloud if *she*'d ever have enough bosom to wear low-cut gowns and declared I looked like a bloomin' duchess, I did indeed.

"Your cousin's goin' to be impressed," she added.

"Do you think so?"

" 'E's certainly a fine figure of a man. Betty's been assigned to do 'is room. 'E was there when she went in to change th' linen, 'n she said 'e was th' 'andsomest devil she'd ever clapped eyes on. 'Course Betty says that about anything in trousers. Funny you never mentioned 'im before, Miss Jenny."

"Didn't I?"

"You never said a word about 'im, never said you'd invited 'im to Mallyncourt. Took us all by sur-prise when 'e turned up this mornin'. Didn't give 'is name or anything, just told Jeffers 'e wanted to see Mister Edward right away."

I refrained from making any comment, and Susie was visibly disappointed, quite plainly hoping to reap more information about the cousin who had materialized so suddenly. I opened a bottle of perfume, applying a touch of scent behind each ear.

"Miss Vanessa seems quite taken with 'im," she remarked idly, brushing a blond lock from her temple. Her blue eyes were deceptively innocent. "They were quite chummy when they came back from their ride this afternoon, ever so relaxed, like they'd known each other for years 'n years."

"Clive makes friends quickly," I remarked.

"So does Miss Vanessa," she said slyly.

I ignored the comment.

"Mister Lyman was in th' stables when they returned. 'E'd just gotten back from 'is row with Anderson and was in a *very* foul mood, George says. George was there, chattin' with one of th' grooms. Anyway, Miss Vanessa 'ad 'er arm linked around your cousin's and they were laughin' and carryin' on ever so chummy like, like I said. Mister Lyman met up with 'em outside th' stables and Miss Vanessa introduced your cousin. Your cousin bowed real polite like and Mister Lyman just scowled and went on 'is way, didn't say 'ow do you do or *any*-thing. Your cousin looked surprised, but Miss Vanessa just laughed."

"Mister Robb isn't noted for his good manners," I said. "It's getting late. I'd better go down."

" 'Ope dinner isn't a complete shambles," Susie remarked. "Cook 'asn't been 'erself since she turned up those cards this mornin'. Death 'n disaster, she keeps repeatin'. 'Course *I* don't put any faith in them cards, but Cook, you see, she actually *believes* in 'em—"

I stepped out into the hall, dreading the ordeal

ahead. It was going to be quite an evening, I thought wryly. Cook was hardly a gourmet's delight to begin with, and the food would probably be inedible tonight. Lyman's foul mood wouldn't help matters. Even though he had been tolerant of Lyle Radcliff and quite plainly couldn't care less about Vanessa's conduct, he had obviously taken an immediate dislike to Gerry and had no intentions of being civil. We were going to be a jolly group at the table, all right. Another pleasant evening at Mallyncourt, I told myself, stepping into the long gallery.

"There you are," Edward said. "I've been waiting for you. I thought we should go down together."

"I'd as soon skip the whole thing," I said bitterly.

Edward smiled. Resplendent in dark suit and a sky blue waistcoat embroidered with black silk, he was the picture of sartorial elegance, cool, composed, his dark blond hair gleaming. It irritated me that he should be so calm, so completely unperturbed by this new turn of events.

"You look upset, Jennifer."

"I've been upset all day long," I snapped.

"Whatever for?" he inquired lazily.

The sardonic amusement was back in his eyes again, and it disturbed me even more than it had this morning.

"Could you possibly still be worried about Prince?" he said smoothly. "I thought I told you I'd handle him. You must learn to trust me, my dear. I sent a letter to my solicitor this afternoon. The money will be here in a few days. There's nothing whatsoever to worry about."

"I wish I could believe that."

"Compose yourself, Jennifer," he said. He wrapped his fingers around my elbow, leading me to the steps. "Come, they'll be waiting for us. You must be very gracious to your cousin tonight—"

As we went downstairs, I kept thinking about Cook and her tarot cards. I didn't believe in such things, of course, but, just the same, I wished Susie hadn't mentioned it. It didn't help at all.

Eleven

I STOOD beside one of the pairs of tall French windows that opened out from the ballroom into the side gardens, temporarily without a partner and glad of the respite. It was gay. It was grand. It was a great success, and I was bone weary after too much dancing, longing ardently for another glass of champagne. Behind me, in the gardens, Japanese lanterns swayed from tree limbs and spread splotches of wavering blue and red and green, and couples strolled along the paths, enjoying the night air, enjoying stolen kisses among the shadows, and here in the ballroom six great chandeliers hung from the ornate ceiling, shedding a brilliant radiance over a dance floor crowded with swirling couples. It was a kaleidoscope of movement and color, men in dark, elegant suits dancing with women whose skirts billowed like colored petals, jewels flashing, dancers bending, turning, abandoned and adrift on a sea of music.

Gilt chairs and Regency sofas had been placed all around the floor for those not dancing. Men stood in scattered groups, discussing politics, and plump matrons gossiped behind fans. Shy young girls sat demurely, casting longing glances at robust young men ill-at-ease in their swell attire. Buffet tables had been set up in the formal drawing room adjoining, laden with gorgeously arranged meats, moulded aspics, pyramids of tiny glazed cakes, presided over by liveried servants who served the guests with stern, impassive faces while others, equally as impassive, circulated with large trays of champagne glasses filled to the brim, going back for more as soon as the tray was empty. A hearty festivity prevailed. Country gentry, I observed, enjoyed themselves wholeheartedly, with a robust zest quite lacking in the formal London society dominated by a prudish Queen.

A gentle breeze lifted the long yellow silk draperies behind me, causing them to billow inward, rustling. I wore a rich gold brocade gown, the skirt very full, the tight bodice emphasizing narrow waist and full bosom, cut low, the puffed sleeves dropping off the shoulder. The rich cloth was embroidered with tiny silk flowers of darker gold. Dancers swept past me. On a sofa nearby two elderly women in old-fashioned gowns waved their dusty ostrich fans and talked about their ailments, and a young girl in white, eyes forlorn, stood beside a pot of tall green plants and watched her sister flirt with a dashing young man in a dark blue uniform with shiny golden epaulets that shimmered when he moved.

The reception line in the great hall had been an ordeal, but, standing beside Edward, I had played my part brilliantly, greeting each and every guest, never once betraying the nervousness inside. I chatted with a cantankerous old duchess who looked like a cracked, aged china shepardess in pink organdy and imitation pearls. I smiled as matrons gushed and tittered, eyeing me with great curiosity.

I nodded and shook hands and made pleasant remarks and prayed for it to end.

It did end, and Edward and I opened the dance. He was perfectly at ease, but I was nervous, knowing all eyes were on us, and when the first dance was over I danced with retired military men, with energetic country squires who talked about horseflesh and hunts, with young bucks who held me too tightly, with a duke, with a parson, with Lyle Radcliff, silent and embittered as he tried to keep his eye on Vanessa in the crush. I danced with Lord Mallyn, who danced just the one dance with me, creaking around the floor with a defiant expression on his face as his doctors watched from the side of the room. Then he took me for champagne, and I had time for just one glass before a ruddy-cheeked squire seized my arm with robust glee and led me back to the dance floor and another round of dancing began.

I finally managed to escape, and now, as I stood beside the tall windows, I hoped no one else would ask me to dance, at least for a while. I could see Lord Mallyn across the room, holding court. Standing with the aid of a silver-headed cane, dressed to the hilt in a tight-fitting black suit and an outrageous magenta waistcoat that would have done justice to a young Disraeli, he was in his element. Rings flashing, dark eyes snapping, he looked like some dry, decrepit old butterfly just recently broken out of a dusty cocoon, and, seeing him, one would never have guessed he had been seriously ill such a short time before. He was enjoying himself thoroughly, preening audaciously, drinking far too much champagne, yawning at bores and chuckling raucously with old cronies.

Glancing around the vast, crowded room, I saw

Lyman standing in a corner, sullen, looking ill at ease in his handsome black suit and a gleaming white satin waistcoat embroidered with darker white patterns. The splendid apparel offset his virility and made him seem even more rugged. His white silk tie was crooked, his raven locks tousled, his eyes dark and brooding, and he was obviously miserable, wishing the ball were over and he could get out of the fancy clothes. As I watched, an attractive, flirtatious blonde in sky-blue organdy sailed over to him, smiling and placing her hand on his arm. Lyman scowled and said something between his teeth and the blonde hurried away, blushing furiously. He scowled again and looked more miserable than ever.

In contrast, Vanessa was radiant, a merry smile on her lips as she swept around the floor in the arms of a tall, handsome youth with brick-red hair and a rakish manner. She hadn't been without a partner since the ball began, and she was quite easily the center of attention in her spectacular silver gown, emeralds blazing at her throat and dangling from her ears. Her ebony hair was superbly arranged. Her cheeks were flushed a delicate pink. Her eyes sparkled, vying with the emeralds for brilliance. The men sought her attention, young and old alike, and she reveled in it, allowing this one to fetch her champagne, permitting that one to bring her a plate, abandoning both to return to the dance floor with yet another. I noticed several of the women whispering behind their fans as they observed her, but Vanessa couldn't have cared less what any of them thought.

As she swirled past, I caught sight of Gerald Prince standing across the room with two pretty girls, one in pink, one in white, both listening with rapt attention as he continued some narrative. Gerry was quite a sensation with the ladies tonight, attentive and gallant to the older ones, jovial and roguish with the younger. More than one matron had told me how much she admired my cousin, and I knew he had received a number of invitations from several with marriageable daughters. The role of Clive Randall, amiable cousin, was one he performed with great aplomb, and I wondered how much longer we would have to suffer his presence at Mallyncourt. As he ended his narrative, the girl in pink giggled and the girl in white looked deliciously scandalized. Gerry chuckled, pleased with himself, pleased with his success.

I wondered where Edward was. I hadn't seen him in over an hour, not since the first dance, the duty dance, Edward Baker and his new bride opening the ball. He hadn't asked me to dance a second time. He had turned me over to the duke, had turned to a pretty girl in lavender, the music beginning again, separating us, and I had lost sight of him, disappointment deepening as time passed and dance followed dance and he didn't seek me out again. He had to dance with all the ladies. It was his duty. Disappointment? Absurd. I didn't care whether I danced with him again or not. I had danced enough already to last a lifetime.

A strapping lad with untidy blond hair and boyish brown eyes came over to me, grinning affably, and I felt my heart sink. He had almost broken my rib cage earlier. He was going to ask me to dance again. He did, and I couldn't refuse without being rude. I smiled. I braced myself. He wrapped his arm around my waist and seized my hand in a bone-crushing grip and propelled me onto the floor, into the midst of the swirling color, the movement, and I continued to smile, enduring his awkwardness, enduring his talk about the county fair and the hog he intended to enter in competition, and when the waltz ended I sighed and turned and found myself face to face with yet another lad, dark-eyed, intense, wickedly handsome, and he pulled me into his arms and the music began again. He danced divinely, smoothly, not awkward at all, and he talked too, not about hogs, but about life and love and poetry, fancying himself a Byronic figure, telling me his life was a perpetual search for a woman who would understand him and touch his soul, and I told him I was happily married and he frowned, disappointed, dancing in silence, and, the dance done, going on with his perpetual search while I danced with another squire, with a student from Oxford, with an aged gentleman with silver hair and rheumatism who looked down at his feet throughout the dance, counting steps, one two three, one two three.

Shortly after nine, the music stopped. The dancers applauded. I applauded, too, in the middle of the crowd, standing with Lyle Radcliff who was still silent and embittered, staring at Vanessa. On their raised platform at the end of the ballroom, the musicians put down their instruments to take a short break, and the crowd began to mix and mingle, voices rising, laughter trilling. Lyle asked me if I would like a glass of champagne, and I shook my head and he thanked me for the dance and walked away looking painfully young, soon swallowed up by the crowd. A general movement began toward the drawing room where champagne was still flowing, the tables still laden, and I moved back toward the French windows, eager for fresh air and another rest, however short.

I stood in front of a set of windows, my back to

the gardens, drapes billowing in the breeze, the air refreshing. The crowd was thinning rapidly on the dance floor now, the golden parquet littered with ribbons and petals and dance cards. Vanessa was standing alone, people moving past her, the skirt of her gown like a great silver bell, the formfitting bodice cut extremely low, emeralds dripping from her throat. She was watching someone approach, an expectant look in her eyes. People passed. I lost sight of her for a moment. When I saw her again, Gerry was with her, and she tilted her head back, looking into his eyes, smiling. He leaned down, whispering something into her ear. She nodded, placing her hand on his arm. They moved toward the door leading into the hall.

And then, suddenly, Edward was standing in front of me, a smile on his lips, his blue eyes filled with amusement. I had been so engrossed in watching Vanessa that I hadn't seen him approach. He seemed in an unusually relaxed mood, almost jolly.

"Hello, Mrs. Baker," he said.

"I—I didn't see you."

"I saw you—standing all alone in your magnificent gold brocade gown, looking disturbed. I dumped Mrs. Crothers. Mrs. Crothers was telling me all about her roses. 'Damn your roses,' I said, 'I've got to go cheer up my wife.' "

"You didn't say that."

"I wanted to. I foisted her off on Colonel Jameson. Colonel Jameson is half-deaf, has an ear trumpet, but he grows roses, too. You look absolutely lovely, my dear. Now you look startled."

"I—I'm not used to compliments from you."

"It wasn't a compliment. It was a statement of fact. You're the most beautiful woman here tonight. Everyone says so. 'You've picked yourself a real stunner, Baker,' Sir Roderick told me. 'That red hair—damned if she doesn't look like Lady Hamilton.' Sir Roderick is ninety-one years old. He was a young diplomat in Naples, knew the lady in question well."

"Why are you doing this?"

"Why am I doing what?"

"Being so friendly. It—isn't like you."

"No?"

"Not in the least."

"Must I have a motive?" he asked, smiling.

"You probably do," I told him.

"Am I such a monster, then?"

"Yes," I said peevishly.

"We'll have to change that image, my dear."

"You've been avoiding me all evening."

"And that upset you?"

"Don't be absurd. I—I was relieved, frankly."

"I've been doing my duty. I've danced with plump, fussy matrons, with blushing, tittering girls. I've charmed garrulous old crocodiles in shabby velvet. I've carried plates of food to the duchess— astounding appetite that woman has, I don't think she gets enough to eat at home. I've fetched shawls and listened to gossip and endeared myself to all the ladies. Now I can concentrate on you."

"I wish you wouldn't."

"Oh?"

"I prefer the—the other Edward."

The smile still played on his lips, and it was warm, an amused smile, and there was amusement in his eyes, too, as though I were a child he found enchanting. The lapels of his dark suit gleamed silkily. His white satin waistcoat was embroidered with black and maroon flowers. An errant lock of heavy blond hair fell across his brow like an inverted comma. I had never seen him so relaxed, so natural, not a trace of the icy remoteness now. He exuded warmth, and charm, such charm, not like the Edward I knew, not at all like the Edward I knew. I was uneasy, unsure of myself, not knowing how to react.

"People are looking at us," I said.

"Naturally. 'What a handsome pair,' they're saying. We do make a handsome pair, you know."

"What do you want, Edward?"

"I want to take you for a stroll in the gardens. They're quite lovely tonight with the lanterns swaying. We'll have time for a leisurely stroll before the music starts again."

"I—I don't want to go."

"But you shall," he said. It was a command.

I looked up at him. The warmth was there, the charm, but so was the steely determination of old. It would be futile to argue. He took my elbow, leading me out through the tall windows. Before us, the gardens were like a fairyland, lanterns rocking gently in the breeze, spilling great blurs of color, intensifying the shadows. It was cool, the air stroking my bare arms and shoulders. I shivered. From the cold? I wasn't sure. We moved down a short flight of flat stone steps, walked along a graveled path with rose bushes abloom on either side, now in darkness, now passing under pools of color, tree limbs creaking, leaves rustling. Others were strolling as well, and there were quiet voices, soft laughter.

"You've made quite an impression on our guests," Edward remarked idly. "You've been superb. They came here tonight consumed with curiosity, eager to find fault with you. They're going to leave praising you. Your dignity, your poise—it's won everyone over, even the most critical."

"Is it so important?"

"It's terribly important."

"I'll be leaving soon. Everyone here tonight will learn I'm not really your wife. I don't see what difference it could make what they think of me now."

"But you're not leaving," he said. "You're going to marry me. I've already made arrangements. We leave for London next week. We'll be gone for two or three days, and when we return you will be Mrs. Edward Baker and no one will be any the wiser."

"I'm not going to marry you, Edward."

"Yes, my dear, you are."

"I—I don't intend to argue about it."

"Fine. I'm in no mood to argue. I'm in a very good mood, as you've no doubt observed. There's a reason for it."

"I surmised as much."

"My uncle's lawyer is here tonight, a decrepit old fossil by the name of Smith. I overheard the two of them talking. My uncle instructed Smith to return to Mallyncourt next Tuesday—prepared to draw up a will. There can be no question of its contents. The old man dotes on you, and, because of you, he's developed a great respect for me. We've won."

He was still holding my elbow, loosely, and now he led me toward one of the secluded spots abounding in the gardens, pale pink and purple-white bougainvillea spilling over the side of a tall stone wall, a white marble bench beneath, all illuminated by a shaft of silver-blue moonlight. Like an automaton, I let him lead me, and I tried not to think, not to feel, aware of the danger, oh so aware of it, afraid not of Edward but of myself. We had come some distance from the house, a great block of darkness behind us with tall golden squares where light streamed out of the windows. There was no one else around, not this far from the house. I was painfully aware of that, painfully aware of his touch, his nearness.

"Everything's worked out just as I planned," he said. "Well, not precisely as I planned—I'm getting a bonus."

"A bonus?"

"You," he said.

"You're quite sure of yourself, Edward."

"I'm sure of you."

"What—what do you mean by that?"

"I think you know."

"No," I said. There was a tremor in my voice.

"You're in love with me."

"That's absurd. I've never heard anything so—"

"You're in love with me," he repeated. "You have been from the first. You've fought it, no doubt. You've tried to deny it, even to yourself, but the fact remains. You love me."

"You're quite mistaken, Mr. Baker."

Edward smiled to himself. He propped one foot up on the bench, placing his hand on his knee, leaning forward a little. His jacket fell open, revealing an expanse of white satin waistcoat. In the moonlight, I could see him clearly, every feature sharp and distinct: the eyes, half hooded by heavy, drooping lids, his cheekbones high, slight hollows beneath, his lips curling with the smile. Behind him, the bougainvillea spilled like a froth of puffy lace, scented. He gazed at me thoughtfully, and I looked away, apprehensive, trying not to tremble. Far away, among the trees, the Japanese lanterns swayed, splotches of color floating in the darkness, and the sounds of the ball drifted out into the night, muted, barely reaching us here.

"That first night," he said, "when I kissed you— I could have taken you then." His voice was a lazy drawl. "You would have struggled, but not for long. I contemplated it, I must admit, but at the time it would only have complicated matters."

"And now—now I suppose it suits your purposes ideally."

"Ideally," he agreed. "It makes it so much easier to have you in love with me."

I looked at him, silent, that tremulous fear strong inside. He was a fascinating man, yes, there was no denying that. He was strong and virile and incredibly handsome, the kind of man women dreamed about, but he was also cold, ruthless, dangerous, and I couldn't love a man like that. He was everything I despised. I *couldn't* love him. I was intrigued by him, for danger is always intriguing, and, too, there was a strong attraction, purely physical, but I was far too intelligent to mistake that for love. I didn't love Edward Baker. I couldn't. Standing there in the moonlight in my gold brocade gown, I told myself that he was wrong.

A gentle breeze caused the bougainvillea to tremble, several blossoms tearing free and floating to the ground. A bird called out in a bush nearby, one sad note, then silence. Edward continued to gaze at me. A heavy blond wave had spilled over his forehead, burnished by moonlight, and his waistcoat gleamed, jacket hanging loose as he leaned on his knee, relaxed, confident that he had only to make a move to have me melt into his arms. I felt cold, and frightened, wondering what would happen if he did make that move, wondering how I would respond. Would I have the strength to resist him, or would I react exactly as he thought I would? I gnawed my lower lip nervously, waiting.

"As Mistress of Mallyncourt, you'll have everything," he said. His voice was silken, caressing.

"You'll have fine clothes, jewels, servants to wait on you, your own carriage to drive. You'll have everything any woman could want, and later on, when the old man dies, we'll sell everything and move to London. We'll have a town house, a box at Covent Garden, and we'll travel—"

"You think you can buy me, don't you?"

"But of course."

"You think I'm as—as venal as you are. I can't blame you. You have every reason to think that. I agreed to this insane charade willingly, for money. You must think—"

"I think we've talked long enough," he said firmly.

"I despise you, Edward."

"No, my dear, you don't."

He took his foot from the bench. He stood up straight, looking at me with a faint smile curling on his lips. He was in no hurry, certain of an easy victory whenever he chose to make his move. I stood very still, like a statue, watching him. I felt cold, so very cold. Music began to drift out into the night from the ballroom. They were dancing again, the break over. Edward reached up to brush the wave back from his forehead, his lips still turned up at the corners. He was amused. I suddenly realized that his eyes were full of amusement. He gave a quiet chuckle and began to straighten the lapels of his jacket.

"You're a stubborn little thing, Jennifer," he said lightly.

"Is that what you think it is—stubbornness?"

"We've settled nothing, it seems, but then I haven't used the—uh—ultimate persuasion. I'm tempted—you're quite fetching with the moonlight streaming over your shoulders—but, unfortunately,

now isn't the time for it. We have guests. I don't
want to start anything that can't be brought to it's—
uh—inevitable conclusion."

"Then I suggest we return to the ballroom."

Head tilted to one side, lids drooping, he regarded me with an expression of idle amusement.

"Alas, I suppose we'd better. We can settle this
at—uh—a more appropriate time. I shall look forward to it."

"You're due a great disappointment."

"I don't think so, luv," he said pleasantly.

Thrusting his hands into his trouser pockets, he
strolled across the damp grass to the graveled path.
On the path, he turned, waiting for me, tall and
handsome, completely at ease, completely confident. I hesitated a moment, then joined him, the
skirt of my gold brocade gown making a soft crackling noise. Silent, we moved up the path, through
alternate patches of moonlight and shadow, soon
reaching the area where the lanterns bloomed red
and blue and green, swaying from the limbs overhead, creaking faintly on their wires. The music
grew louder and louder as we neared the house and
there were others around us now, couples strolling
hand in hand, talking quietly. Reaching the low flat
steps, Edward sighed and took his hands out of his
pockets, wrapping one of them around my elbow in
the old, familiar way, guiding me up the steps as
though I belonged to him. Light spilled out of the
ballroom onto the terrace in brilliant pools, turning
the flagstones gold, and through the tall French windows I could see the dancers swirling in a blur of
shifting colors.

We stepped back into the ballroom, pausing in
front of the windows for a moment, Edward's hand
still gripping my elbow. The chandeliers shed daz-

zling light, crystal pendants glittering, and the
drapes behind us swelled like sails, billowing inward. Dancers swept past us, whirling, turning,
swaying with the music, skirts belling out, and I noticed Lyman standing in the corner, arms folded
across his chest, watching the two of us with dark,
brooding eyes. I felt disorientated, unnerved by
what had happened in the gardens—what had almost happened—and everything seemed unreal. I
had been calm enough there in the moonlight, but
now that the danger was past a curious reaction
was setting in and I felt giddy and light-headed.

Edward seemed to be looking for someone,
holding my elbow but totally unaware of me as he
searched the room with his eyes. That chilly remoteness was back, and I suddenly realized that I didn't
exist for him as a person at all. I was merely a tool
he was using and planned to use again, not a human
being with human emotions. He didn't spot the person he was looking for. A slight frown creased his
brow. He sighed, noticing me again, remembering I
was beside him and we were in the ballroom and
dozens of people were watching us. He smiled. He
took my hand. He led me into the sea of dancers and
curled his arm around my waist and swung me into
motion, and we danced, sweeping along through
the crowd, music lilting, rising and falling in me-
lodic waves. He looked deep into my eyes, playing
his part, and I smiled, playing mine, and we were
the handsome pair everyone said we were.

The waltz ended. There was a scattering of applause. A woman in pink velvet smiled at Edward,
toying with her fan. A hearty squire in tall brown
boots made his way toward me. He said he thought
this dance was his. Edward nodded and stepped
over to the woman in pink. The music started again,

and we were separated, Edward and the woman moving in one direction, the squire and I in another, dozens of couples coming in between. I lost sight of him. I smiled at the squire. He stumbled. I continued to smile. When the dance was over he gave me up to a student I had danced with earlier, and the student turned me over to a tall man with a pearl stickpin in his black stock, and dance followed dance, time passing, my feet aching, and I was trapped, but still I smiled, still I danced.

It was an hour later before I managed to excuse myself. I moved toward the drawing room, nodding to people I passed on the way. My head was splitting. I hadn't eaten a bite, but I didn't intend to eat. I caught a glimpse of myself in one of the mirrors in the drawing room. My cheeks were flushed. My eyes were bright. The coiffure Susie had worked so hard on was beginning to come undone, titian waves slipping a little in attractive disarray. A footman passed bearing a tray of champagne glasses. I reached for one. I drank it rapidly and set it down. The old duchess was at the table heaping her plate with food. There was a guilty expression on her face as she looked up. I smiled at her. Another footman passed. I took another glass of champagne. The room was crowded. I spoke to several people, names forgotten, and everything was pleasantly blurred. I felt much better now. I drank a third glass of champagne, quickly, and I was reaching for another when a hand clamped tightly over my wrist.

"You've had enough," he said brusquely.

"Lyman! Hello! My, you're scowling again. Don't you ever smile? Do you know, I've never seen you smile, not once. I wonder how you'd look? I can't imagine—"

"Come with me!" he muttered.

"You're abducting me? That's enchanting. I've always wanted to be abducted—"

We moved down a long, narrow hall, the sound of music growing fainter and fainter as we moved. I tripped along beside him, his hand holding my wrist securely, and I was still enchanted and delightfully bewildered, everything hazy. Lyman walked briskly, angry. I wondered why he was angry. We turned down another hall. It was in darkness, a shadowy void, and we moved down it, eventually reaching the long back hall. It was gilded with moonlight, the tapestries like ghostly shrouds on the walls. Lyman was silent, grim, leading me to the back door, leading me outside. The night air was cold, unpleasant. I protested, trying to pull away, but he paid no attention at all, forcing me to follow him across the veranda and onto the lawn.

We walked. We walked for a long time, passing the shrubs, passing the tall, broken statues that watched us with sightless eyes. The lights and music were far away, and here there was only the silvery sheen of moonlight and shifting shadows, black, blue-black, gray, no sound but the sound of our footsteps and the rustle of leaves. Lyman didn't speak. He held on to my wrist, forcing me to walk. The sky overhead was ashy gray frosted with stars that glimmered like gems. I closed my eyes, stumbling along, hating him because the pleasant haze was going away and my head was beginning to hurt worse than ever. I don't know how long we walked, but when he finally stopped the haze was completely gone and I felt wretched, ashamed of myself, ashamed he had seen me like this.

"Ready to go back now?" he asked. His voice was indifferent.

"I—I suppose so. Why—why did you do it?"

"You were on the verge of making a spectacle of yourself, Mrs. Baker. I felt someone should step in."

"Why should it have mattered to you?"

Lyman didn't answer. He gave a curt nod of his head, indicating that I should follow, then started back toward the veranda, moving in long, brisk strides. His shoulders rolled, the tail of his jacket flaring out behind him as he walked. He stopped at the veranda and turned to wait for me with his mouth set tight, his eyes dark with impatience. I stood in the middle of the lawn for a moment, my bare shoulders trembling with cold, and then, wearily, I went to join him. My head throbbed furiously, as though brutal fingers pressed against my temples, but all the dizziness was gone now. I looked at Lyman, trying to regain some semblance of dignity.

"I don't—usually do things like that," I said.

"You were upset when you came back in from the gardens with Edward. I kept my eye on you, suspecting something was wrong. *Is* something wrong, Mrs. Baker?"

"Of—of course not. I was merely—over stimulated."

He was silent, studying my face with a dark, intense scrutiny I found extremely disconcerting. It was almost as though he were reading my mind, as though he knew everything. His sullen manner and rough-hewn exterior were quite misleading. Lyman Robb was a highly intelligent man, and he was altogether too observant. I brushed at my skirt nervously, avoiding those probing brown eyes.

"I spent an hour with Lettice this afternoon," he said in a matter-of-fact voice. "She showed me the doll clothes you'd made for her. She chattered like a magpie, singing your praises. I've never seen her so natural, so vivacious. She was like a completely different child. You're responsible for that."

I looked up at him, startled by the abrupt change of subject.

"I—I've done nothing," I said.

"On the contrary, you've done quite a lot. You're the first person who has ever shown a genuine interest in the child, and it's made all the difference in the world—already. I appreciate that, Mrs. Baker. I'm beginning to think I may have been wrong about you."

I made no reply. There was another long moment of silence. The veranda was spread thickly with shadows, only a few rays of moonlight spilling over the stone balustrade. It was cold and damp here under the low ceiling. I shivered. Lyman continued to stare at me, as though waiting for some sort of confession. He must think I was a scheming trollop who had married Edward for money, I thought, and he must despise me for it. The truth was even worse. What would he think if he knew that? Another long moment went by, the silence broken only by the raspy whir of crickets in the cracks of the flagstones, and then Lyman scowled, brows lowered, and said tersely that we'd better get inside.

Skirt rustling softly, I followed him down the veranda. He opened the door for me. I preceded him into the long hall. He closed the door quietly and took my arm in his hand, guiding me toward the hall that led back to the front of the house. He stopped, abruptly, his fingers tightening painfully on my arm. I was startled. I started to protest, and then I heard the footsteps, too. Lyman pulled me over to the back wall, into the nest of shadows between two windows. This side of the room was shrouded with thick layers of blue-black darkness, while the moonlight, seeping through the windows, brushed the tapestries on the opposite wall with a misty light and coated the wide stone steps with a dull silver-blue sheen. Someone was coming down. The footsteps rang loud and clear in the silence. Lyman was tense, standing rigidly against the wall, his fingers biting into the flesh of my arm. My heart pounded. The darkness was so dense here that I couldn't even see him beside me.

Gerald Prince came slowly down the steps, a thoughtful expression on his face. In the shaft of moonlight gilding the steps, every detail was quite distinct. He stopped two steps from the bottom and smiled. Locks of glossy brown hair lay across his forehead. He reached up to brush them back and then tugged at the lapels of his jacket, shifting his shoulders around until the hang was right. His stock, so carefully folded against his neck earlier on, looked rumpled, carelessly tucked into the top of his elaborate satin waistcoat. I realized I hadn't seen him since he and Vanessa had left the dance floor at the beginning of the break. There were more footsteps, light, tapping ones this time, and he turned, looking back up toward the landing.

Vanessa came down leisurely, her great silver skirt sweeping over the steps with a crisp, silken rustle. She paused halfway down to fasten one of the emerald pendants back on her ear, and then she sighed. She had never been lovelier. The gown was only slightly crushed, and her ebony waves were still flawlessly arranged. She smiled at Gerry. A warm glow seemed to suffuse her. Moving down the remaining steps, she touched his cheek with her fingertips, rubbing the skin with gentle strokes. He made as if to gather her into his arms, but she held him off, shaking her head.

"We've been gone long enough as it is, love. We'd best join the others now. There'll be other times."

Leaving the steps, they walked to the door of the hallway and disappeared down it. We could hear their footsteps echoing for a moment or two, and then there was silence. Lyman said nothing. Neither did I. We continued to stand there in the darkness for what seemed an eternity, and then Lyman released my arm. I rubbed it. There would probably be a bruise tomorrow. Still not speaking, he started toward the doorway, moving across the darkness until he reached the misty silver light. He paused at the doorway and turned to wait for me. His face was like granite, impassive, his eyes flat and expressionless. I joined him. We went down the hall. I could hear the music, far away, and as we turned down the second hall it grew louder, a merry, lilting waltz, and I could see the lights ahead, and, a moment later, we were back in the drawing room, mingling with the crowd.

We weren't going to discuss what we had seen. That was plainly understood. Lyman was frightfully composed, far more composed than I was. One of the squires came over to him and said something about crop rotation, and the old duchess, eyes slightly glazed, tapped my arm and indicated I should join her over in front of the white marble fireplace. When I complied, she looked around the room like a conspirator and told me in a low confidential whisper that the pâté was almost gone and I'd better get some right away. She bustled off, and I shook my head. Lyman had left the room.

A short time later, I went back into the ballroom. My head was still throbbing, and I felt dazed, wondering how I was going to endure the rest of the evening. The candles in the great chandeliers were half burned down now, and there weren't nearly so many people dancing. Those who lived some distance away were already leaving. Lord Mallyn stood near the door, shaking hands. Although his eyes were as bright and lively as ever, he looked weary, his face sagging, his shoulders slumping a little. I went over and stood beside him and, when we were alone, told him that Edward and I would see the rest of the guests off and suggested that he call it a night and go up to his room. He snapped and fussed and called me a spoil sport, a nagging hussy, a wet blanket, but that was merely for show. Summoning George to assist him, he took his leave, holding onto the husky footman's arm for support.

Another hour passed. The crowd thinned even more. I hadn't seen Lyman since he'd disappeared from the drawing room, but I saw Gerald Prince, chatting with a cluster of matrons, dazzling them, his manner as florid and dramatic as ever, and, later, I saw Edward standing beside one of the tall French windows with Vanessa. That rather surprised me. Head cocked to one side, he smiled a tight, humorless smile, his blue eyes cold as she spoke to him at length. Then he nodded and made some short remark which seemed to amuse her. She laughed and moved away to be immediately claimed by a young man in uniform who swept her back onto the dance floor. The tight smile remained on Edward's lips, and I could see that he was angry about something. I wondered what Vanessa had said to him.

The candles burned down even more, sputtering, and more guests departed. Edward joined me in the front hall, and we made farewells and shook hands and exchanged pleasantries, and, finally, the last guest had gone, the last carriage had pulled away from the drive. I sighed, weary through and through, filled with relief. Beside me, Edward was silent. He seemed unaware that our duties were over, a grim, distracted look in his eyes as though he were contemplating some problem. I wondered if it had anything to do with what Vanessa had said to him. After a moment he looked up, becoming aware of his surroundings again. It was at this point that Gerry sauntered into the hall. His cheeks had a ruddy glow. He seemed to be in a jovial, expansive mood, regarding the two of us with mocking brown eyes.

"Quite a show you put on tonight," he remarked amiably. "First rate performances from both of you. You look a bit flustered, Jenny, but radiant—as always."

"Save your gallantry for someone else," I said coldly.

"I say, you're not still resentful, are you? I thought I'd been a most engaging fellow these past few days." He grinned and then stiffled a yawn with his hand. "A delightful evening, this. Wine, music, sparkling companions. This is the life—I could grow quite accustomed to it."

I glared at him with open hostility, but Gerry's baiting didn't seem to bother Edward at all. In fact, he seemed almost pleased to see him. To my surprise, he asked Gerry to join him in his study for a nightcap.

"Hunh?" Gerry seemed as surprised as I was. "I say—that's a ripping idea, old chap. You—uh—have some good news to impart?"

"I had an interesting communication from London this afternoon." Edward replied. "I'd like to settle things tonight."

Gerry extended his arm toward the door with a dramatic flourish. "After you, my good man," he said, "after you."

They left, and I returned to the ballroom. There was no sign of Vanessa or Lyman. I supposed both of them had already gone upstairs. The ballroom looked vast and empty as footmen swept up the litter with long-handled brooms and housemaids gathered up dishes and stacked them noisily on trays. The great chandeliers had been lowered until they almost touched the floor. George and another footman snuffed out the candles one by one. All brightness and gaiety was gone now, the tattered remnants of the night being removed with swift efficiency. The ball was over, at last. Weary, I went up to my room, too tired even to think about all that had happened during the course of this eventful night.

Twelve

$\mathcal{I}$ WAS tired, but it was a pleasant tiredness, a relaxed, rather languorous feeling after having walked for what must have been miles. Two days had passed since the ball, and this afternoon, after sewing with Lettice and taking tea with her in the nursery, I had simply left the house and started walking with no particular destination in mind. Past the stables, down the long avenue of lime trees, over the empty fields beyond, I walked, enjoying the solitude and the exercise, enjoying the wind whipping at my skirts and tossing my hair, enjoying the smell of the countryside and the arching gray sky that stretched endlessly above. Perhaps it was foolish to go so far afield after what had happened that afternoon when I was returning from the village, but I gave no thought to that.

I had walked over the fields to the sloping knolls beyond, then over the moors, a vast sea of land covered with thick, dry, grayish-brown grass only faintly brushed with green, a vague blue-green. There were shales of crumbly gray rock as well, and, here and there, strangely shaped black-gray boulders that seemed to grow out of the earth. I walked, thinking of all that had taken place over the past weeks, trying to resolve the dilemma I felt inside, and, as I started back, nothing was resolved. It was as though Mallyncourt had cast a spell over me, becoming the only reality. My life before seemed dreamlike, insubstantial, and I couldn't visualize a future away from the great house. I had become inextricably involved with the people there, and although I told myself I would be leaving soon, that I must leave before it was too late, I couldn't visualize that either.

I had grown fond of Lord Mallyn, very fond, and he had come to depend on me. He didn't know what he would do without me. He said that repeatedly. Could I leave him? I had grown fond of Lettice, too. The child was gradually blooming, thorns softening into petals, and what would happen to her if she discovered my deceit? What would it do to her? And there was Edward. Yes, there was Edward. There was no moonlight now, no frothy bougainvillea, no tremulous fear inside, and my mind was clear. Perhaps I didn't love him. What is love? I asked myself. How does one know it? I told myself I didn't love him, and I believed that most of the time, yet Edward Baker had become the center of my world, his presence so strong that it effected my every thought, my every action, and even though I knew him, even though I might even actually despise him, I couldn't visualize a life without that strong central force.

What was I going to do when he made his next move? I had been so sure there in the moonlit gardens two nights ago, but now I wasn't sure at all. I told myself I couldn't leave Lord Mallyn, couldn't fail Lettice, but perhaps that was merely a subterfuge on my part, something to hide the unpleasant fact that it was Edward I couldn't leave, couldn't fail. Here, with the wind tearing at my hair and the moors stretching bleakly on every side, I could be entirely honest with myself for the first time.

Tired, filled with a weary languor, I climbed a slope and, leaving the moors behind, started back across the fields. They were empty, too, but rich and loamy underfoot, covered with green. They had brought in a great yield before and would again in the future, but Lyman respected the land he worked and rotated the crops to keep it vital and productive. It was late now, the sky a lighter gray, turning yellow, and on the horizon orange and golden banners blazed, spreading, fading. There was a faint haze in the air and soon, I knew, as soon as the last banner faded, the sky would lose all color and gradually blacken and the haze would take on the purple tints of twilight. Across the fields I could see the avenue of limes, a narrow passageway opening through the woods. The rooftop of Mallyncourt reared up over the leafy trees beyond, the ornate pinnacles bathed in sunlight.

I thought about the house, about that dusty east wing, closed up and given over to decay except for that one bizarre room with its many reds and the erotic bronzes. Events and emotions following one right after another had temporarily eclipsed that mystery, yet mystery there was. What secret did that room hold? What caused the noises the servants spoke of? Why had Edward been so alarmed when he found me in the room, and why had Lyman been lurking in the hall that night before Gerry's arrival? Why had he told me to keep quiet about that midnight encounter? I had been too occupied with other things to give much thought to that room and the mystery surrounding it, but I thought about it now, strolling toward the avenue of limes, and I had the disconcerting feeling that I should *know* the answers to all those questions, that it was something quite obvious, something I should have realized immediately. It was as though the answers were there in the back of my mind, half shrouded in mist, striving to break through, but no matter how hard I tried to summon them they continued to elude me.

One problem, at least, had been solved. Gerald Prince was no longer at Mallyncourt. He had left the morning after the ball, long before anyone got up. His sudden, abrupt departure had been puzzling at first. I knew a train left the station at six o'clock in the morning, but how had he gotten to the station? There had been no one to drive him there, not at that hour, and when the stable boys got up they reported that all the horses were still in their stalls. Did he walk two miles, carrying his bags? That wasn't like Gerry, not at all. I had been extremely mystified until Edward informed me later on in the day that he had seen Gerry off himself. Immediately after they had their nightcap in the study, Edward had given him the money, Gerry had packed his bags and, while everyone else was asleep, Edward had saddled two horses. They had ridden to the station together, and then Edward had led Gerry's horse from the station, arriving back at Mallyncourt just before dawn. Gerald Prince had gone, ten thousand pounds richer, and Edward assured me he wouldn't be back to bother us again.

I had explained to the others that Clive had had an urgent appointment in London and had to leave suddenly. Lord Mallyn expressed relief. Lyman was indifferent. Vanessa, though, had been acting most strangely these past two days. She had been moody, upset, her temper flaring on several occasions. She was more openly resentful of Edward, almost as though she knew he had been the cause of Gerry's departure. Yesterday, sitting in one of the window recesses with a book in my lap, I had happened to glance out at the back lawn. Edward and Vanessa had been together near the back hedge, and she seemed to be berating him furiously, her eyes flashing, her cheeks flushed a bright pink. Although naturally I couldn't hear anything, I could sense her fury. Edward had been cool and remote, untouched by her words, and Vanessa had finally stormed back to the veranda, leaving him alone. He had watched her departure with indifferent blue eyes, then shook his head and strolled calmly across the lawn and out of sight.

She had been petulant and sulky at dinner last night, snapping at one of the servants, glaring at the rest of us, her remarks even bitchier and more scathing than usual. Her effervescent spirits were completely missing, her gaeity gone ever since the night of the ball. Was it because Gerry had left without telling her? Of course, I told myself. Vanessa was a tempestuous creature, all fire beneath that lovely surface, frustrated now because her lover had deserted her without an explanation. Edward had probably made some taunting remark about it that had caused her to lash out at him so vindictively. She had always resented him, and now she simply wasn't bothering to hide it beneath a civilized façade.

She had even more reason to resent him in the past day or so, for Lord Mallyn had made certain everyone knew his lawyer was coming next Tuesday to draw up the will, and he had dropped several broad hints that Edward would be his heir. Lyman smoldered in silence, and his loss would be Vanessa's loss as well. If her bright scintillation had been replaced by temperament, it was no wonder. Oh well, I reflected, she would soon enough find another man. A woman like Vanessa couldn't be without a man for long. Gerry would be replaced, as Lyle Radcliff had been, and even though Edward might inherit Mallyncourt, Lyman would still continue to handle the estate, she would still have a place. Until Lord Mallyn died. Would Edward really sell the house and farms then? Somehow I couldn't believe that.

Leaving the fields behind, I started down the avenue of limes. It was long, several hundred yards, leading from the stables to the fields, and narrow, perhaps twenty feet across. The limes grew tall on either side, and the ground was hard and uneven, the grass sparse and half dead, for, leading directly to the open fields as it did, it was used as a shortcut by horseback riders who preferred not to follow the formal drive around to the gatehouse. Lyman rode down the avenue every morning on his way to the tenant farms, and Vanessa frequently charged up and down it to exercise her horse when she wasn't in the mood for a long ride. It was spread with thick shadows now, and the sky overhead was darker, the yellow fading. A brisk wind had sprung up, causing the limes to stir and groan like live things. Leaves rattled crisply as I passed.

The light was beginning to go as I reached the stables. The low brown stone buildings were coated with shadows, and, beyond, Mallyncourt towered darkly, brown and black, sunlight burnishing the pinnacles a dark orange. I would just have time to wash and dress for dinner, I reflected, listening to the horses stamping and neighing in their stalls. A stocky, brown-eyed groom perched on a stool in front of one of the stalls, tattered red locks falling over his brow as he mended a harness, and another lad carted a load of hay across the cobbled yard. I recalled that the last time I had been here Lyman and I had come through the woods from another direction, the afternoon I had gone to the village to buy Amanda. We had run into Vanessa, and she had made a suggestive remark about the two of us. So much had happened since that afternoon. It might have been an eternity ago.

As I approached the side door, it opened. Edward stepped outside and stood on the walk, waiting for me. He wore tight brown breeches and a beige silk shirt open at the throat, the full-gathered sleeves billowing in the breeze. The breeze ruffled his thick hair as well, and with his tall brown boots turned down just below the knees he needed only a cutlass to make him the very image of a ruthless blond pirate ready to loot and plunder. I put the picture out of my mind, irritated with myself for such fanciful thinking. Edward observed me with heavy-lidded eyes.

"So there you are," he said in a lazy drawl.

"Hello, Edward."

"I've been looking for you. You've been gone for hours."

"I was—walking."

"I see that. You look wonderfully windblown and radiant, my dear."

I ignored the compliment. "You said you were looking for me. Was there something you wanted?"

The minute the words left my mouth I regretted them. Edward looked at me with eyelids drooping and smiled, his lips curling slowly at one corner. I didn't like that smile, nor did I like the look in his eyes. He wanted something, yes. His manner made that perfectly clear.

"What did you wish to see me about?" I asked stiffly.

"I wanted to remind you of our date."

"Date?" I didn't know what he was talking about.

He nodded slowly. "I promised to show you that old Roman fort, remember? I thought we might go tomorrow."

"I—I had forgotten all about it. I'm—really not all that interested, Edward."

"No?"

"Besides, I have things I must do. The fort is five miles away, you said. We'd be gone most of the day. I—I promised Lettice I'd help her with some embroidery, and Lord Mallyn will want me to—"

"In other words, you're afraid."

"I—"

Edward came closer, stopping not more than a foot away from me. Lips curling, eyes hooded, he rested his forearms on my shoulders, and I looked up at him. I could smell the male, leathery smell, and the smell of slightly damp silk, and I could feel the throbbing warmth of his body. Beneath the chilly, remote façade, he was an intensely sensual man. I had always known that. The façade was missing now. Now he was simply male.

"You're afraid," he repeated.

"Edward, I—"

I couldn't finish my sentence. The words seemed to catch in my throat. I felt weak, trembling inside, and I despised myself for that weakness and despised him for knowing it was there.

"Why deny the inevitable, Jenny? Why put it off any longer? It's something both of us have known would happen, something both of us have wanted to happen."

I looked into those incredibly blue eyes, and I knew that he was vile. He was perfectly aware of the power he had over me, and I was aware of it, too. I couldn't deny it any longer. I fought it, even now, but I knew I wouldn't be able to fight much longer. Edward seemed to sense my thoughts. The smile broadened on his lips.

"Good," he said.

"I despise you, Edward."

"Tomorrow I'll prove otherwise."

"I—I don't intend to go."

"You'll go."

Edward continued to gaze into my eyes, his forearms resting heavily on my shoulders, his body inches from my own. His magnetism was almost overwhelming, that lazy sensuality he could turn on or off at will, and I felt helpless under the force of it. He cared nothing for me. I was merely a tool, some-one he intended to use to further his own ambitions. I knew that, but the knowledge didn't help at all, not now, not with his eyes gazing into mine and the weight of his forearms bearing down on my shoulders. Intellect and instinct told me to pull away, to demolish him with some scathing remark, but I couldn't.

Several long seconds passed, each one tormenting. The sun was sinking rapidly now, tinting the air with a blazing orange light that would be gone in minutes. Shadows moved like black veils drawing over the dark brown wall behind us. Edward finally stepped back, dropping his arms.

"Tomorrow," he said.

He took my elbow and led me into the house. The side door opened into a long, narrow passage that led directly to the back hall. Strong rays of bright orange light spilled through the windows,

lmost as soon as they touched the opposite
ur footsteps rang on the bare stone floor. I
w. ent, a battle raging within me, and Edward
still smiled, the confident, victorious male, so
pleased with himself, anticipating what he knew
was to come. We stepped into the back hall. Almost
all the orange light was gone now, and the long hall
seemed to be filled with a misty blue-gray haze that
deepened even as we passed down the length of it.
Edward stopped a few yards from the wide stone
steps.

"I'll have Cook pack a picnic basket," he said.
"As you don't ride one of the men will drive us there
and come back for us a few hours later. We'll leave
around, say ten o'clock in the morning. It should be
a most enjoyable day—"

He cut himself short as footsteps rang above us.
We both looked up to see Vanessa descending. She
wore a gown of cream-colored satin printed with
delicate pink roses and tiny jade leaves, the small
puffed sleeves dropping off the shoulder. The low
cut bodice left half of her bosom bare, and the skirt
belled out in rich, creamy folds. Her hair was loose,
spilling down in lustrous ebony waves. Seeing us,
she hesitated for a moment, her cheeks rather pale.
Edward wrapped his arm around my shoulders,
pulling me against him and holding me in a loose,
affectionate grip almost as though he wanted to
flaunt our closeness for her benefit. Vanessa came
on down the stairs, slowly. She was completely
poised now, but her violet-blue eyes were dark with
an animosity she didn't even try to conceal.

"You're dressed for dinner," Edward remarked
lazily. "Is it so late? I had no idea."

"It would appear you had other things on your
mind," she said acidly.

least, but I was also relieved. The sensual, romantic
Edward Baker of yesterday might have been a fig-
ment of my imagination. He was like a stranger,
remote, hardly aware of my presence as the carriage rumbled along.

This morning he had been crisp, snapping instructions to the servants, having the carriage
brought round, the picnic basket placed in it, and he
had ignored me then, too, handing me into the carriage without a word, his blue eyes frosty. I told him
I would just as soon not go. "We're going," he retorted, and that was that. I wondered what had happened to put him in such a foul mood. He seemed to
seethe with suppressed anger. *Had* something happened, something I didn't know about? Edward had
gone to his study immediately after dinner last
night. Restless, worried, plagued by doubts and apprehension, I had been unable to sleep, and I had
heard him coming to his room at two thirty in the
morning. He hadn't had a good night, either, but
that was hardly enough to explain the stony silence,
the grim expression on his face as he sat beside me
in the carriage.

I turned my attention to the countryside. We
had come a long way from Mallyncourt, and although there were low gray stone walls on either
side of the lane, the rolling fields beyond were un-
planted, covered with dark emerald-green grass.
There were hills and slopes rising like dark green
mounds on the horizon, divided into sections by the
gray walls, and when I saw the flocks of sheep in the
distance I realized that this was grazing land. The
wind grew brisker. The sky, it seemed, was already
a darker gray, and the clouds were massing together, scuttling across the sky and causing deep
blue-black shadows to scuttle across the fields, mak-

Thirteen

THE SKY was a pale, pale gray, almost white, mottled with faint blue-gray clouds sent scurrying across the surface by a brisk wind. I had learned to read the weather in this part of the country, and I feared we would have a storm before the day was over, but Edward had insisted on our going to the ruins just the same. Despite the rather ominous signs, it was warm today, extremely warm, and I hadn't even brought a wrap. I wore a light jade-green muslin frock printed with miniscule emerald flowers and tiny black leaves, the square-cut neckline modestly low, the puffed sleeves dropping just off the shoulders. My glossy auburn locks tossed and tumbled in the wind as we rode down the lane in the open carriage.

The coachman perched on the front seat, clicking the reins to urge the grays on at a spanking pace, and, beside me, Edward sat silently, his profile stony. Deeply immersed in his own thoughts, his manner grim, he hadn't said a word since we left the house. It was as though this were an unpleasant obligation he was being forced to fulfill, something he would much prefer not to do. Under the circumstances, I found his attitude surprising, to say the ing the green darker, making patchy, moving patterns. There was a distant rumble. Thunder? Hardly a suitable day for a picnic, I thought wryly, but Edward must have his way. He always did.

Always? No. Today he wasn't going to have his way. Today he was going to experience his first failure.

Yesterday, when he had come out of the house to meet me as I returned from my walk, Edward had made it quite clear why he wanted the two of us to spend the day together, alone, away from Mallyncourt. The visit to the ruins was merely an excuse. He intended to convince me that I loved him. He intended to employ all his considerable masculine charms, convinced seduction would be a simple matter. This morning seduction seemed the last thing on his mind. Rarely had he been so cool, so stern. I was glad. That would make it all the easier for me to stand firm.

There was another distant rumble. The noise broke into my revery and brought me back to the reality of here and now. Silky auburn waves sprayed across my face. I brushed them back. The sky, now, was the color of slate, and the wind seemed stronger than ever. The countryside was like one of the new impressionist paintings, all done in varying shades of green and grays, slate gray sky, dark green hills, darker black-green patches where ominous shadows moved, low gray walls intersecting the green, everything beginning to blur in the misty light. The clouds, blue-gray before, were gradually changing to an ashy black.

"It's going to storm, Edward," I said. "We'd better turn back."

"The storm may hold off for hours," he said dryly. "Besides, there's shelter at the ruins."

"It's madness to think of a picnic on a day like this."

"Relax, Jennifer. A little bad weather shouldn't disturb you."

"It's grown much worse since we left. I think we should—"

"I told you to relax," he said crisply.

I sat back against the padded leather seat, irritated, almost hoping we were caught in a deluge. It would serve him right. The grays skittered nervously down the narrow dirt-brown lane, made uneasy by the weather, and finally the driver brought them to a halt. Edward climbed out of the carriage and reached for my hand. I alighted, stumbling against him. Edward took the picnic basket from the floor of the carriage and stood back. The driver turned around to face us, looking uncertain.

"Come back for us at three," Edward ordered.

"Yes, Sir, but—uh—Sir, the weather—"

"You have your instructions, man! Obey them!"

The driver clicked the reins. The carriage pulled away and, making a difficult turn on the narrow road, headed back in the direction from which we had come. Directly behind us, there was a small gate in the low gray wall. Beyond there was a wide, flat field that gradually began to slope up to the crest of a hill that loomed high on the horizon, the climb becoming steeper and steeper as it neared the top. Clusters of trees grew on the crest of the hill, looking like mere sprigs from this distance, and I could see broken blocks of gray-brown forming ragged squares, barely visible from where we stood.

"It's a long climb," Edward said, holding the gate open, "at least half a mile to the top. There's part of an old Roman wall on the other side of the crest, then a sheer drop to the valley below. Good site for a fort, ideally located."

"I suppose so," I replied, not at all enthusiastic.

We crossed the field and began to trudge up the slope. A worn footpath wound about the side of the slope, and it was easy going at first, becoming more and more difficult the higher we got. Gripping the handle of the picnic basket in one hand, Edward strode along at a brisk, athletic pace a little distance ahead of me, not at all bothered by the climb, but I soon found myself short of breath. The wind tore at my hair and sent skirt and petticoats spinning and flapping. I paused, hand against my breast. Edward turned and looked down at me with a faint smile flickering at one corner of his mouth. He wore shiny black boots, close-fitting black trousers and a loose white silk shirt with full-gathered sleeves ballooning at the wrists. A long black cloak was fastened about his shoulders, and it fluttered like demonic wings behind him, crackling in the wind. His hair whipped about his head, waving like short blond banners, and his blue eyes were filled with a kind of detached amusement as he regarded me.

"What's taking you so long?" he inquired in a lazy drawl.

"You go ahead," I said acidly. "I'll catch up."

There was a frightening noise. I was horrified to see three huge brown and white cows cantering around the slope toward me. The horror must have registered on my face. Edward chuckled. I hurried up the path to join him as the cows continued on their way, lowing threateningly. Edward took my arm, pulling me up to his level. The cows glowered at us belligerently and lumbered rapidly on across the side of the slope.

"All this land belongs to a chap name of

MacLean," Edward explained. "His farmhouse is a little further on, beyond that cluster of trees on the left. He keeps cows."

"Will—will there be more?"

"Probably. They frequently graze among the ruins."

"Wonderful," I said petulantly.

Strangely enough, my petulance seemed to restore Edward's good humor, or at least it caused that earlier grimness to disappear. We climbed on up to the top, moving at a far more leisurely pace now. Although rocky, the crest of the hill was mercifully flat, perhaps an acre across. The trees that had looked like sprigs from below were oaks, quite large, lifting heavy boughs overhead. The ruins spread out at our feet, enormous, crumbling brownish blocks sinking into the ground in spots, half walls remaining in other places. A labyrinth of connected square holes, ten feet in diameter, formed a kind of basement. This, I knew, would have served as a heating system for the now nonexistent rooms above. There would have been vents opening into each room through which the steam of a central fire would rise and warm the whole building.

"Careful," Edward warned. "One could easily have an accident."

"They're fascinating," I cried, all else forgotten. "Look, that must have been the bath—"

"Undoubtedly."

"And over there—the graneries. This—why, this must have been the barracks. Look, that part over there is still standing, ceiling and all. It must have been one of the corner towers—"

"You're quite knowledgeable, it seems."

"Can't you just see them in their shining breastplates and plumed helmets, reigning like haughty lords over the downtrodden natives? They were quite militant, you know, the early Romans, I mean. Look, over there in front of those trees. That would have been the parade grounds—"

Edward was quite tolerant of my effusive remarks, setting the basket down and following me around the ruins like a patient parent indulging his child. I couldn't help my enthusiasm. The ruins were indeed fascinating, and I wanted to see each stone, explore each room. Skirting around the deep square holes, climbing over tumbled walls, we walked from one end of the fort to the other while I tried to reconstruct each chamber in my imagination. The wind didn't bother me now, and I paid no attention to the darkening sky or the clouds that gathered in ponderous black masses. The light had grown dimmer, and the air seemed to be tinged with a light purple tint as at twilight. The ruins were grayish-brown, streaked with dark gold and rust-colored stains, and the grass here on top was dry and stiff, greenish-brown. A solitary cow ambled leisurely along the crest, the bell hanging around its neck clattering. It paused to stare at us curiously, then mooed defiantly and ambled on out of sight beyond the trees.

Almost an hour passed. Satisfied now that I had explored the ruins as thoroughly as it would be possible, I was ready to examine the old ruined wall running along the edge of the crest. Somewhat wearily, Edward suggested we eat first as it was after noon now and both of us had worked up quite an appetite. I agreed, and, taking the basket, spread the tablecloth out on the grass near one corner of the ruins. The wind had died down now, completely. Everything was still, silent, as though the elements were poised on the verge of chaos. The clouds hung heavy, ponderous black masses that seemed to sag down with their own weight, and the dark gray sky was smeared with purple. It was going to storm, no question about it, but perhaps it would continue to hold off until we got back to the house.

Cook had done herself proud with the picnic lunch. There was crisply fried chicken, cold and meaty, and various sandwiches, hunks of cheese, boiled eggs, a large, dusty bottle of amber colored wine and, for dessert, tiny brown cakes thick with raisins and nuts. Pouring wine into two sparkling crystal glasses, Edward admitted that he had chosen it himself, bringing it up from the cellar this morning. It was a light wine, delicious with the chicken, not at all inebriating. We sat on the tablecloth with the basket between us, and as we ate four cows strolled past the ruins, one of them stopping a few feet away to regard us with an inquiring stare. I was a bit nervous until it finally went away, and Edward chuckled, refilling my glass with wine.

"Harmless creatures, quite tame. They won't hurt you."

"They're so large—"

"I'll protect you," he promised smiling lazily.

We ate leisurely, sipping our wine, both of us completely relaxed. It had been glorious once we arrived, and I wondered idly why I had been worried earlier. Edward sat with his legs folded in front of him like a Red Indian. The cloak hung about his shoulders in limp folds, spreading out on the ground behind him like a silky black pool, and, tearing the meat from a drumstick with his teeth, he looked like anything but a predatory seducer. In fact, I felt closer to him than I had ever felt before, more at ease with him, and I had been afraid I would have to fight for my virtue. Perhaps he had given up that idea. Perhaps he had realized how futile it would be to try and bend me to his will. I let him refill my glass a second time. The wine had a wonderful taste, rather like olives, quite mild, with none of the heady dangers of champagne.

Finishing up, I set the glass aside and placed one palm on the ground behind me, leaning back to peer up at the sky. The clouds looked even lower, so low it seemed I could almost reach up and touch them, and the patches of sky visible behind them were a watery purple. It was incredibly warm, almost sultry, and that brooding, tension-filled calm still prevailed, not a single breeze blowing, not a leaf rustling, everything still and silent, so silent we could hear the cow bells clanking almost a mile away. I felt wonderfully indolent, wonderfully at ease, and I wondered if the wine might have been stronger than I thought. No, of course not. My head was perfectly clear. I felt a curious sensation inside, and I suddenly realized that it was happiness. I was happy, all worries and cares temporarily forgotten, happy to be here, happy that Edward was with me.

"You look pensive," he remarked.

"I was thinking."

"Oh?"

"I—I was thinking how—how different you are now."

Edward reached for another piece of chicken. "Different?"

"You seem—almost nice, almost human. This morning when we left you were so—so stern, as though you were angry about something, as though you were contemplating a brutal murder. Now, though, now—you're not the Edward I know."

"Which Edward is that?"

"Cold, remote, unscrupulous, unfeeling."

"You think I'm like that?"

"You are. Most of the time you—are like that."

"I'm sorry I've given you that impression, Jenny. I've been under a great deal of strain since we arrived, surely you're aware of that. I won't pretend I'm a hearty, affable, outgoing chap, but I—uh —I'm sorry you think I'm unfeeling."

"I—I don't think that. Not now. Not at this moment."

Edward finished the piece of chicken and threw the bone aside, then he climbed slowly to his feet. The cloak swirled about his shoulders in silky folds. He placed his hands on his thighs and spread his legs wide apart, looking down at me. I leaned back on my palm, so indolent, gazing at him. His loose white silk shirt was slightly damp with perspiration and his hair was slightly damp, too, several blond locks plastered across his brow. Heavy lids drooping, blue eyes thoughtful, he lifted one corner of his mouth in a twisted smile, standing there like some mighty conqueror of old. I was vaguely alarmed, but only vaguely, too indolent to feel anything stronger. A long moment passed. A sudden streak of lightning flashed across the sky veining it with dull silver, then disappeared. It was warmer than ever. My skin felt moist. The bodice of my dress seemed to cling wetly to my bosom. A gust of wind suddenly swept over the hill, causing Edward's long cloak to bell out behind him in fluttering waves.

He reached for my hand. He pulled me to my feet. I felt weak, disturbed by the feeling. The wine, I thought, it must be the wine making me feel this way.

"You're lovely, you know," he said huskily.

"Edward—"

"You wanted to see the wall. Come along, we'll look at it. It's going to rain soon."

He was still holding my hand as we skirted the ruins, but that seemed perfectly natural. The contact of palm against palm was intensely pleasant. Once, when I stumbled, he squeezed my hand tightly, pulling me upright, and that brief instant of crushing pain was pleasant, too. Leaving the ruins, passing under a group of oak trees, we reached the old Roman wall. It was surprisingly wide, over six feet across, heavy stones on either side. The center of hard-packed earth was uneven, worn down by the sandaled feet of Roman warriors walking guard duty centuries ago. Edward helped me up onto the wall, climbed up behind me.

"It only stretches a short distance," he said. "The rest has crumbled away. Not as impressive as Hadrian's Wall in Northumberland, I'm afraid, but interesting nevertheless. Want to walk a bit?"

I nodded, and we began to walk along the wall, stooping occasionally to pass under low-hanging oak boughs that reached out over it. The wall was perched on the very edge of a sheer cliff that dropped in a cascade of jagged gray rock to the floor of the valley below. The valley was dark, dark green, treetops a blacker green, and it took me a moment to realize that those fluffy white spots scattered about over the grass were sheep grazing. From this height they looked like tiny white daisies. We walked for several minutes, finally stopping when the wall ahead disintegrated into a heap of dirt and broken stone. I stood looking out over the valley, dim and blurry in the purple-gray light, and Edward stood directly behind me, his body almost touching mine.

"It's beautiful," I said quietly.

"Beautiful," he agreed.

He wrapped one arm around my waist, pulling me back against him. He curled his other arm loosely around my throat and leaned his head down, and then his lips were on my earlobe, warm, moist, caressing it. Fear swept over me. I tried to protest. He held me closer, his forearm firmly across my throat, his lips on my temple now. Sensations awoke, tight buds exploding into blossom inside, and I tried to ignore them, tried to hold on to the fear. Edward whirled my body around with one quick turn, and before I could even think coherently his mouth was covering mine. Bending me at the waist, he swung my body around, and I had to cling to his shoulders, arms holding tightly for support. His mouth worked urgently, and I responded, I couldn't help but respond, and when he released me I was thoroughly shaken, conflicting emotions warring inside.

"Today," he said tersely.

"No, Edward. I—I can't—"

"It's what we came for."

His voice was stern, his features hard, blue eyes burning with fierce determination. I shook my head, denying it, trying to deny the sensations surging inside.

"Don't do this—" I pleaded.

"It's what we both came for!"

A clap of thunder exploded, rumbling violently. The whole earth seemed to tremble. Lightning flashed, ripping at the sky with merciless silver claws. Raindrops began to pelt down, staining my skirt, streaming over my upturned face as I looked at him, entreating him. His mouth was a tight, grim line. His nostrils flared. His fists were tightly clenched, and his eyes were like blue fire. Raindrops continued to fall, faster now, heavier, splattering loudly all around us.

"We've had this appointment from the first," Edward said harshly. His chest heaved. "From the moment we met there on the promenade, we've had this—"

The clouds seemed to burst. The rain came down in sheets, soaking both of us instantly. Edward leaped down from the wall, pulled me roughly down into his arms, set me down beside him. Holding my wrist in a savage grip, he began to move rapidly through a splattering, swirling, blinding world of rain, and I stumbled along beside him, slipping on the now muddy ground, my heart pounding. Lightning flashed over and over again in blazing silver-blue explosions. Thunder rumbled, louder, louder. The ground seemed to rock with rumbling fury as we hurried toward the ruins as though through crashing waterfalls.

Stumbling himself, Edward pulled me into the corner of the ruins where part of a roof offered some little shelter. Rain slashed violently against the walls and pounded on the jagged stone roof projecting several yards out into space. It was dark, purple-black, but the lightning continued to flash repeatedly and I could see him in those explosive silver bursts. His features were taut, granite-hard as he ripped off his cloak and spread it out over the ground. His shirt was plastered against him in a solid mass of wet white silk. His hair clung to his skull in flat, wet locks. I backed up against the wall, my bosom rising and falling, my throat tight with fear. Rain swept in through the opening, spraying over us in furious showers. Edward turned to me, standing with fists planted on his hips.

"You're going to marry me," he said harshly.

I nodded. I knew that he was right. I knew what he was, and I knew he was using me, yet I knew I was going to marry him. He had proved what he had set out to prove. There was another blinding flash of lightning. Another violent gust of wind hurled sheets of rain through the opening. Observing my expression, Edward scowled angrily.

"You love me," he said in a tight voice. "You're going to marry me. Does a ceremony make so much difference? Does a slip of paper? Are you so bloody conventional you must have that before—"

I didn't answer. I couldn't. Edward turned away angrily and stalked over to the opening, standing there tensely as the rain slashed and splattered. Several moments passed, and then I drew myself up and began to wipe the wet auburn tendrils from my temples. The storm would be over soon, and in just a few days I would be Edward Baker's wife. His victory today hadn't been total, but if he hadn't turned away when he did it might easily have been. I was fully aware of that. I tried not to think of it.

Fourteen

$\mathcal{I}$ CAME downstairs unusually early the next
morning. It was just after eight o'clock, half
an hour before the maid usually woke me up
with my breakfast tray, but I knew Cook placed an
early buffet breakfast in the drawing room for
Lyman and I hoped there would be toast and coffee
left. Lyman left for the tenant farms at eight, so
there was no danger of encountering him. My hair
brushed smoothly, my tan and brown striped muslin
skirt rustling over billowing petticoats, I moved
down the hall, completely composed. I felt more at
east than I had for some time. I was going to marry
Edward, and it would probably be a disastrous mistake, but at least that tormenting indecision was behind me.

I stepped into the drawing room, startled to
find Lyman leaning over the sideboard, pouring coffee into a lovely Spode cup. He looked up, as startled as I, and then, without a word, reached for another cup and filled it as well. He was wearing
highly glossed black boots, a handsome navy blue
suit and a black satin waistcoat. His sky blue ascot
was impeccably folded, and his hair, for once, was
carefully combed, although an unruly raven wave

was already beginning to spill over his brow. He handed me the coffee with a curt nod.

"There are eggs and kippers under the covers," he said gruffly, "and toast in the rack. You're up early."

I nodded, standing by the table and sipping my coffee.

"Shall I get you a plate?" he inquired.

"This will be fine for now."

"You didn't come down for dinner last night," he remarked. "Hope you weren't ill."

"No. I—Edward and I went to the ruins yesterday. We were caught in the storm. I was rather tired when we got in and went to bed early. That's why I woke up so early this morning, I suppose."

"It's just as well you didn't come down. My—uh —my wife was in one of her moods, one hateful remark after another all through the meal. Your husband was in an unusual mood, too, almost jovial. That didn't help Vanessa's disposition at all. In fact, it made her worse."

"I'm sorry."

"Edward seemed inordinately pleased with himself."

"Did he?"

"Inordinately. He mentioned that the two of you were going to London. Made a point of mentioning it, in fact, though he didn't say *why* you were going."

"We—decided to have ourselves a holiday."

Lyman was watching me closely, and I had the peculiar feeling that he was baiting me, trying to spur me into making some specific response. Taking my coffee cup over to the window, I peered out at the front gardens. The sun wasn't fully out yet, and a faint mist hung in the air. The thick multicolored flowers were a soft pastel blur, blues, reds and golds half seen through the shimmer of mist. When I turned, I found Lyman still looking at me with dark eyes, a crease between his brows. He seemed to be contemplating some grave question. Once again I had the feeling that he knew far more than he let on. I was vaguely uneasy, irritated with him for making me feel this way.

"You're quite spruce this morning," I remarked. "That isn't what you usually wear to the fields."

"I don't spend all my time behind a plow, Mrs. Baker." He curled one corner of his mouth up in what may have been a half smile, acknowledging my bitchiness. "I manage the estate, and that entails considerably more than just manual labor. I frequently conduct business with grown-up men in real offices."

"Do you indeed?"

"As surprising as that may sound. I'm leaving for London on the nine thirty train. I'll be gone all day, getting back sometime around ten in the evening."

"Have a pleasant day," I said, ever so sweet.

Lyman set his coffee cup down, scowling. The elegant clothes seemed to emphasize his virility, the cut of the jacket making his shoulders seem broader, his waist leaner. I found myself wondering how Vanessa could ever have looked at another man while she had this one at home. He might have a crude, rough manner, he might lack polish, but his intense vitality more than made up for that. Too, there was a staunchness about him, a kind of fierce integrity that made him all the more appealing. Lyman Robb might resort to violence, but he was incapable of deceit. This was the man I intended to help Edward cheat out of an inheritance. I looked away from him, disconcerted by the thought.

"Is something wrong, Mrs. Baker?"

"Wrong? Of course not."

"For a second there you looked almost as though someone had stepped on your grave."

"What an absurd thing to say."

"Jenny—"

I looked up, surprised. His dark eyes were grave, and he seemed to be struggling with himself, debating whether or not to reveal what was on his mind. The frown dug deep between his brows, a worried frown. Why should he be worried? My coffee cup began to rattle in its saucer. I set it down on the table, disturbed.

"What is it? What—what were you about to say?"

His mouth tightened. He grimaced, turning away. A pair of black leather gloves and a riding crop set on top of the sideboard, beside the silver service. Ignoring me, Lyman began to put the gloves on, pulling each one tight, flexing his fingers to get a proper fit. He picked up the riding crop, and when he turned back around his expression was severe. The moment of near-revelation was past. His manner was abrupt.

"I'm on your side," he said tersely. "I want you to know that."

"What do you mean?"

"Exactly what I said! I hate like hell having to leave today, but it's absolutely necessary I go to London. You'll be safe enough. The time isn't ripe yet."

"I—don't know what you're talking about."

Brows lowered, dark brown eyes glowering, he stared at me, the corners of his mouth tight. "No," he said, "I don't believe you do. You're a bloody, naïve little fool, but under the circumstances that's just as well."

"What—"

"I have to leave now, Mrs. Baker," he said abruptly. "I want to get to the station in plenty of time. It's a long ride."

He strode briskly out of the room before I could question him further, and as his heavy footsteps rang loudly down the hall I had a moment of complete frustration, a moment of tremulous fear, and then common sense came to my rescue. I had no earthly idea what he had been talking about, but I had no intentions of letting it upset me. Lyman Robb was an enigma, and I had enough on my mind at present without trying to figure out the meaning of his terse, cryptic remarks. Stubbornly, perhaps unwisely, I poured another cup of coffee, determined to forget about it.

I had just entered the back hall some thirty minutes later when George came clumping down the stairs, looking unusually robust in his dark blue livery. His blond hair was shaggier than ever, his brown eyes more roguish. He nodded to me as we passed, grinning a sly grin, and I noticed a bright pink hand mark burning on his left cheek. I wasn't at all surprised to find Susie upstairs in the long gallery, looking for all the world like a mischievous pixie with her upturned nose and merry eyes.

"Oh—*there* you are, Miss Jenny," she cried. "I've been lookin' for you."

"Indeed?"

"I was sidetracked," she confessed. "I guess you must-a met George on th' stairs. I declare, Miss Jenny, a girl idn't *safe* any more. 'E tried to drag me into one of th' window recesses, said 'e was sick an' tired of playin' games. I gave 'im *such* a slap!''

I smiled, amused at her pretended outrage. She would have been much more outraged, I knew, had George *not* tried to molest her.

"I 'appen to know 'e was in th' village day before yesterday," Susie continued. "'E was at th' jewelers', pricin' plain gold rings. Bob told me about it—Bob's one of th' grooms, an' 'e an' George are thick as thieves. I reckon I'll be gettin' that ring any day now," she added.

"You said you were looking for me," I reminded her.

"Oh yes. Th' old—uh—Lord Mallyn, 'e wants you to come to 'is room right away. I was passin' down th' 'all, mindin' my own business, when 'e flung th' door open an' poked 'is 'ead out, glarin' at me with those eyes. It gave me *such* a start! 'E said for me to fetch you. I declare, now that 'e's up an' about 'e's worse than ever—"

Lord Mallyn was indeed in a testy mood, complaining because his breakfast had been late, his valet had been all thumbs, his boots hadn't been properly glossed and that wretched dog, Ching, had had an accident all over one of his best Persian carpets. Wearing a dark brown suit and embroidered plum waistcoat, topaz and turquoise rings on his fingers, he bustled about like an irritable grasshopper, complaining bitterly and paying me no mind at all. Although his illness was firmly behind him, he still needed a great amount of rest, and the spurts of excessive nervous energy invariably left him weak and depleted. I waited patiently, standing in front of one of the vivid Chinese screens, examining the brass and jade ornaments on the table beside me.

Lord Mallyn finally stopped bustling and fixed me with an angry stare, his brows lowered fiercely.

"Took your own sweet time gettin' here," he snapped. "I get no cooperation, none whatsoever! I'm surrounded by incompetents! Just because I've been ill and out of commission for a few weeks everyone thinks they can run right over me, ignore my orders, make cheeky remarks—"

"You wanted to see me?" I interrupted.

"Why else would I *send* for you!"

I gave him a long, cool look, totally unperturbed. "If you're going to shout, Lord Mallyn, I'll leave. I have no intentions of being bullied by a nasty-tempered old man."

Lord Mallyn glared at me as though on the verge of apoplexy, and then the fierceness vanished and he looked thoroughly delighted, emitting a dry, raspy chuckle that caused the three Pekinese to burrow under the bed covers in alarm. The old man grinned, regarding me with adoring eyes.

"Ah, Jenny, you do know how to set me down," he said fondly. "I don't know what I'd do without you."

"I—I do wish you wouldn't keep saying that."

"Why shouldn't I? It's perfectly true. If it hadn't been for you—" He paused, frowning. "I have a confession to make, girl: I was much sicker than I ever let on. I was damn near the point of death, and, like a ruddy old fool, I refused to obey the doctors' orders. I wouldn't take my medicine, I insisted on havin' my port, no one could do a thing with me. If you hadn't come when you did, if you hadn't defied me and forced me to take my medicine and give up my port and do what the doctors said—"

"That's nonsense," I told him.

"I know what I'm talkin' about!" he said

crossly. "If I'd kept on at the rate I was goin' I'd already be six feet under. You're responsible for my recovery, girl, you and you alone."

"That's rather an exaggeration, Lord Mallyn."

"Don't contradict me!" he snapped. "I think I know a bit more about it than you do. You're an exasperating vixen, totally disrespectful, totally infuriatin', but I owe you a great deal. Don't go makin' faces! It's the truth—you think I'd admit it if it *weren't?*"

"I think this conversation has become a bore. I've got better things to do than—"

"There's something I want you to have," Lord Mallyn interrupted. "I was prowlin' around the room this morning, opening drawers, looking at some of my treasures, and I found something—"

Lord Mallyn moved nimbly across the room, pulled open the drawer of a tall ebony cabinet inlaid with mother-of-pearl and, poking about irritably, finally located a small, dusty bag rather like a woman's reticule. Nodding with satisfaction, he slammed the drawer shut and came back over to where I was standing, swinging the bag by its worn drawstring. The contents clattered noisily as he moved.

"Got 'em in India—must-a been thirty years ago. Clean forgot I had 'em. Here, take a look!"

There was a gleam of anticipation in his eyes as he thrust the bag into my hands. It was surprisingly heavy, as though filled with rocks. I sat down in one of the worn Chippendale chairs and, holding the bag in my lap, struggled with the drawstring. It was tied tightly, the knot almost impossible to loosen. Lord Mallyn stood watching me, a wicked grin on his face, and I knew he must have re-tied the knot this way just to aggravate me. I threw him an irritable look and continued to struggle, and the knot finally gave. I shook the bag. Chunks of glittering green fire spilled heavily into my lap. I stared, too stunned to speak.

"Belonged to a Rajah," the old man informed me. "I did a little piece of business for him—nothing illegal, mind you, but it saved him a considerable amount of embarrassment. He gave me these as—uh—a token of his esteem. I figure you'll want to have 'em set into a necklace. Well, don't just sit there, girl! Say something!"

I stared down at the lapful of emeralds, emeralds that sparkled with green and blue-green flames, vividly snapping fires that would surely burn one's fingers if touched. The smallest were the size of peas, the largest as large as grapes. They slipped and rolled over my skirt, glittering with incredible brilliance.

"Well!" he cried, bristling with impatience.

"I—I couldn't accept them," I stammered.

"Stuff and nonsense! Of course you can! Vanessa got the family diamonds, Sarah's emerald necklace, the rubies. She went through the collection like a greedy child, grabbin' up everything in sight. It amused me to let her have 'em—baubles, didn't mean a thing to me after Sarah's death. I never let on about these, though. They're worth more than all the rest put together. You'll take 'em and be grateful!"

"I can't, Lord Mallyn."

"Dammit, girl! Must you always try to thwart me! I *told* you, Vanessa got the others. These are yours by right!"

I looked down at the flashing, sparkling green splendor in my lap, and I shook my head. I was touched by his gesture, so touched there were tears

in my eyes, but I couldn't accept the stones. There
were so many reasons why I couldn't accept them.
Never before since I had arrived at Mallyncourt had
I felt so treacherously dishonest. I had deliberately
come here to deceive this marvelous old man, and
he wanted to repay my treachery with emeralds.
One by one, I dropped them back into the bag. Lord
Mallyn glared at me with an appalled expression. I
re-tied the drawstring, composed now, the tears
forced back.

"What are you *do*ing!" he exclaimed. "Blast
you, Jenny! You're the most infuriating minx I ever
clapped eyes on! You're going to accept those emeralds, you hear! You're going to keep every last one of
'em!"

"You're wrong," I said.

I stood up. I set the bag on top of the ornate
teakwood table nearby. Lord Mallyn seemed about
to dance a jig, his eyes flashing angrily. I met his
infuriated glare with a calm, level gaze. I had
wronged him, I had wronged everyone at Mallyncourt through my deception, and I resolved now
to make up for it. As Edward's true wife, I would be
in the position to do so. I could continue to look
after Lord Mallyn. I could continue my work with
Lettice. Perhaps I could even help eliminate the
contention and rivalry between the two cousins.
Perhaps out of all this deception and dishonesty
some good might come.

Lord Mallyn scowled. His anger vanished. He
shook his head.

"You're sure?" he asked.

"I'm sure," I said.

"I think I understand, Jenny." His voice was
quiet, his expression grave now. He frowned
slightly, staring down at the carpet. "I'm an old fool

full of bluster and brass, selfish, cantankerous, thoroughly miserable to be around. Everyone thinks I'm going through my second childhood, but I still have my wits, I'm still able to put two and two together. When Edward left Mallyncourt some weeks ago, it was with the express purpose of finding himself a wife, someone who would please me, impress me, influence me to draw up the will in his favor. I knew that, and I wasn't at all surprised when he brought you back—"

He paused, looking up at me. I was extremely uncomfortable, but I didn't look away.

"Yours wasn't a love match," he continued. "That was obvious from the first. I've no doubt the marriage was little more than a bargain struck up between the two of you—you both had much to gain. Edward must have explained everything, told you what you must do. Am I right? Yes, I can see that I am. Well, Jenny, you've done your job—you've done it damned well. Despite any ulterior motive you may have had for agreeing to marry my nephew, you've proven yourself worthy over and over again. You can fake a lot of things, but you can't fake sincerity, you can't fake genuine concern. You've given a doddering old man a new lease on life, and I appreciate it. I bloody well intend to *show* my appreciation, too!"

"I won't take the emeralds, Lord Mallyn."

The old man grinned. It was a wicked, mischievous grin. "I know that. I knew you wouldn't even before I offered 'em to you. You might say the emeralds were a final test—you passed with flyin' colors, girl. You proved I was right about you. You're going to get a damn sight more than emeralds, Jenny— that's a promise."

"Lord Mallyn, there—there's something I want to tell—"

"I don't want to hear another word! There's nothing you could tell me that'd change my mind now, girl. You'd just be wastin' your breath and *my* time. Go on, get out of here now! I've got things to do! Where did that wretched valet put my quizzing glass? By the bed? On the table? Damn! What—are you still here? Out, girl. Out!"

I left. I went out to the back lawn and walked for a long, long time, thinking about what had happened, thinking about all the old man had said. He was going to make the will in Edward's favor. I should have been elated by this knowledge, but I wasn't. I kept thinking about Lyman, his love of the land, his hard work, and I was filled with remorse. Why? Why should I feel this way? Lyman was the enemy, and I was going to marry Edward, yet for a moment there I had been on the verge of confessing everything to Lord Mallyn, simply because of Lyman. I doubted now that my confession would have made any difference, and perhaps it was better this way. Perhaps after I married him I could persuade Edward to do right by his cousin. Perhaps I could make him see that Lyman was entitled to a rightful share. . . . Yes, I would do that. Somehow or other I would make up for the wrong I was doing. I would see that Lyman eventually got what he was entitled to. Why should I be so concerned about Lyman? Guilt. It must be guilt. It couldn't be anything else. . . .

"Good morning, Jenny."

I had been so immersed in thought that I hadn't heard Lettice come out of the house. She strolled across the lawn toward me now, her white dress billowing, her long hair glistening golden-brown in the sunlight. Demurely, a bit shyly, she joined me by the marble bench and, taking my hand, smiled a shy smile, her gray eyes shining. Could this be the same sour, hostile child I had seen that first night? It hardly seemed possible that such a change could take place, yet it had. The proof was right here before my eyes.

"What are you doing?" she inquired.

"Nothing in particular. Just—thinking. What are *you* doing? I thought you and Partridge had history lessons at this time of day."

"We do," she confessed. "Partridge has one of her migraines, and she went to her room for a short nap. I'm supposed to be reading about Richard III, but I skipped—Partridge would be very upset, but I'll be back before she wakes up. I wanted to talk to you about my plan, Jenny."

"What plan is that?"

Lettice released my hand, a trifle irritated.

"My plan to be beautiful," she said. "Don't you remember? You told me all about that woman— Mary Ann Evans. I found one of her books in the library. It had a picture of her. She *was* plain, Jenny, much plainer than I am, but she was beautiful, too. Only a beautiful woman could have written that story. *The Mill on the Floss*. I read it straight through."

"Did you enjoy it?"

"I cried," she said.

She frowned, and, avoiding my eyes, stepped over to the back hedge, idly stroking the leaves with her fingertips. "I plan to be beautiful, too, just like her. I couldn't ever write *books*, but maybe I could learn to know people and understand them like she did. That's what being beautiful is—understanding people, liking them, accepting them no matter what faults they might have."

"That's—that's very wise, Lettice."

Lettice turned around, a rather peevish frown creasing her brow. "I'm a very *bright* child. I told you that a long time ago. Jenny, I—I know I can't change overnight—I still feel very hateful at times, I still want to lash out at people and make shrewish remarks—but I—I *am* going to try to be different. I want to like people. I want them to like me." Her expression was intense, her eyes determined.

"I'm sure you'll succeed," I told her.

"Last night I put away my dolls," she said matter-of-factly. "I put every one of them in the bottom drawer of the chest. I shan't take them out again—" Her voice trembled just a little, and I realized how painful that ceremony must have been for her. "I—I loved them, and I still do, but from now on I'm going to concentrate on real people."

"That's an—admirable resolution."

"My birthday's next month. I've decided to have a party. I'm going to invite all the local children—even Squire Brown's twins, and they're *horrible* boys, mean and rowdy, both of them. I—I'm going to have a party, and I'm going to be polite and gracious no matter how detestable the others are. I'm going to make friends with Lyle Radcliff's little sister. She's just my age. It's going to be hard, but—will you help me, Jenny?"

"Of course I will."

"Mother wouldn't, I know. She couldn't be bothered. But Daddy'll let me have the party, I know he will, and if you're there to help—" Lettice looked up at me with a worried expression.

"I will be, dear. I—I promise. You're growing up, Lettice. You're going to be a beautiful young lady. You're going to have lots of friends, dozens of them."

"I don't expect miracles," she said quietly, "but at least I'm going to try. I'd better go back in now before Partridge wakes up. I—I love you, Jenny. There, I've said it!"

Shoulders squared, she marched briskly back across the lawn. Her white skirt fluttered as she stepped onto the shadowy veranda, and then she disappeared. I stood there by the leafy back hedge, refusing to give in to the emotion welling up inside. I wouldn't cry. No, I wouldn't. I was going to be very firm and resolute. Something good had come from my dishonesty, and I vowed there would be even more to come in the future. Lettice, Lyman, Lord Mallyn: All of them were going to benefit by my decision to marry Edward. I vowed that. I was going to make up for the wrong I had committed. Mallyncourt hadn't been a happy place these past weeks. There were brooding undercurrents, tensions, an atmosphere of bitterness and strife, but the future was going to be different.

I intended to use everything in my power to see to that.

It was almost eleven when I finally went back inside. Vanessa was coming down the steps as I entered the back hall. Wearing a lovely pearl-gray velvet riding habit with tailored jacket and wide skirt, she carried a hat with three long dark blue plumes curling about the gray velvet brim. There were faint mauve shadows etched over her lids, and her mouth drooped down at the corners. She looked troubled, I thought, her violet-blue eyes dark with some private anguish. Was she still brooding about Gerry's departure? Had it affected her so deeply? Seeing me, Vanessa paused at the foot of the stairs. Her features tightened, eyes hostile.

"Hello, Vanessa."

"Hello, luv," she said. "I'm glad to see you up and about. I missed you last night at dinner."

"Did you indeed?"

"Edward said you weren't feeling well. I imagine you were just *tired*. He said you two were planning a trip to London."

"That's right."

"Don't count on it, luv."

I gazed at her, too startled to reply.

"I saw you coming back in the carriage yesterday afternoon," she said in a flat voice. It was almost as though she were making an accusation. I found her attitude totally perplexing. Why was she using that tone and why was she looking at me with such intense hatred?

"You looked *so* disheveled," she continued, "— you and Edward both. I suppose you had a divine time."

"It was quite satisfactory," I replied.

"No doubt," she snapped. "Did he make love to you?"

The question startled me. "I—I'm afraid that's none of your business, Vanessa."

Her nostrils flared. I had never seen such hatred.

"Is something *wrong*, Vanessa?"

"Yes, luv, something's wrong. I think it's about time you know that—" She broke off abruptly as Edward strolled into the hall. Her cheeks flushed a vivid pink.

Edward paused a few feet away, gazing at the two of us with an ironic expression, one brow arched, the other straight. He sensed the tension immediately, of course. The air was charged with it. Resting his hands on his hips, he lifted one corner of his mouth in a wry smile as though appreciating some private joke. The flush had gone from Vanessa's cheeks. She looked pale now, and worried.

"What a lovely pair you make," Edward remarked. "Am I interrupting something?"

Neither of us replied. Vanessa glared at him with pure venom.

"Uh—I believe you were about to say something, Vanessa."

"It can wait," she said coldly.

"I rather fancy it can. My, what a lovely outfit you're wearing this morning."

"I'm going riding," she said stiffly. "I—I intend to ride over the moors. I shan't be here for lunch. I don't imagine I'll be back until two or three o'clock —" She turned to me, all icy dignity now. "You and I can continue our little discussion then, Jenny luv. I think you'll be extremely interested in what I have to say."

Moving past us, Vanessa walked briskly down the hall, the long gray velvet skirt trailing behind her. Edward stood beside me, watching her with that same ironic expression, the smile still curling on his lips, and when the door slammed behind her he shook his head in mock dismay.

"Such an unpredictable creature," he remarked. "Vanessa has her problems, no question about it."

"She seemed terribly upset about something."

"Oh? What did she say?"

"It wasn't what she said, it was the way she said it. She mentioned seeing us returning from the ruins. She—she seemed almost to be accusing me of something."

"You probably imagined it," he said dryly.

"No—no, I didn't. Something is bothering her. I suppose I'll find out what it is this afternoon."

"No doubt you will." Edward shrugged his shoulders, bored with the subject now, indifferent to Vanessa's woes. "I've finished in the study for the morning—I think I'll take a long walk. Lyman keeps complaining about the crows. I may fetch my pistol and try to pick off a few. Care to accompany me?"

"I think not, Edward."

"Suit yourself," he said.

Edward hadn't returned from his walk at lunch time, and I ate alone. I was in a distracted mood, strangely disturbed by the encounter with Vanessa and unable to put it out of my mind. What had she been about to tell me? No matter how I tried, I couldn't forget that look of venomous hostility in her eyes. Vanessa had been cool and bitchy to me from the first, but it was only since Gerry's departure that her hatred had become so open, so obvious. She had every reason to resent me, of course, but somehow or other I felt that there was another explanation, one that should have been quite clear. I had the feeling I had missed something, something that would have answered a number of questions that kept recurring in my mind. It was similar to the feeling I had about that bizarre red room. I felt I should know the answer to that puzzle, too.

Despite my intentions to forget about it, I found myself thinking about this morning's encounter with Lyman in the drawing room. I remembered his cryptic remarks: *I'm on your side. I want you to know that . . . the time isn't ripe yet . . . You're a bloody, naïve little fool, but under the circumstances that's just as well.* I found them even more puzzling than I had when he first uttered them. Lyman's remarks, Vanessa's attitude . . . there was a connection. I felt sure of that. I remembered his curious manner that night when I discovered him in the east wing, remembered Edward's anger when he found me in the red room. That was all a part of it as well. It was like a great jigsaw puzzle, various pieces floating around disconnected. If only I could fit them all together. If only . . . I left the dining room, trying to put it all out of my mind. Everything would be explained in due course. Everything would be resolved. I mustn't brood about it. That would accomplish nothing.

The afternoon seemed long, endlessly long. The old house was strangely silent, the servants moving about their duties quietly, unobtrusively, like phantoms. I wandered from room to room, restless, uneasy without knowing precisely why. My earlier confidence had evaporated, and try though I might I couldn't shake the feeling of apprehension. I went to the library. I tried to read. I couldn't. I went to my room, thinking I might rest, but the lovely room seemed like a prison, confining me, the walls pressing in on me with steady malevolence. Lyman was gone, and Vanessa, and Edward still hadn't come in from his walk. Lord Mallyn was in his room, taking his afternoon nap, and Lettice would be napping, too. The house seemed empty, desolate, so still, so silent, yet the very air seemed to be charged with tension, like the still, silent tension before a storm. I passed down the long gallery, moved slowly down the wide stone steps, and for some reason I kept remembering Cook and her tarot cards. Death and disaster. That was nonsense, of course. I . . . I was merely restless. The encounter with Vanessa had disturbed me and, unwisely, I had dwelled on it, had dwelled on those other disturbing incidents. I must pull myself together.

I paused at the foot of the stairs, frowning, and when the scream came I wasn't really surprised. It was loud and shrill, muted by distance, coming from outside. I stood there for perhaps half a moment, perfectly still, my heart pounding, and then I began to run.

A deafening explosion sounded as I hurried outside. It came from the avenue of limes. I ran, stumbling past the cobbled yard, past the stables, and then I was on the rough, uneven ground and the lime trees were on either side and I saw the excited figures at the end of the avenue. I saw the grooms, the head coachman, Anderson the gardener. I saw the still thrashing body of the horse, and the blood, bright scarlet blood, and I saw the other body, too. The long gray velvet skirt was twisted under her, and her head was at such a peculiar angle, all limp, hanging to one side, ebony waves spilling over the grass. I stopped, paralyzed, unable to move any closer.

My heart was still pounding. My breath came in short, painful gasps. Edward looked up. He saw me. He broke away from the group at the end of the avenue and hurried toward me, clutching a still smoking pistol in one hand. His face was ashen, his high cheekbones chalky white. I shook my head, denying it, knowing it hadn't happened, knowing it couldn't have happened. Edward dropped the pistol. He seized me. I was trembling violently, still shaking my head. Edward said something, but I didn't hear. I cried out, and he tightened his arms brutally, turning me around, turning me away so I couldn't see that grotesque tableau that was all too real.

Fifteen

IT WAS over now. The doctor had come and examined the body and signed the death certificate. They had come with their wagon for the body, taken it to the funeral parlor in the village, and Edward had gone along to talk to the constable and explain the accident and take care of the necessary formalities. It was almost seven, and I felt weary, so weary. I had gone up to the nursery. I had explained the accident to Lettice. The child had been stunned, too stunned to say anything, and I had persuaded her to take the sedative the doctor had left. Lord Mallyn had been thoroughly shaken when I told him what happened. He had his own sedative, a bottle of port. Silently, defiantly, he took it out of the chest of drawers by his bedside, and I left him with it.

I was in the drawing room, waiting for Edward to return. After that first outburst of hysteria immediately after the accident, I had been surprisingly calm, a well of calmness, doing everything it was necessary to do, helping wherever I could, but it was a peculiar calm, a numbness that left me curiously detached. Ever since I had seen the body, the blood, the cluster of excited men, it was as though I

were two people: the Jenny who spoke and moved
with admirable self-control, and the Jenny who
stood outside, watching from a distant vantage
point, still unable to believe it had really happened.
I knew I had to keep tight rein on myself. I knew
that if I ever once let go I would fall to pieces, and I
couldn't. Someone had to tell Lyman. When he returned late tonight someone would have to tell him
his wife was dead. Lord Mallyn would be in no condition, Edward would be too terse, and it wasn't
something one of the servants could do.

I stood at the window, watching the shadows
spread, watching the final rays of sunlight gilding
the flowers with splendor, their colors vivid and
sharply defined. Was it only this morning that I had
seen them through a haze of shimmering mist? That
might have been a century ago. I let the drape fall
back in place and turned away. I could see my reflection in the mirror across the room. My auburn
hair spilled down in untidy waves, framing a pale,
oval face, green eyes dark and troubled, mouth
tremulous. I was still wearing the tan and brown
striped muslin, the square neckline cut low, the
waist tight, the skirt very full, billowing over my petticoats. I should change into something more appropriate, I thought, but I hadn't the energy. I sat down
and gazed at the empty fireplace. Beams of wavering sunlight slanted through the windows, gleaming
on dark, polished woodwork and making pools on
the faded gray and maroon Aubusson carpet. In my
mind I could see it all happening again, exactly as
Edward had described it.

He had spent more than three hours out in the
fields, shooting at crows. He had killed several and,
strolling back toward the house down the avenue of
limes, had been pleased with himself, satisfied that

he hadn't lost any of his prowess with a pistol. He had heard the hooves thundering loudly across the fields behind him, had turned in time to see Vanessa come charging down the avenue, riding like a mad woman, slashing the horse with her riding crop, urging it on. The horse stumbled and fell, breaking its leg with a loud splintering of bones, hurling Vanessa into the air. She let out one shrill scream, then died instantly, landing on her head, her neck breaking. Edward hurried over to her, saw that she was dead, and the horse was kicking and thrashing and neighing in agony. He raised his pistol and put the beast out of its agony just as the servants came hurrying down the avenue. I had arrived a few seconds later.

I looked up as Jeffers solemnly entered the room. He asked me if anyone would require dinner, and I shook my head. Jeffers said Cook would have a cold meal on hand should anyone feel hungry. He asked me if I needed anything. I shook my head again. Jeffers slipped silently out of the room. Since the accident, the servants had been even quieter than before, moving on tiptoes, it seemed, speaking in hushed whispers, and the house was like a great silent tomb. I could almost feel its heavy weight pressing down on me, tons and tons of stone hovering overhead, ponderous. Mallyncourt had never seemed so vast nor so lifeless.

What was keeping Edward so long? I stood up, unable to sit still any longer. There had been things to do, and I had done them, and I had been able to hold back the horror, maintain that numb detachment, but inactivity was taking its toll and my composure was wearing thin and shadowy questions were beginning to take shape in the back of my mind. I couldn't ask myself those questions. The horror was there, and it involved much more than Vanessa's accident, and I didn't want to look too closely. I didn't dare. I couldn't ask the questions, because I knew instinctively that the answers would materialize this time and I couldn't face them.

I left the drawing room. I moved slowly down the narrow passageway and stepped into the great front hall with its high gallery and Brussels tapestries and the collection of ancient weapons. The candles in the huge brass chandelier were unlighted, and the immense, ornate chairs cast long shadows over the black and white marble floor. Only a few nights ago Edward and I had been standing here, bidding guests farewell, but now the room was like a museum room, stately, cold, without personality. I pulled open the heavy front door and stepped outside, and I stood on the steps for a moment looking at the untidy, riotously colorful gardens beyond the drive, blazing now in the last burst of sunlight. The shadow of the great house was gradually creeping over them, quenching the colors, those flowers nearest the house already drab under the blue-black pall, those further away still flaming in brilliant hues of red and purple, yellow and gold.

I moved down to the drive and turned to look up at the house. The huge brown stone walls loomed up in stolid, ponderous majesty, the heavily-leaded windows gleaming an opaque blue-gray. The immense columned portico seemed to be waiting solemnly for someone to pass under it. Mallyncourt stood heavy and impassive, guarding its secrets. I turned away, walking slowly around the drive toward the stables. No grooms were in sight. The horses moved uneasily in their stalls, restless, as though fully aware of that one empty stall and knowing the reason for it. As the end of the drive the carriage house stood, half in sunlight, half in shadow, the great doors open to reveal the gleaming vehicles within. I headed toward it, moving over the crushed-shell drive, and then I turned, crossing the cobbled yard, passing down the side of the stable buildings, and a moment later I was at the top of the avenue of limes.

I paused, staring down that long, narrow expanse of uneven ground, the trees tall and close on either side. It was spread with flickering patterns of sunlight and shade, and at the end, far away, I could see the fields bathed in light. I hadn't intended to come here. I hadn't even intended to come outside. It was . . . it was almost as though something had drawn me here, some inexplicable force that compelled me to obey. I didn't want to be here. I didn't want to go further. I wanted to turn and rush back to the house, for I was afraid, my nerves taut, voices inside warning me that I mustn't look too closely, I mustn't ask those questions again. There was something else inside, too, something hard and determined, something icy cold. I had to see. I had to know.

I stood there with my brow creased, the wind fluttering my hair, and I was torn by the conflict inside, not wanting to obey that compelling force, wanting to deny the truth and hold the horror back, yet knowing I couldn't, knowing the questions had to be answered. Several minutes passed. The sky was a dark slate gray now, the sunlight a deep, deep orange, fading. The shadows over the ground were thickening, spreading rapidly. I squared my shoulders. I took a deep breath. Slowly, calmly, I started down the avenue of limes. Tree boughs groaned mournfully in the wind. Leaves rustled with a stiff crackling noise. My skirt and petticoats billowed as

I moved, and strands of auburn hair kept blowing across my face. I brushed them away impatiently, continuing toward my destination.

I was wrong. I had to be wrong. It was the sheerest folly even to consider it. It wasn't possible. There was no way. Was there? How? How could it have been arranged? I gnawed my lower lip, hoping I was wrong, knowing I must be. I would find nothing. Of course I wouldn't. I merely had to put this treacherous doubt to rest once and for all. Her death had been an accident. Of course it had. The horse had thrown her. Her neck had been broken. An accident. The wind grew stronger, whipping my skirts into a frenzy of flapping cloth. I stopped. I stood staring down at the ground.

They had taken the horse away, but the blood was still there, dry now, rusty brown, caked thickly on the grass, and there was a splinter of bone, too. I shuddered, horrified by the sight, unable to look away. I could see the clods of earth that had been torn up when the horse stumbled, and over there, several yards away, the grass was flattened, crushed down when her body fell. An accident. It couldn't have been anything else. I felt a great wave of relief, that horrible doubt vanishing. How could I possibly have entertained it even for a moment? I turned away from the grisly scene and started back up the avenue, and it was then that I caught sight of the gray velvet hat with its long curling blue plumes.

It was on the ground, among the trees on the left side of the avenue, undoubtedly thrown there when she fell. I went over to pick it up, and then I saw the cord tied around the trunk of the tree, perhaps a foot from the bottom. It was tightly knotted, one frayed end dangling down to the ground. I stared at it, comprehending immediately, expecting great waves of emotion to sweep over me. None came. I knew now, and the certainty was strangely calming. I crossed the avenue and bent down to examine the tree trunks on that side. There was no cord, but the bark of one of the trunks had a deep ridge scratched around it where the cord had been. If I looked, I would probably find the whole length of cord hidden in the woods, but there was no need to look. I knew. I think I had known when I was standing there in the back hall, when I first heard the scream.

Wearily, I started back to the house. The shadows were deeper, the wavering rays of sunlight a darker orange. I had rarely been so calm, so completely in control of myself. The questions came, and there was an answer for each. Each piece of the puzzle materialized in my mind, each fit into place, making a complete picture. Lyman had called me a naïve little fool. He was right. He had known. He had known all along. That was why he had been lurking in the hall of the east wing that night. He had wanted to make sure. I had to make sure, too. I passed the stables and crossed the cobbled yard. Moving up the walk, I opened the side door of the house and started down the narrow passageway leading to the back hall. I had to go to the east wing. I had to see the proof with my own eyes, and I was certain now that I would find it.

The back hall was dim, filled with shadows. My footsteps echoed as I walked down it. There was no other sound. That tomblike atmosphere still prevailed. I might have been completely alone in the house. I turned at the well and moved slowly up the wide, flat steps, the steps built to accommodate the horses of those long-dead equestrians who had galloped up and down the gallery on wintry days. The gallery was a vast, shadowy cavern, only a few rays of orange light slanting through the recesses, fading almost as soon as they touched the mat of woven rushes. No one was about. The servants, usually so much in evidence, might all have disappeared. I crossed to the door leading into the east wing. It should have been locked, but it wasn't. I turned the handle, and the door opened, squeaking rustily on its hinges. Closing it behind me, I started down the narrow hall.

It was much darker here, everything a hazy blue-gray, and dustier even than I remembered. Cobwebs billowed from the ceiling, swaying to and fro in the currents of cold, fetid air. The tomblike atmosphere was even more pronounced here, augmented by the smell of decay, a strong, sour smell of mildew and yellowing paper. The silence was unbroken except for the sound of my footsteps. The noise echoed disturbingly, reverberating against the close walls and making it sound as though someone followed close behind me. I refused to let it bother me. I refused to give way to the nervous apprehension building up inside. I had to see. I had to know. I couldn't give way to nerves, not now.

I passed into the big room with the great chandelier dangling from the high, flaking ceiling. Dim orange sunlight streamed through the curtainless windows, giving a pinkish cast to the dust sheets covering the furniture, making pools on the bare parquet floor. There was a low creaking noise. I stopped abruptly, my pulses leaping. The noise had come from the hall I had just passed down. It . . . it had sounded like someone stealthily opening the door. I peered down the hall. It was a long nest of blue-black shadow, and I couldn't see the door. My heart seemed to stand still, and I waited, listening, but there was no repetition of the noise and I knew it must have been something else. No stealthy footsteps sounded. No floorboards groaned. Relieved, I moved on toward that other hall that would take me to the room with the red walls.

There were doors on either side. With no windows to let in even what little sunlight was left, the hall was almost pitch black. I stopped midway, trying to remember which door opened into the red room. The first two I tried were securely locked, but the next one swung open almost as soon as I touched the handle. Taking another deep breath, I stepped into the room, leaving the door open behind me. It was so dark I could barely make out the shapes of the furniture, but I remembered seeing a tall jar on the mantle that had contained matches. Groping in the darkness, I found it and struck a match. The stem exploded with fizzling yellow-orange fire, and I lit the candles in all the brass wall sconces. I wanted plenty of light. I intended to search until I found what I was looking for.

Tossing the burned match into the black marble fireplace, I turned to examine the room, illuminated now with warm golden light. The small, erotic bronze pieces on the mantle and low ebony tables gleamed darkly. Candlelight reflected on the rich old mahogany wainscoting. The reds seemed even richer, embossed scarlet silk on the walls, scarlet hangings on the large mahogany bed, rich crimson carpet on the floor. I felt the same disturbing atmosphere I had felt the other time I had been here, but now I recognized it for what it was: an aura of opulent sensuality. It was as heady as perfume, as real, clinging to the walls, filling the air. I knew what the room had been used for, and I knew who had used it. There could be no doubt now.

Ghosts? Hardly. The pair who had met here after everyone else had gone to sleep had been all too human. Here, far away from the others, they had felt free to indulge their passion, and if the servants heard noises it was convenient to let them think the wing was haunted. I had heard a noise myself that night when I had come to fetch a book in the long gallery, and I knew now that it had been laughter, husky, sensual laughter. I had been blind, from the first I had been blind. This explained so much. I understood it all now, and I was strangely unmoved. I should have been shocked, appalled, horrified, yet I felt nothing but a grim determination to carry through with my plan, find definite proof.

That wasn't at all difficult. Moving over to the huge mahogany wardrobe, I pulled open the heavy doors. There were only two garments inside: a nightgown and a man's dressing robe. The nightgown was a diaphanous white silk with long, full-gathered sleeves and a billowing skirt. The robe was a sumptuous garment of heavy navy blue satin. Edward had worn the robe the night he had come into my bedroom, the night he had kissed me with such lazy expertise. I stared at the garments, again expecting great waves of emotion to overwhelm me, yet there was nothing but this curious calm and something strangely like relief.

I closed the wardrobe doors. I felt his presence there in the door behind me, and I turned, so calm, insanely calm. I wasn't even surprised. He would have to kill me, too, now, I thought idly. He stood in the doorway, leaning forward a little, one hand on either side of the frame. His blue eyes were cool and detached, his features impassive. His thick blond hair was windblown, heavy locks tumbling over his brow. We stared at each other, silent. I realized I should be trembling with fear. I should feel faint. There were no feelings whatsoever. My nerves seemed paralyzed. He arched one brow, sighing.

"So you know?" he said.

"I know."

"I had just come back. I was still in the stables when I saw you coming from the avenue of limes. I waited, watching, and then I followed you. I had a feeling you'd come here. You—uh—saw the cord, didn't you?"

"I saw the cord."

"I barely had time to tear it loose and hurl it into the woods. I knew one end was still fastened to the tree, but there wasn't time to unloosen it before the others arrived. I intended to do that tonight."

"You killed her," I said.

"I had to, luv. There was no other way. She came charging down the avenue just as I told you. She didn't see the cord. It was stretched tightly across the avenue, practically invisible against the gray-green grass. She never knew what happened. She died instantly."

"You and she—"

"Vanessa and I have been lovers for well over a year and a half. The other men were merely a smoke screen to divert suspicion. We needed a place to meet, and what better place than this room? It was the only room still in good condition, and with a little work—done secretly, of course—it made a perfect love nest."

"The servants heard noises—"

"That was inevitable, I'm afraid. They're a superstitious lot, and we played on that. One night we heard someone coming up the back stairs. Vanessa started down the hall in her white nightgown, moaning softly, and the girl was frightened out of her wits."

"Betty's ghost," I said.

"No ghost at all, but at least it kept any of the servants from nosing about in the east wing. No one else knows about this room."

He was wrong about that. Lyman knew, but I didn't intend to tell Edward that.

"We had everything carefully planned," he continued. "My uncle was on the verge of death, and it was imperative that I inherit the estate. I had to have a wife—not a real wife, of course, because I intended to marry Vanessa as soon as the old man died and I inherited."

"What about Lyman?" I asked.

"Oh, we planned to pay him off. If he would agree to a divorce, we would give him so many farms as payment. He would have accepted. Lyman had no love for Vanessa, but he has an insane fixation about the land."

"So—so you brought a make-believe wife to Mallyncourt, but the situation altered. Lord Mallyn started recovering—"

"That changed things," Edward agreed. "It needn't have, not really. Vanessa was firm about that. As soon as he drew up the will, he could have a sudden relapse—she even described the drug we could use to bring it on. Everything was still the same, she insisted, but, unfortunately, it wasn't. Something unforeseen came up."

"Oh?"

"After a year and a half I began to see Vanessa for what she was—a tiresome bitch. Beautiful, fascinating, incredibly passionate, true, but in the long run—tiresome. And, my dear, there was you. I wasn't simulating my attraction to you, Jenny."

"You—you're trying to say you fell in love with me?"

"Let's just say that I found marriage to you a more attractive alternative."

"I—I see."

"She didn't like it, of course. She didn't like it at all. When I told her she was quite livid."

"You told her that afternoon after the ball. I saw the two of you out on the back lawn. She was berating you—"

"Yes, I had just informed her. She took it quite hard."

"And I thought she was upset about Gerry."

Edward smiled, his mouth curling slowly at one corner. His eyes were amused now.

"Poor chap," he said. "He never had a chance."

"What do you—mean?"

"Gerald Prince was out of his league. Vanessa kept her eye on him all the time he was here—she had as much to lose as anyone if he made a slip. She bedazzled him, and Prince was quite smitten. On the night of the ball they went upstairs together. Vanessa was—uh—extremely thorough. While they were together he told her why he was here and said I was going to give him ten thousand pounds, said that was just the first installment. I'd be a constant source of revenue in the future, he claimed, and the two of them could go away together, live off the blackmail money. Vanessa told me about it after they came back downstairs."

I remembered seeing them together in the ball-room, standing in front of the tall French window, Edward in his elegant formal attire, Vanessa in her spectacular silver gown and emeralds. I remembered his tight, humorless smile as she spoke to him. He had been distracted the rest of the evening, until the ball was over, until Gerry had come strolling into the hall. His manner had changed abruptly. He had been almost friendly, suggesting that the two of them have a nightcap. I looked at the man standing in the doorway, his hands still resting on either side of the frame, his expression utterly calm, blue eyes rather thoughtful now.

"Gerry never left Mallyncourt," I said.

"No, my dear, he never left. After our nightcap in the study I said I needed a bit of fresh air, suggested we take a stroll in the gardens and discuss the—uh—financial details. He was cocky, quite sure of himself, never suspecting a thing. We walked through the water gardens. Prince kept saying how sensible I was, how much he admired my attitude, said we were both civilized chaps, no reason why we couldn't continue to do business together. As we neared the end of the gardens I moved back to let him step in front of me—"

Edward paused, his lips twisting in a wry smile, his eyes alight with cynical amusement. "I slung my arm around his throat and jerked back hard. He thrashed and struggled, making frantic gurgling noises. A minute later he was a limp heap of flesh. I dragged him to the old abandoned well and pried the wooden cover off and dropped him inside. Vanessa arrived a few minutes later with his bags. I dumped them in, too, and nailed the cover back on with a heavy rock. The next morning Prince was gone, and no one ever doubted he took the six-thirty train."

He gazed down at the deep crimson carpet, smiling, and then he looked up at me. I was still standing by the wardrobe, completely composed, but that was merely on the surface. Horror, sheer, stark horror gripped me. I was in the middle of a nightmare, and there was a hazy, dreamlike quality about everything: the wavering golden light, the dark gleaming woods, the vivid reds, the man standing in the doorway. He was totally amoral. He had committed two brutal murders, and he had thought no more about it than he would have thought about swatting a gnat or stepping on an ant. A third murder would mean nothing whatsoever to him.

"The next afternoon I told Vanessa it was over between us," he continued. "I reminded her that she was an accomplice to murder and suggested she keep her mouth shut. However a woman scorned—I had to kill her, too. Surely you see that?"

I looked at him, and I seemed to see him through a fine, shimmering mist, the mist that half veils a dream landscape. None of this was real. It couldn't be. This man intended to kill me—why else would he have revealed so much—and I couldn't grasp it. This bizarre red room with golden light gleaming on bronze and mahogany was a nightmare room and the man with tumbled blond hair and thoughtful blue eyes was a nightmare figure. I would wake up, and none of it would ever have happened. Everything was beginning to blur. The man in the doorway stood up straight and folded his arms over his chest, looking at me.

"So it's settled," he said.

"Set-settled?"

"We'll go to London. We'll be married."

"You—you think I could—"

"You have no choice, luv. Oh, I can see how you might have a few reservations—you're such a moral little thing—but you stand to gain a fortune. Soon, too. I've decided the old man is going to have a relapse after all. I don't fancy waiting until he dies of natural causes."

"You're insane," I whispered.

"I'm a highly sensible man. I think you should be sensible, too, Jenny luv. I really don't want to kill you—another death would be rather inconvenient at this point, but I've no doubt I could explain it satisfactorily enough."

"Lord Mallyn—he hasn't made his will yet. If I die—"

"If you die, I'll be a bereaved widower, bowed with grief, a highly sympathetic figure. My uncle will be bowed with grief, too, and he and I will sit together and talk about you. We'll be closer than ever, your death a bond between us."

"Edward—"

"What shall it be, luv?"

I didn't answer him. I couldn't speak. Edward waited, growing more and more impatient. Still I didn't speak, but the answer was there in my eyes. He saw the horror there, and he knew that I could never marry him, never willingly be a part of his heinous plan. He frowned deeply, and then he shook his head, exasperated, resigned to doing what he knew he must do. He stepped fully into the room, and that calm, resigned expression on his face was far more horrifying than a menacing leer would have been. He would kill again, casually, without a qualm. I backed against the wardrobe, the dream mist shimmering, my head whirling.

"Sorry about this, luv," he said lazily.

He stopped a few feet away, looking at me thoughtfully.

"You were depressed by Vanessa's death," he told me, "distracted and not in your right mind. Restless, you wandered into the east wing, and when you reached the back stairs you stumbled against the railing. The railing is rotten. It gave way against your weight. You fell hurtling down to the landing forty feet below—a distressing accident, doubly distressing after what happened to Vanessa this afternoon.''

It was a nightmare. It had to be a nightmare. The horror was too great to be real, too overwhelming. I prayed I would wake up. I prayed the humming inside my head would stop and the mist would clear and reality would return, quickly, quickly.

Edward glanced down at his hands. ''I think it would be much easier to break your neck here,'' he said thoughtfully. ''Yes, much easier than dragging you to the stairs and shoving you over—'' He flexed his fingers, and then he looked into my eyes. ''Relax, luv. There'll be one moment of exquisite pain, then darkness, then oblivion—''

He smiled. There was a gleam of anticipation in his eyes. He was going to enjoy killing me, just as he had enjoyed killing the others. I saw the perverted madness, and I realized that it had been there all along beneath the remote façade. He was mad, quite mad. I shook my head. I tried to scream, but no sound would come, and that was part of the nightmare.

''As I said, I'm sorry about this, luv—''

Edward moved toward me, the smile twisting on his lips, his blue eyes glittering with anticipation, and there was a thundering noise and the mist shimmered and the room whirled, a blur of revolving red streaks, and I saw his hands lifting, fingers curled, and dark wings fluttered in my mind and I closed my eyes. I heard him cry out in agony and heard a heavy thud and when I opened my eyes again the two of them were grappling and pommeling at each other, and I realized the thundering noise hadn't been my heart pounding, no, it had been thundering footsteps, and Lyman had come, somehow or other he had come, and Edward was trying to kill him now.

The room was still revolving, and the mist was brighter than ever now, and through it I saw them fighting, and I felt nothing, no relief, no horror, because it still wasn't real. They were locked together, reeling, and they fell against the wall with a deafening thud and, still locked together, tumbled to the floor. Edward had his hands around Lyman's throat, and he was crazed, blond hair spilling over his eyes, mouth stretched back over his teeth. Lyman threw him off and Edward leaped to his feet, standing in front of the fireplace. He drew his leg back. He delivered a savage kick to Lyman's ribs, but Lyman rolled out of the way and Edward's foot met nothing but air and he lost his balance and threw his arms out, one of them hitting against the erotic bronze statue of centaur and woman sitting on top of the mantle. He fell to the hearth, and then I screamed. I screamed as I saw the heavy bronze piece tipping, tottering, tumbling off the edge of the mantle and falling. Edward screamed too, just once, and I heard the crushing impact of bronze and bone and knew that his skull had been cracked open even before I saw the grotesque mass of blood and gore.

"It's over, Jenny. Jenny—it's over—"

He was holding me and looking down into my eyes, his own eyes full of anguish, and I was trying to speak, but I couldn't. He put his hand behind my head and shoved my cheek against his chest, and he held me, tightly, so tightly that my bones seemed about to crack, and, finally, I began to sob. Lyman held me, stroking my hair as he had done once before, and I realized that it was truly over at last, and

I realized something else, too, and it was sad, so sad, because it was too late now. Now that it was too late I realized something I should have known a long time ago.

Sixteen

THE SALARY was one pound a week less than I had been making with the Gerald Prince Touring Company, and I would be a supporting player, not the leading lady. The company itself was even shabbier than Gerry's had been, but I had to work and this was the only work I knew. I told Ian Bartholomew I would accept and he told me he would have a contract ready the next day and said the company would be leaving for Bristol at the end of the week. Grimly resigned, I left his small, cluttered office and walked down the dark, narrow stairs and stepped out onto the pavement. Carriages rattled noisily up and down the street. Hawkers shouted their wares from behind pushcarts. A group of tattered, dirty-faced boys chased a yowling dog. A girl wearing a light summery dress strolled by on the arm of a sternly handsome youth in a brand new army uniform, and across the street a plump woman argued vociferously with the butcher in front of his shop. Midmorning London was full of noise and bustle and color, life abounding in riotous profusion.

I was discouraged at the thought of two more years of touring, but if I was careful I would be able to add enough to my savings to finally open a dress shop at the end of that time. I had left Mallyncourt without a penny. I had left four days ago, early, early in the morning, having arranged with George the night before to take me to the station. There had been no good-byes, for no one had really believed I would go. I had done so surreptitiously, knowing I wouldn't be able to face Lettice and Lord Mallyn, knowing I had to go. I couldn't stay, no matter how much Lord Mallyn blustered and pleaded. He knew everything, of course, knew I had been an impostor all along, but that didn't matter one jot, he claimed. He and Lettice needed me, my place was at Mallyncourt and I'd bloody well stay and that was that. Quietly, calmly, I had talked to Lettice, explaining everything as best I could. I had expected her to draw away from me, but she hadn't. She had been stubborn and defiant, saying it didn't matter, saying I could stay on as her companion, begging me not to go.

And Lyman . . . Lyman hadn't said anything. He had held me in his arms and he had comforted me, but afterwards he had been as terse and sullen as ever. If he had asked me to stay, would I have left Mallyncourt? I didn't know, and it was foolish to speculate. George had come to my room to fetch my bags, and Susie had been there, in tears despite the new gold ring on her finger, and I had left the great house while the mist still hung heavily in the air, shrouding everything in clouds of vaporous white.

Turning a corner, leaving the busy thoroughfare behind, I walked down several streets, moving toward the square where Laverne's flat was located. Brassy, outrageous, still fond of gin, still as fussy as an old mother hen, Laverne had been wonderful these past four days, taking me in with her and setting out to help me find work with crisp determination. As the wardrobe mistress at the Haymarket she heard all the theatrical news and knew everything that was going on. When she learned that Ian Bartholomew was hiring new people for his touring company, she hurried home with the information, insisting I apply at once. Tomorrow I would sign the contract. Even though I might dread what was in store, I knew I was exceedingly fortunate to have obtained work so soon, for any kind of job in the theater was hard to come by. At the end of the week I would leave for Bristol. Perhaps then I could begin to forget.

I walked down the street past quaint, narrow shops. Tall slender trees grew along the side of the pavement, their boughs reaching out to touch the slanting slate roofs and squat black chimney pots. Customers sauntered in and out of the shops, and a woman selling violets stood at the corner, her shabby cart brimming over with purple and purple-blue flowers wrapped up in bouquets with twists of lacy paper. From the bakery there came the heavenly smells of freshly-baked bread, and the grating noise of a knife sharpener rang in the air. I stepped aside to make room for a little girl who was gleefully rolling a hoop down the pavement, her pigtails flying, and a huge dray came clattering down the street, rumbling heavily over the cobbles. I was oblivious to all of it, thinking about those weeks at Mallyncourt and the events that had happened there.

I had never loved Edward. I had been fascinated by him, and I had been strongly attracted to him, but love had never entered into it. That night after the horror was over and Lyman Robb was holding me and speaking tender words and stroking my hair, I had realized what love was, and I realized I had never felt anything remotely like it for Edward Baker. During the week that followed I had seen very little of Lyman. I saw him at the funerals, and I saw him when he and I together explained things to the man from Scotland Yard who had come to sort things out and prepare a statement to be signed. Those dark events had never become public knowledge, for Lord Mallyn was still a very influential man, and only a few people knew that Vanessa's death hadn't been an accident and that Edward had died while trying to commit yet another murder. Only a few people knew that I had never been Edward's wife.

Lyman had known it almost from the first. He had been aware of the affair between Edward and Vanessa for some time, and when Edward had brought me back to Mallyncourt he had been suspicious, for on that very first night he had heard his wife leave her room and go to the east wing. He had mailed a letter of inquiry to a certain firm in London, and in less than a week he received information that a marriage between Edward Baker and Jennifer Randall had never taken place. He made further inquiries, learned that I was an actress, learned of my background, and, suspecting some devious plot, had decided to play a waiting game, convinced Edward and Vanessa would make no move until the will was actually signed.

Although he knew there was friction between Edward and Vanessa, Lyman had no idea Edward had broken off with her, and as he knew the lawyer wasn't due at Mallyncourt until the following Tuesday he felt it was perfectly safe for him to spend a day in London on business. However, he had been unable to concentrate. He had felt a curious premonition that something was going to happen. He took an early train back and arrived at Mallyn Green at seven and hurried back to the house, finding it strangely silent, sensing immediately that something had indeed happened. Jeffers told him about Vanessa's "accident," and Lyman asked for me. No one knew where I was. Lyman was frantic, and then he saw that the door to the east wing stood open. If he hadn't arrived when he did . . . but I wasn't going to think of that. I was going to try never to think of that again.

I crossed the street, walking slowly past a block of flats, the white stone a dingy gray now with soot, the marble portico worn smooth with age, red and purple geraniums growing in flower boxes in many of the windows. A group of children were playing noisily on the steps. I could see the square at the end of the street, trees dark green, shading the pavements and the small park enclosed by an ancient wrought iron fence. Laverne's flat was in the building on the other side of the square. She didn't have to report to the theater until three, so she would be in, waiting eagerly to hear the outcome of my interview with Ian Bartholomew. She would be pleased, for I was indeed fortunate. I only wished I didn't feel such grim resignation at the thought of two more years of touring. The two years would pass, I knew, and then, God willing, I would have my shop.

The future . . . I had to think about the future. Mallyncourt was the past. Walking toward the square, I felt tremulous emotions swelling up inside, and suddenly I was on the verge of tears. Brutally, I forced them back. I had to be very hard on myself. I knew that. I had to forget. I was a grown woman, not a romantic schoolgirl, and life was hard, life was not a story-book with storybook endings.

Lyman Robb must despise me. He had every right to despise me. Blinded by my fascination with Edward, I had been totally unaware of those other feelings growing inside, and now it was too late. I would forget, in time. In time he would become a distant memory, and in the interim I would work, I would build a new life.

By the time I reached the square I was in complete control again, my features composed, emotions contained. The small park was spread thickly with cool blue-gray shade, and leaves rustled overhead as I crossed through it. An old man sat on one of the benches, reading a newspaper, and a stout nanny stood in front of a bed of marigolds, holding the handle of a large black perambulator and gossiping idly with a strapping middle-aged bobby in helmet and cape. The square was quiet and peaceful, as it always was, the tall brown stone buildings mellowed with age. A large carriage stood in front of our building, horses standing patiently in harness, and Laverne was just coming out the door as I crossed the street. Plump, untidy, she looked a bit startled to see me, and then she smiled an enigmatic smile, her eyes full of mischief.

"Oh, there you are, luv," she clucked. "I was just steppin' out for a pint. Didn't expect you back so soon."

"I got the job, Laverne. I'll be leaving for Bristol in—"

"Never you mind, ducky," she interrupted. "We'll talk about it later. You run on up to the flat now, do. I'll be back before you know it. Oh, Jenny, I'm so *pleased*—"

Laverne folded me into her arms and gave me a quick, affectionate hug, and then she chuckled to herself and scurried on across the street before I could say anything else. I frowned, watching her pass through the wrought iron gate and hurry across the park. She hadn't been herself, not at all. She had been extremely excited about something, and it wasn't the news of my job. That mischievous twinkle had been in her eyes even before I told her about it, and that enigmatic smile had been like the smile of a jovial conspirator. Something was afoot. I was certain of it.

Still puzzled, I went inside and wearily climbed the stairs with their threadbare blue carpet. I walked down the hall and opened the door, and as I closed it behind me he turned around to face me. He was standing in front of the small gray marble fireplace. He was wearing his handsome navy blue suit and black satin waistcoat, and his raven locks were unruly. His face was expressionless, lids drooping lazily over dark brown eyes. He looked bored and impassive, totally indifferent.

"It's taken me three whole days to find you," he said in a flat voice. "I had absolutely nothing to go on but the fact that you bought a ticket to London and the knowledge that you worked on the stage. For three days I've been trouping through every theater in London, speaking to everyone I could grab hold of, trying to find a lead."

I looked at him, unable to speak.

"Early this morning I went to the Haymarket. It was shut up tight, but I rapped on the door until someone came. It was the stage manager. He told me the wardrobe mistress had a friend visiting her, said she had red hair. He was highly suspicious, didn't want to give me the address—I practically had to throttle the fellow before he gave it to me."

I set down my reticule, brushed a lock of hair

from my temple, praying I'd be able to maintain my composure.

"Why did you come?" I inquired.

"I came to take you back," he said, bored.

"You needn't have bothered," I told him. "I'm not going back to Mallyncourt."

Lyman ignored my reply. "That was a damnfool thing you did, going off like that." His voice was weary now, slightly impatient. "When they discovered you'd gone, my daughter was dazed, my uncle in a flying rage. He had to be given a sedative."

"I can't help that."

"My uncle has grown to depend on you, Miss Randall. He needs you, and so does Lettice. She kept talking about a birthday party, said you'd promised to help her with it. She refused to believe you'd gone, refused to believe you'd break your promise."

"I—I'm sorry."

"Are you?" he inquired lazily.

"Lord Mallyn will simply have to learn to get along without me, and so will Lettice. I—I have my own life to live."

Lyman Robb lowered his brows, scowling. Here in the confines of the small room he seemed even larger, more powerful, exuding strength and a potent virility. His expression was grim now, his mouth set in a tight line. I could sense the anger welling up in him. He had come to take me back to Mallyncourt. He had come because his uncle had forced him to come, and he intended to accomplish his mission. Lyman controlled his anger and grimaced and sighed heavily, looking stern and harsh, his dark brown eyes full of steely determination.

"Pack your bags, Jenny," he said. "The train for Mallyn Green leaves at noon."

"I'm not going back to Mallyncourt! How many times do I have to tell you that? I—I've just been hired by Ian Bartholomew. I'm joining his company. At the end of the week I leave for Bristol, and—"

"You can forget that nonsense," he interrupted.

"I won't be bullied, Lyman! I—I know what you think of me. I know you only came because he sent you. Well, I won't go back with you! You can tell him that. You can—"

"You bloody little fool! Is that what you think? You think I came because he *sent* me?"

"Of course he sent you! Why else would you come?"

Lyman shook his head in angry dismay. "You actually believe I'm asking you to come back merely because my daughter needs a companion, my uncle a nurse? You can't be *that* blind."

"What other reason could there be?"

"A very selfish reason," he said grimly. "If you expect me to play the gallant and spout poetic phrases, you're due a disappointment. I wanted you from the moment I saw you—" He glared at me with fierce, smouldering eyes. "I wanted you in the worst way, and then—then I fell in love with you and I wanted you even more!"

"I—I don't believe you. You're just—"

"And now, by God, I intend to have you! I'll use force if necessary, but I intend to take you back with me, back where you belong! Do you plan to come peacefully, or do I have to drag you to the station?"

Lyman Robb glared at me, standing there in front of the fireplace with his legs spread wide apart and his fists clenched, looking like some rugged prizefighter about to launch into battle. I wanted to laugh, and I wanted to cry, too, but I did neither. I looked at him, and there was so much I wanted to say, yet in the end I said nothing. Lyman waited for my answer, but words weren't really necessary. Calmly and with great dignity I went into the next room and began to pack.